THE
ROMANCE
OF CRIME

DOCTOR WHO – THE MISSING ADVENTURES

Also available:

GOTH OPERA by Paul Cornell

EVOLUTION by John Peel

VENUSIAN LULLABY by Paul Leonard

THE CRYSTAL BUCEPHALUS by Craig Hinton

STATE OF CHANGE by Christopher Bulis

THE
ROMANCE
OF CRIME

Gareth Roberts

DOCTOR WHO

THE MISSING ADVENTURES

First published in Great Britain in 1995 by
Doctor Who Books
an imprint of Virgin Publishing Ltd
332 Ladbroke Grove
London W10 5AH

ISBN 0 426 20435 2

Cover illustration by Alister Pearson

Typeset by Galleon Typesetting, Ipswich
Printed and bound in Great Britain by
Cox & Wyman Ltd, Reading, Berks

Special thanks to the special Rupert Laight

1

The Killings

It was not a planet for humans.

Steaming blue slime shifted constantly, the top layer of the boiling sludge that coated the planet's compacted core. Bogs gulped, fermenting pools in which chemicals combined oddly, below treacly inflammable gases. Patches of the gas cleared occasionally and revealed bright near stars. The growls and belches from the ground accompanied the low note of the slow wind.

Three figures appeared through the thick screen of gases, tramping with difficulty through a mire. They wore bulky black atmosuits, rubber-jointed at elbows and knees. A range of equipment was slung over their shoulders and strapped to their sides in metal webbing pouches. Tiny sprinklers sprayed their faceplates every fifteen seconds. Their bearded faces were uplit inside their helmets.

The oldest of the men, their leader, stepped forward and pointed to a nearby ridge of rock. 'I was right. It's behind there.'

One of his companions unpacked a large communicator from his equipment pouch, sprayed its indicator panel clean with the sprinkler on his wrist unit, and punched in a recognition code on the panel below with slow, metal-gloved fingers. He waited a few seconds. The others heard his sigh over their radio links. 'Still no response.'

The third man said, 'There has to be a fault back at base. I still think so. I reckon a storm or something knocked down the communicator aerial. I think that's what must have happened.'

The leader did not comment. He had heard a number of the young man's theories in the three days since contact with base had been lost, and contributed several of his own. None of them were convincing. The base had been constructed to stringent standards and its power source, external transmat link and communication systems were backed by infallible failsafe mechanisms.

So why had they lost contact?

It had baffled the expedition from the start. They had sunk a deep rig in the wasteland as intended and collated results for two uneventful days. Early on the third day of the mission, the hourly check call from base had not come. Moments later the guidance line had snapped out.

The team had assumed the fault was with their equipment, possibly influenced by a small increase in local magnetism, but a thorough check on systems and back-up components confirmed that these were functioning normally in the circumstances.

They had waited a few hours, continuing with their work in the belief that this was only a temporary error. At any moment the communicators would crackle back to life, and a voice from base would appear to explain everything. After all, this planet was renowned for the ability of its superdense atmosphere to muffle signals and baffle sensors.

But no reply came, and the leader decided to turn back. Without the guidance line the team were forced to rely on their own sense of direction and a flimsy, grime-coated metal map. It had taken three days to retrace their route. The outward, computer-aided journey had been covered in one. On a shorter journey, they would have used the base's skimmer, but the board had not wanted to risk flying it over uncharted territory.

Now they were back at last. Over the ridge was the deep valley of solid ground selected by McConnochie Mining for the establishment of its base.

The leader squared his shoulders inside his atmosuit.

'Right. Over we go.' He took a leap forward and scaled the ridge in three jumps. The others followed.

The base consisted of three low, rectangular outbuildings, housing storerooms and laboratories, connected by narrow walkways to a central dome. Windows lined the walls. The wind had covered the base's metal plates with dark blue dirt. An aerial, which served to carry radio, video and transmat information, stood unbowed next to an emergency launchpad. There were no signs of activity inside or outside the base.

The survey team padded down the sides of the valley and leapt over to the dome's entrance.

The team leader flicked open his personal radio channel. 'Survey team to base. This is Hogan. Request entry.'

There was no response. He stepped forward and keyed his emergency entry code into the panel next to the air-lock.

The youngest man shuddered. 'If that door won't open,' he said, 'we'll be trapped outside.' He looked behind him at the barren surface of the planet. 'What a place to die.' He raised his hands to his helmeted head and took deep breaths. Hogan recognized that as a training exercise that was supposed to quell claustrophobia. It didn't work.

The panel beeped its agreement, and a few seconds later they heard bolts drawing back automatically. The air-lock shield swung open and the team clambered through into the base.

The shield swung shut behind them, and the compression process began. An indicator on one wall of the small chamber clicked from red to green as oxygen was released. The three men stood in silence, obeying drill. A minute passed.

The internal door opened. The youngest man reached for the seals of his helmet. 'I've got to get out of this thing.'

Hogan stopped him. 'Wait.' He carried out a sensor check using his wrist unit. A red light winked.

'Life support's gone. No oxygen, temperature a hundred below zero.' He lifted a leg. 'Grav field's off, too.'

'They must have been holed,' said the third man. 'Hope they got out in time.'

Hogan shook his head. 'No. It's a vacuum. The support systems have failed.'

He stepped through the internal door.

The base was unlit, and the bodies were revealed in beams cast from the team's helmets. Their twenty friends and colleagues lay frozen in small groups. Frosty white bile was spattered around their blue-lipped mouths. Their limbs were twisted, the fingers of grasping hands outstretched like claws.

The youngest man was crying. He was crouched against a wall. Nearby was Doctor Couper, who often used to sit with him in the refectory and who had beaten him in a poker game only last Friday night. Her face was lit by the report she had been compiling.

PLANET ELEVEN MINERAL SURVEY
Month Three, Day 3
Relative Date 28/2

The board may be interested in the results transmitted by the survey team. Their deep mini-rig has uncovered only a small seam of iron ores, as expected, together with the anticipated excess of low value minerals, including goominum, portizol and a trace deposit of helicon. We must assume that the Jilharro mountain range beyond will provide similar findings, and this will be confirmed by the end of next week.

So, finally, we have reached our conclusion. Planet Eleven is further from the company's standard exploitation threshold than we might have hoped. It remains the board's decision whether to move in, but I would remind the directors that although a full mining option is obviously unfeasible, limited exploitation ma

A cursor flashed at the end of the report.

The young man pressed a button on his wrist unit and a mint-fragranced coolant was released into his helmet. He looked up as he sensed a presence. His colleague had returned alone.

'Where's Hogan?'

His colleague's face was pale under the faceplate and there were blobs of vomit in his beard. His voice was cracked. 'Gone to check the life support unit. He reckons Karl went crazy and turned off the life support himself.'

'Karl?' The computer operator and life support technician had been one of his closest friends. 'No, I don't believe that.'

The other man's face dropped. 'Hogan says only Karl had the know-how to override the safety checks. Lots of the other computers have gone crazy as well. Everything's gone from survey records.'

'What about the transmat?'

'Disaligned. But we've counted the bodies. Everyone but Karl accounted for. Nobody else had the time to get to the transmat, or even to send the distress beacon.' He put his hand on his colleague's shoulder. 'It must have been over in under a minute.'

The voice of Hogan crackled in their ears. 'Davis, Wilkin. I'm at life support. Get over here.'

The two younger men stepped nervously into the humming life support chamber. Rows of neons bathed it in amber. Their leader stood in the centre of the large room. His head was lowered. At his feet was an oddly shaped bundle.

'Mr Hogan?'

He looked up. 'It wasn't Karl who did this.' He indicated the bundle and turned away, sickened. 'That's Karl.'

The younger men looked down. They saw that the bundle was a set of overalls containing a flattened mess of skin, bone, hair and blood. The body of the systems operator had been compressed.

Hogan walked over to a panel in a corner and pressed his thumb down on a button marked EMERGENCY DISTRESS. A light next to the button started to flash. He crossed over to a window and looked out onto the surface of the small, worthless planet.

The youngest man spoke. 'Somebody got in, then. From outside.'

Hogan nodded. 'But how? Why?'

The base shuddered as the distress beacon, flaring red, shot from its mooring on the topside of the dome. The three survivors watched as it sizzled up and away through the gas clouds.

2

Sentence of Death

Humanity is an industrious species. In the early years of the first great break-out, humans came to the Uva Beta Uva system, a complex of fourteen planets that sits near the centre of the Milky Way. The explorers discovered that the fifth planet was capable of supporting human life, and after a few years of tinkering with its polar caps to improve the temperature, settlers started to arrive. They brought with them idealistic visions of escape from life on Earth, which was becoming grubbier and crowded. The planet was green and pleasant and for a few years they lived there, undisturbed. Their only major dispute was over what to call their beautiful new world. Uva Beta Uva Five was not only long and clumsy, it lacked poetry and vision, something of the pioneering spirit. Such a title reeked of bureaucracy and red tape, the old way. The council of settlers plumped eventually, with a pitiful lack of originality, for New Earth. At the same time, they declared their independence.

Not long after, an agent from one of the big mining companies came for a sniff at Uva Beta Uva Five. He was sent away with a bloody nose by the citizens of New Earth, who were happy to sacrifice their principles when it suited them. Rather than return home empty-handed, the agent took a quick look at a couple of the other, inhospitable planets. Just to be sure.

So it was discovered that Uva Beta Uva Three was a solid giant composed almost entirely of belzite, then fourth in the league of precious non-terrestrial minerals posted by Earth Government.

This being the case, the settlers of New Earth suddenly found all their legal rights rescinded under a little-known sub-clause of the Intergalactic Mineral Exploitation Act of 2217. The mining companies blundered in, and the Uva Beta Uva system became the centre of a rush unparalleled in cosmic history.

A hundred and fifty years later, things were very different. The belzite was long gone, the third planet ripped apart. Almost all the other worlds in the system had been drained of whatever wealth they possessed. Planet Five, as it came to be known, remained populous and industrialized, but money was running out. Tourism and service industries boomed, as the colonists attempted to glamorize their past with tales of ore pirates and ghost bases.

Then came the galactic recession, crippling the central markets on Earth and sending waves of financial discontent through the optic beams the length of its influence.

Somewhere between the erratic, spooling orbit of Planet Two and the graceful arc of the gutted Planet Three, an object was moving. It ploughed through space on a direct course, but it was not a spacecraft.

An asteroid, two miles wide. It had been plucked from its natural home and converted to a specific purpose. It was propelled by gigantic rocket ports bolted to its rear.

A magnificent building sprawled over the asteroid. Had it been built on a planet, it might have been taken for the residence of an eccentric billionaire with a fascination for the Gothic. Its stacked storeys and array of turrets and towers appeared to be made of stone but were not. Light poured from windows in the vaulted halls and high-ceilinged chambers that led away from the central block, and through them a mass of people could be seen rushing about inside. Barristers and their clerks, solicitors, law students, ushers, administrative workers, psychologists, wardens, security operatives, criminals. Each had a place somewhere along the nine miles of coiled corridor.

Other features included a concealed docking port, unused since the construction of the building, and a laser cannon, ceremonially ornamented, and still primed for the unlikely event of an attack. An aerial whirled on top of the central tower, providing a constant link to the civilization that had deemed it necessary to build such a place as the Rock of Judgement.

All in Courtroom One stood as the door to the debating chambers opened with a theatrical creak and High Archon Pyerpoint returned to pronounce judgement. The defendant, a thin, sharp-featured man in his early thirties, dressed in grey coveralls, got to his feet. His knuckles whitened as he gripped the handrail of the dock. Two burly security officers in full dress uniform, red frockcoats with black edging and gleaming gold buttons, stood on either side of him.

Only feet away, High Archon Pyerpoint cleared his throat and settled into the red leather upholstery of his chair. 'You may be seated,' he mumbled. Everyone apart from the defendant and his guards sat.

Pyerpoint's lined face was expressionless, but his stare was penetrating and swept the large room. Seated on the bench below him were counsels for the defence and prosecution. They wore the fleecy wigs and black gowns that had symbolized their profession for centuries. Beneath them were court officials and a stenographer typing the details of the hearing into a small terminal.

The recess had lasted three hours and the tension in the courtroom was reflected in the absolute silence observed by its occupants. Motes of dust drifted down slowly through square shafts of light cast by artificial skylights mounted in the high vaulted ceiling. After four days of debate, counter debate and wrangle, the truth had been decided.

'The State of Uva Beta Uva Five versus Jarrigan Voltt,' Pyerpoint began, reading from a prepared statement scrolling up on a screen before him. His sonorous tones echoed dramatically around the courtroom. 'I have accepted the evidence submitted by counsels for the defence and prosecution. I have studied the computer records supplied by prosecuting counsel for the night of November third last. They indicate clearly that the accused Voltt entered the premises in question,' he consulted his notes, '503 Winter Street, Coppertown, and there, in a state of intoxication, raised his vibro-knife and murdered the unfortunate Viktor Stott.'

Voltt's face flushed. 'No!' he shouted. 'Them records were fakes! I never went nowhere near Stott that night!'

One of the security men laid a restraining hand on his shoulder. The High Archon ignored the interruption. 'I do not accept the defence's contention that the security records for Stott's premises were inadmissible under Section 5 Para 2 (a) of the Computers and Cybernetic Systems Act of 2265.' He sent a withering look down at the defence counsel. 'I would refer counsel for the defence to the case of the State versus K. Archibald, 23 and 5, on the matter of admissibility of privately registered information.'

Defence counsel nodded.

'Furthermore, three witnesses of good character testified to separate sightings of the accused in the area of Stott's premises not ten minutes afterwards. I have therefore concluded that the charge levelled against the accused, Jarrigan Voltt, is tested and true, and I find him guilty on both counts, of forced entry and murder.'

Voltt leapt forward. 'This is a frame-up!' he screamed as the guards twisted his arms behind his back. 'They've done me in good and proper!'

High Archon Pyerpoint looked down at him. 'Does the accused wish me to add a charge of contempt to the indictment?'

Voltt stopped struggling. He sneered. 'What does it matter? You're gonna have me frazzled, anyway! Frazzled to a cinder!'

The High Archon maintained his level gaze. 'I have yet

to pronounce sentence.' He glanced down at some papers on the desk before him. 'Voltt, you were given the opportunity to rebuild your life and your position in society following several lengthy periods in prison. Your talents as a mineralogist made you a valuable asset to the company that chose to employ you. But you betrayed the trust they had placed in you and became involved in what can only be described as a drunken brawl. Such behaviour cannot be excused.'

He gestured to an aide, who stepped forward and placed a square of black fabric over his wig. 'Jarrigan Voltt, you will be taken from this place to an area of close confinement. From there you will be led in due course to a justice chamber, where your particles will be reversed until they have dispersed into the atmosphere. May the Lord have mercy upon your soul.'

'I never did it!' Voltt screamed as he was led from the dock. 'I never killed Stott! It's a frame-up!'

The square of black fabric was removed from the head of Pyerpoint, and he stood and left the courtroom for his chambers. The counsels for prosecution and defence shook hands and started to gather their papers together. It had been a long Thursday.

The cells beneath the courtrooms were metal-walled and brightly lit. Each of the barred spaces contained a human occupant, caged by an electronic lock.

Death Corridor, as it had become known, looked exactly the same as the others in the detention area, but the prisoners were quieter and their wardens friendlier. At the end of the row of condemned men and women stood a shelf that overflowed with religious and philosphical texts. The door next to it led to a dark tunnel, at the end of which lay the justice chamber and the particle reversal apparatus.

Something peculiar was happening in one of the condemned cells. An elderly lady dressed in vivid green sat still on a stool. An easel and canvas had been erected before her. An extraordinary figure was dabbing at the canvas with a brush that he replenished regularly with paints from the palette held in his left hand. His name was Stokes. He was forty-three, completely bald, and his hulking frame was covered by a long black coat. He wore a cravat and a dark blue beret. His shiny head and fussy hand movements gave him the aspect of an agitated egg. At the moment he was enjoying himself rather more than usual.

'Splendid, splendid,' he told his model. 'You sit so well, my dear.' He gave the canvas a broad upward stroke of mossy green and his thin, bloodless lips curled into a smile.

The elderly lady remained inert as she spoke through a tiny gap in her lips. 'Oh, it's nothing. Gerald had me sit for portraits a dozen times. All of them turned out a fright, of course.'

'Gerald?' Stokes pondered a moment. 'Now, which one was he? Number three, wasn't it? The little something extra in the sandwiches?'

The elderly lady shook her head slightly. 'No, dear, no, no. Gerald was number five, I pushed him off that high speed train. You're thinking of young Arthur.' She smiled wistfully. 'A sweet boy, Arthur. I almost felt guilty on that occasion. Fussy little thing, though. Wouldn't eat his crusts, and if I left them on he'd leave them behind or tip them away.' Her eyes lit up. 'Do you know, I think that must have been how I got the idea.'

Stokes chuckled. 'You wicked creature. But I'm sure it was Gerald who was sandwiches.'

She shrugged. 'You may well be right. My memory isn't what it was. I even got myself confused at the trial.' She settled herself back into position. 'Now, Mr Stokes, tell me, how's it coming along? I'm so looking forward to the end result.'

Before he could answer, the electronic lock of the cell bleeped. The bars were slid back and two officers stepped in. They were dressed in full ceremonial uniform. The first was a middle-aged woman whose features were stern and unpleasant. Stokes recognized her immediately. Margo, chief of security. She always made him feel uneasy, as if she was about to arrest him.

'Mrs Naomi Blakemore,' she said. 'It is time for you to face judgement.'

The elderly woman's face crumpled with disappointment and she turned to Stokes. 'Oh, surely not already!' she protested. 'Mr Stokes hasn't had time to complete his portrait!'

The artist put aside his tools and wrung his hands. 'Another hour is all I need,' he pleaded. 'Please, Margo.'

The woman was clearly irritated. 'You should know procedure by now,' she told Stokes. 'Termination has been scheduled and cannot be delayed.'

Naomi Blakemore tutted. 'How uncivilized. Typical of you young people nowadays, it's rush, rush, rush.' She slipped from her stool, brushed the creases from her dress, and, to his surprise, took the male warden's arm. 'What a lovely moustache you have, dear,' she told him. 'My fourth husband had one just like it. Bristly kissy, I used to call him. Or was it the fifth?' She shrugged again and held out a hand to Stokes. 'So nice to have met you.'

He took and kissed it. 'The pleasure is mine alone. Taste and refinement are qualities I am not accustomed to finding in these parts.'

She winked. 'Goodbye, then.' With a giggle and a nervous wave she and her escort were gone in the direction of the justice chamber.

Stokes started to pack away his things. 'I suppose,' he murmured as he covered the canvas, 'I can complete it later, from memory.' He shook his head and sighed. 'Still, it will lack the essential verisimilitude.'

Another warden passed the cell and tapped on the bars. 'Hurry up in there, Mr Stokes,' he said, 'or I might mistake you for one of your subjects and lock you in.'

Stokes gave him a playful punch on the shoulder with one of his pale, long-fingered hands. 'Oh, you!'

13

As he left the cell, carrying the canvas under one arm and his paints in a box under the other, shouts came from the far end of the corridor, and the door that led to the courtrooms above. Stokes watched as a burly man in grey coveralls was brought into view. 'It's a fit-up!' he was shouting. 'It's a conspiracy! They've got it in for me!'

The wardens broke open a cell, bundled the man inside, and slammed the bars closed again. 'I want to see my lawyer!' the man screamed defiantly. 'Get him, I want to see him! It's a fit-up!'

Stokes rolled his eyes heavenward. He hated the drab ones. 'Oh, how tedious,' he said. 'Still,' he told himself as he strode over to the new arrival, 'duty beckons ever on.'

He stood before the man and bowed before the cell. 'My friend,' he said, 'Menlove Ereward Stokes.'

The man, identified by a collar around his neck as Jarrigan Voltt, looked him up and down. 'Who the dark mine might you be?'

'I imagined I had made that perfectly clear,' Stokes said. 'I have come to offer you my services as an artist.'

'Oh yeah?'

'Quite so,' Stokes went on. 'For no charge, I offer you, as I offer every wretched soul that finds his way to this, the darkest of all destinations, the opportunity to endure forever in my work.' He flung his laden arms as wide as he could and his eyes bulged with enthusiasm. 'Name your choice of materials. Chalks, clay,' he looked down sadly at the covered canvas, 'oils. I am expert in the use of these and many others.' His voice dropped to a whisper. 'Your essence will endure long after your physical envelope has been snuffed from our miserable sphere.'

Voltt shook his head in disbelief. 'You sick maniac,' he snarled. 'Get away from me!' He shouted up the corridor at the warden. 'Get this scumball away from me and get me my lawyer!'

Stokes backed away. He knew when he was not wanted. And the fellow would have been difficult to get an accurate likeness of. His features were lumpy, undistinguished and charmless.

He waited for the lift at the end of the corridor and tried to ignore the deluded ramblings of Voltt. 'It's a fit-up, I tell you! Someone's got it in for me. Calls himself the Sentinel. He wants me out of the way. I want to talk to my lawyer! Get him!'

The lift arrived and Stokes climbed in. The doors closed and Voltt's shouts were cut off. 'Thank heaven for that,' Stokes said to himself. 'The effrontery.'

He found himself longing for some novelty in his life. Some really splendid crime, deviously and expertly hatched by a clutch of cunning masterminds. But there was little chance of that. After all, the really impressive criminals were the ones who didn't get themselves caught.

The time-space vortex is an area of existence that no two academics can agree upon. Much doubt remains as to whether it is an area at all, or indeed if it can be said to exist. What laws govern the lives of the creatures that inhabit it? Is it distinct from or parallel to dimensions such as hyperspace or phenomena such as black holes? Is it best to visualize it as a corridor, an impossibly twisted strip or an infinite ceiling? While the debate rages on throughout the universe, the academics and their publishers will be happy.

Somewhere in the time-space vortex span a time-space machine that had got stuck in the disguise of a blue police box. This was the TARDIS. Aboard the TARDIS, which was bigger inside than out, a game of Monopoly was in progress. And the Doctor was losing.

He was sitting next to the board, in his shirtsleeves, facing Romana and K9 and shaking the dice. His counter, the ship, was trapped in jail again, powerless to impede his opponents' steady accumulation of cash and property. A combination of personal pride and lack of funds prevented him from buying his way out. He blew into the tumbler for luck.

15

'Right,' he said. 'Now, listen Romana, according to all the laws of probability, this throw has to be a double.' He threw the dice. They landed with one and two spots facing upward.

'Hmm. Improbable,' Romana observed.

The Doctor looked crestfallen, but before he could comment, K9 piped up. 'Dice, Mistress.'

The task of shaking for K9, whose lack of arms prevented him taking on a more physical role in the game, had fallen to Romana. She shook the tumbler and rolled a double six.

The Doctor shook his curly head. 'I don't believe it.'

'Counter, Master. Dog,' K9 prompted him.

'I know, I know, K9, keep your sensors on,' the Doctor said churlishly. He reached for K9's counter and moved it around the board. 'Hah!' he said gleefully as it completed its journey. 'The water works! As I own both utilities, that'll be a hundred and twenty pounds, please.'

K9's ear sensors swivelled. 'Correction, Master. Twelve moves places dog counter on Community Chest square.'

'Does it?' the Doctor said innocently.

Romana studied the board. 'K9's right, Doctor.'

He shrugged and moved the counter on a square. 'Oh, yes. Well, all these distractions, pressures . . .' He waved his arm airily. 'Great green ambassadors almost flattening me in their enthusiasm. I can't be expected to get everything right.'

Romana smiled. 'No, of course not, Doctor.' She reached for a card from Community Chest. 'Congratulations, K9, you have won second prize in a beauty contest. Collect £10.' She allocated a note to his mounting pile.

'Congratulations appreciated, Mistress.'

Romana rolled seven and moved her counter, the top hat, on. 'Ah. Northumberland Avenue.'

'Ah!' crowed the Doctor, pleased to be reminded of one of his earlier successes. 'Which I own.'

Romana reached for some money. 'But which I am going to buy.'

The Doctor looked scandalized. 'You can't do that!'

'Why can't I? You're in jail and I have the funds.'

'K9, tell her she can't do that!'

The robot dog clicked and whirred. 'Negative, Master. The Mistress is proceeding according to the rules you established earlier.'

Romana handed him the dice and tumbler. 'A bad loser, eh, Doctor?'

'Loser?'

'Well, you've been in jail for most of the game.'

The Doctor cleared his throat. 'Listen, Romana, when you've been locked up as often as I have, perhaps you'll learn not to –'

Fortunately for Romana, he was interrupted by an unearthly trumpeting noise from the central console. The centre column, upon which the Doctor's hat was presently resting, wheezed to a halt. The Randomizer, linked up to the TARDIS navigation controls by the Doctor in an effort to safeguard his location from the vengeful Black Guardian, had activated. They had materialized.

Glad of the diversion, Romana sprang up and made for the console. 'I'll take a look at the scanner, shall I?'

The Doctor seemed barely to have noticed the change in their circumstances. 'Hold on, hold on, one thing at a time. We're in the middle of a game, in case you hadn't noticed.'

'It'd be safer to check.'

He looked up at her. 'You know your trouble, Romana?'

'Not yet.' She studied the console read outs. The TARDIS's base was firm and there were no traces of harmful substances in an atmosphere that was almost sterile.

'Your trouble is that you can't keep your mind on one thing at a time. Your mental processes are all over the place.'

'Are they?' She turned the scanner control.

The shutters parted to show what appeared to be nothing more nor less than a small cave. The beacon on the roof of the TARDIS swept about, casting blue light over a wall of rock. 'Hmm,' she surmised. 'A cave. Doesn't look very promising.' She closed the shutters.

The Doctor huffed and turned away. 'Really. K9, I suppose you'll just have to play for her.'

'Master.'

Romana unhooked a grey woollen jacket from the hatstand and shrugged herself into it. She was wearing a white cloth shirt, a bootlace tie, knickerbockers and black boots, an outfit dredged from a remote recess of the TARDIS's enormous wardrobe room. She looked rather like a Victorian street urchin. 'I'm going to take a look outside.'

The Doctor did not reply. Romana shrugged, popped a cap on her head, and pulled the big red lever on the console. The double doors swung open with a soft hum. She walked through and they closed automatically behind her.

Romana emerged into the cave, which was as unremarkable as the scanner had suggested. She dug into the pocket of her jacket and produced the Doctor's yo-yo. She flicked it up and down and frowned. 'Definitely a simulated gravity field.'

She exchanged the yo-yo for a small torch and looked about. About twenty feet ahead the cave ended suddenly in a metal wall. She walked up to the wall and rapped on it. There was no trace of a hidden opening mechanism, and she'd left her sonic screwdriver in another coat.

She looked back at the TARDIS. 'I suppose I'll just have to wait, then.'

The game was progressing. The Doctor's ship was still in jail, and K9's turn had ended in the acquisition of both Whitechapel Road and King's Cross station.

'That girl's got no sense of priority,' the Doctor

mumbled. 'Rushing from one thing to another.' He rolled the tumbler for Romana and a total of nine appeared.

K9 twittered. 'Hat, Master. Mistress Romana acquires Fleet Street and places a hotel.'

The Doctor shook his head in amazement. 'How can she be winning? She's not even here!'

He got to his feet and checked a few instruments idly. 'I suppose I'd better get after her,' he said. 'She's probably already got herself into a mess and needs rescuing.'

'Negative, Master,' said K9. 'Prognosis based on my observation of previous incidents indicates that you are two point four nine five times more likely than the Mistress to need assistance upon leaving the TARDIS.'

'Oh, shut up, K9.' The Doctor jammed his hat on his head, put on his long, oatmeal-coloured coat and wound his trailing scarf around his shoulders. 'When I want your opinion I'll ask for it.' He operated the door and the metal dog trundled forward eagerly. 'Stay, K9,' he ordered. 'I want you on guard.'

K9's tail sensor drooped. 'Affirmative, Master.'

The Doctor nodded and left the TARDIS. A second later there was an alarming crash and a muffled cry. K9 moved forward to investigate. The Doctor reappeared, dusting himself down. He wagged an accusing finger at his computer pet. 'I don't want to hear you say I told you so, K9,' he said and stalked out. The doors closed behind him.

K9's sensors chirped. 'Instruction noted, Master. This unit will never say "I told you so." Linguistic sequence erased from phraseology bank.'

The Doctor joined Romana in the dark cave. He licked a finger, ran it along a wall, and sniffed at the deposits it collected. 'Hmm. Carbonaceous asteroid, I'd say. Traces of refractories, accelerated decay of aluminium-26, et cetera.'

Romana nodded her agreement and produced the

yo-yo. She executed an elaborate double loop. 'And we're on the fringe of a simulated gravity field. I'd say they're using remote gravitic excitation.'

The Doctor frowned. 'Would you?' He snatched the yo-yo and returned it to his pocket.

Romana crossed over to the metal panel in the wall and rapped on it with her knuckles. 'This must be the outer wall of their living space. It's duralinium, so this is possibly an Earth colony.'

The Doctor was dubious. 'On an asteroid? I think even the human race'd have more sense than that.' He started to tap the wall.

'It's all right, Doctor, I've already tried that.'

He stopped tapping and turned to face her. 'I think I'd better come out first next time, yes?'

'If you say so.'

He ferreted in his pocket and pulled out the sonic screwdriver. A couple of adjustments converted it into a powerful cutting tool. The sonic beam started to cut a sparking line through the metal.

Pyerpoint sat behind his desk in the spacious, oak-panelled office of his chambers. Spread before him were a variety of reports and papers awaiting his attention. A small desk lamp illuminated the pinched features of his heavily lined face. He was a tall, distinguished-looking man in his late fifties. Now out of his wig and gown, he wore a glistening gold blouson with elaborately puffed sleeves beneath a dark brown tabard. A skullcap of golden beads had been woven into his uplifted peroxide blond hair. As was the custom for the senior echelon of society at this point in history, his high cheekbones were dabbed with a hint of red cosmetic.

The office reflected his personality. The drinks cabinet, leather-buttoned chairs and green carpet were all spotlessly clean. A tall grandfather clock ticked noisily in a corner. Volumes of law were ranged against a far wall.

The only other ornamentation was a bronze figure

beneath a glass dome, which had been brought from Earth. It depicted Liberty as a woman balancing the scales of justice. A window carved into the back wall displayed the infinite shifting starscape.

Pyerpoint inspected a chart marked for distribution to senior staff only. It showed the course suggested by the station's security computer for the days ahead. This would take them close to Planet Four before veering off to the outer worlds. He took a fountain pen from a drawer in his desk and signed his approval.

There was a knock at the door. 'Come,' he ordered.

Margo entered the office. If anything, she looked even more efficient than Pyerpoint. She was tall and dark-haired. Her hair was braided with silver beads and she wore the long red coat and black trousers of the security division. A sparkling green sash tied about her waist indicated her rank as chief of security. Her face was stern and unattractive. She carried a bundle of papers bound with green string under one arm.

'Sir,' she began. 'Today's terminations. The notice requires the seal.' She handed him the papers.

He unpicked the green string with accustomed ease and flicked through the papers. 'Naomi Blakemore, Seldin Vranch. And Jarrigan Voltt. Yes, that all appears to be in order.'

'Voltt was sentenced only this afternoon, sir,' Margo said with a hint of puzzlement.

'I pronounced sentence myself. There is a problem?'

'It is irregular for termination to be scheduled so soon after sentence, sir,' Margo pointed out. 'There may be religious objections from Five.'

'There was a gap in the schedule,' Pyerpoint said smoothly. 'I ordered Voltt's termination brought forward to fill the gap. And you know well that I have little time to spare for liberal opinion. The victims of crime have no time to reflect. You have an objection?'

Margo smiled. 'No, sir. I am impressed as ever by your devotion to the efficiency of the station.'

21

Pyerpoint took a large stamp from his desk, rolled it in an ink pad, and thumped it down over each name on the list. The stamp left the seal of the Rock. He replaced the tape and handed the bundle back to her. 'Thank you, Margo.' He picked up the course chart. 'And these are the new course details, approved and signed.'

She took them. 'Very good, sir. And there's a Mr Spiggot waiting to see you in the lobby, sir.'

Pyerpoint frowned and looked up. 'Spiggot? I've never heard of the fellow. Has he an appointment?'

'No, sir,' said Margo. 'He is an agent of Five police.'

Pyerpoint sighed and slapped his palms on the desk. He was accustomed to police officers appearing unexpectedly, usually with a warrant to interview somebody in custody. 'Tell him to wait. I'll send for him when I've finished with these reports.'

Margo nodded and left the office.

A few minutes later, the door of Pyerpoint's office was thrown open and a man entered. He wore a fashionably cut black suit, a black sweater, and expensive black shoes with pointed heels. His long dark hair flowed over his collar. His face was long, scarred and stubbled, with a prominent broken nose. He carried a thin plastic case.

He extended a hand to Pyerpoint. 'Spiggot. I'm with capital police on Five.' He spoke with a broad North Nation accent. His manner was conspicuously informal.

Pyerpoint looked up from his work and tapped his pen on his blotter with irritation. 'My chief of security instructed you to wait in the lobby, Mr Spiggot.'

The Doctor and Romana had emerged from the cave into a long metal corridor, at the end of which they found a door. The sonic screwdriver made short work of its electronic lock and they walked through into a crowded concourse. The walls and floor appeared to be made of stone. People dressed in simple coveralls and tabards chattered in small groups. Some were seated on leather sofas and nibbled at bowls of nuts, others sucked at frothing drinks through curled straws. The revellers' skins were pasty and pale. On the far side of the large room was a long bar. Ambient music was being piped through concealed speakers.

'A recreational area,' surmised Romana. She wrinkled her nose. 'Rather drab.'

The Doctor pushed through the crowd to the bar. 'Two glasses of water, please,' he ordered. The barman nodded pleasantly and broke open two bottles of mineral water.

'No till,' the Doctor whispered to Romana as he took the drinks. 'No point of exchange.'

They made their way to a vacant couch. 'Should that matter?' asked Romana as she brought her glass to her lips.

The Doctor stopped her. 'Wait, wait.' He sniffed suspiciously at his own drink and then looked around at the cheerful chatting crowd. 'How very odd. They haven't even noticed us. Don't touch the nibbles, Romana.'

Romana dipped a finger in her water and dabbed it on her tongue. 'A suppressant? Some sort of neural inhibitor?'

The Doctor nodded. 'Has to be. The question is, who's doing the drugging?'

'And why.'

He put his glass down. 'We'll worry about why later. First things first. I'd still like to know where.' He stood and tapped one of the other drinkers on the shoulder. 'Excuse me, yes, hello. I'm a stranger to these parts and I was wondering if you could perhaps remind me of the name of the nearest star.'

In a small darkened room on a higher level, a range of monitor screens relayed images from cameras positioned at points around the complex. Deputy security officer Shom was on duty, eating a nutrition bar and reading a bookscreen. He was a young man, bright, alert and destined for promotion. Only occasionally did he look up to check that all was proceeding smoothly, as always, within the Rock of Judgement.

Something odd caught his eye in the refreshment zone. He put down his book and squinted at the screen. What he saw was impossible. He reached for a communicator button and opened a channel to his superior.

'Ma'am,' he reported urgently. 'There are two unauthorized personnel in the refreshment zone.'

The voice of Margo asked, 'Intruders?'

'Yes, ma'am. A man and a woman. They're talking to the admin staff.'

The man the Doctor had chosen to talk to stared back at him with large dulled eyes. 'You don't belong,' he said slowly. 'I don't recognize you.' He smiled at Romana. 'Either of you.'

The Doctor shrugged. 'Well no. As I said, we're travellers.'

The man shook his head and laughed. 'Don't be silly. There are no travellers here.'

'Really?' said the Doctor. 'How unwelcoming.' The man smiled again and wandered off to join one of the small chatting groups.

'That wasn't very productive,' Romana observed as he rejoined her on the couch. 'If this is a relaxation centre, what work do these people do? Could they be miners?'

'Oh no, no, no. Look at their clothes, their hands, their posture.' He broke off and stared more closely at the nearest group. 'Yes, their posture. Slumped shoulders, cricked necks, knock knees.'

'So they are miners.'

'Office workers, more like. These people have been sitting behind desks all day. In uncomfortable chairs. It's really very unhealthy.' He smiled at her. 'Romana, do you realize that we're surrounded by doped civil servants?'

Before she could reply, a gong sounded and the lights in the large room dimmed. The crowd quietened. The wall facing them slid open slowly with a low hum and two figures, a man and a woman, emerged. They wore blank red masks and skin-tight red leotards. The ambient music was replaced by a tribal drumbeat. The two figures began to strike poses as the rhythm changed.

The Doctor grimaced. 'This must be the turn. I don't like it.'

Spiggot ran a glance over the High Archon, whose duties also made him station administrator. The file on him back at HQ had got him right. He was a man accustomed to being bowed and scraped to. Called to the bar at twenty, first brief at twenty-one, criminal barrister of repute for twenty years, confirmed as High Archon aged forty-five. A man used to giving orders. Well, in Spiggot's line of work, there was no time for that sort of thing. He treated everyone the same, beggar or minister. Gave them the same chances, dealt to them from the same deck. That was how he got results. By breaking the rules.

And, dammit, that was how he'd lost Angie and the kids.

Spiggot settled himself in the chair opposite Pyerpoint. 'This is a serious business,' he said. 'Something big. See, there's something I need from you.'

'What, exactly?'

Probably doesn't like my accent, thought Spiggot. Can't handle the idea of a lad from North Nation making it big. 'Your security computer net. I need to take a look at it.'

Pyerpoint put his pen down and frowned. 'For what purpose? We have a team of skilled technicians working on all of our systems constantly.'

Probably doesn't like my hair either, thought Spiggot. Can't handle the idea of a lad with looks and long hair getting on in life. 'Afraid I can't disclose my reasons, sir. I just need to inspect your security net.' He leant forward on the desk and scratched at his itching chin. 'Then I can be on my way and be out of your life, yeah?'

'May I see your warrant?' asked Pyerpoint.

Spiggot took a slim black plastic wallet from an inside pocket and handed it across the desk. He watched as Pyerpoint flipped it open and inspected it. The small photo inside was one of Spiggot's favourites. It showed him with an expression that was both tough and wounded, displaying the qualities of strength and vulnerability, the unconventional good looks that had brought him results at work and in the bedroom. And, dammit, those were the maverick qualities that had lost him Angie and the kids.

'This does not allow access,' Pyerpoint said severely. 'Your rank is only grade three. Without a special warrant I cannot provide what you ask. I presume you have one?'

Spiggot sighed and took back his identification. 'Listen, mate,' he said. 'You and I both know that rules are there to be twisted. I'm on the trail of something hot. Something big. I need to get in to that computer.'

Pyerpoint stood. 'Your suggestion is impertinent. Now, if you have nothing further to add, I must request that you depart and allow me to continue with my work.'

The old guy was really rattled, thought Spiggot. Not used to having his authority challenged. Well, he had some surprises coming now that Five police had sent their top investigator up to the Rock of Judgement.

The doped workers clapped politely as their evening's entertainment came to a close. The red garbed dancers bowed and returned through the wall, which closed up after them. The lights in the bar came up.

'Well, that was interesting,' the Doctor said. 'In a tedious and incomprehensible sort of way.'

Romana nodded. 'If what you've reasoned is correct, these people's lives must be exceptionally unfulfilling. This kind of recreation releases accumulated tensions in a controlled environment.'

'Yes,' said the Doctor. 'Doesn't stop it being boring,

though.' He yawned. 'The Randomizer really does lack discretion. How about a trip to Transycaster?'

'What, next to the black hole of Dehara?' Romana said doubtfully.

The Doctor stood up. 'Well, it's got to be better than this. At least there you can get a decent drink.' He sat back down again suddenly and jammed his hat down on his tangle of thick curly hair.

Romana was alarmed. 'Doctor, what's the matter?'

'We've got company,' he whispered. 'Over there.' Romana glimpsed men in red uniforms pushing through the crowd. Some of them were carrying blasters.

The Doctor took her hand. 'Follow me, we'll go out the way we came in.' They attempted to tiptoe back towards the door, but as the Doctor was six foot four and was wearing a multi-coloured scarf that was twenty-six feet long, his attempt to appear inconspicuous failed.

A voice cried 'There they are!' and the uniformed officers burst into the open. Their leader, a woman with stern and unattractive features, stepped forward. 'You! Remain still!'

The Doctor indicated the door. 'Yes, well, we were just going, charming place you have here —'

The woman raised her blaster and pointed it between his eyes. 'You are unauthorized personnel. I have the authority to shoot you if you do not comply with my instructions. Raise your hands.'

'Well, if you put it like that,' said the Doctor. He and Romana raised their hands.

'You will follow me in single file and will not attempt to communicate with each other,' the woman barked. 'Make an attempt to escape and you will be executed immediately.' She turned away. The Doctor and Romana were hustled away through the crowd by her officers.

As he passed the bar on the way out, the Doctor called cheerfully, 'A pint of whatever that lady's been drinking, please.'

3

Suspicion

Stokes emerged from a lift on the basement floor of the station. He attempted to balance his covered canvas and box of equipment while closing the lift's gridded metal shutter, failed and dropped everything. He grunted with anger, slammed the shutter, picked up his belongings and set off along the long corridor to a large door at the far end. He shuffled about in his pockets, produced a set of keys, and let himself in to his gallery.

The designers of the Rock of Judgement had intended the basement to be used as a storage area, but it had been empty until Stokes had succeeded in persuading the Legal Chancellery Division back on Five that his project was a worthy one, and that he was in possession of the funds to proceed with it privately. The gallery consisted of a dimly lit central chamber, its high ceiling supported with fake oak beams, and several small annexes partitioned off by broad stone pillars. Positioned about the gallery were representations of many of the criminals executed aboard the asteroid in the last seven years. These included sculptures, photographs, a couple of masks, and some holograms and abstract studies. Stokes's style, if he could be said to have one, was needlessly extravagant. Red was his favourite colour and he applied it liberally to many of his compositions. An observer taking a quick glance at Stokes's works might have found them intriguing and original, but a closer inspection would have revealed a lack of detail and, as his old tutors at the Gelheissen School of the Arts had despaired of telling him, an inability to capitalize on his ideas.

Stokes put down his things and looked over to an aged couch that was propped against a wall. Foam spilled from its torn upholstery and it was marked with burns and stains. Spread across it was a dark-haired young man with an insolent expression. He wore denims and a leather cap and was smoking a flavoured cigarette. This was Zy, a student sent by the education authorities on Five to join Stokes on attachment, a condition of their contract.

He blew a large yellow smoke cloud over at Stokes. 'You're back early, Men.'

Stokes slipped off his beret and patted his smooth shiny head. 'I had work to do and petty officialdom prevented me from completing it.' He stuffed the beret into a pocket. 'Whereas you have obviously been wasting yet more of your time and the state's money festooned there in a state of pacific inertia.'

The young man sat up. He flicked off a cloth that covered an object on a nearby stand. A cartoon was revealed, a caricature of Stokes that exaggerated his large nose, domed head and thin wet lips even more than nature had.

Stokes sneered and took the drawing from the stand for a closer inspection. 'You flatter me,' he said. 'It's a fair likeness. But your technique!' He replaced the picture. 'Dated and strangely timid. What's wrong with young people nowadays? You have all the daring of a hibernating burrow worm.'

Rather pleased with this turn of phrase, Stokes crossed to a sink and started to wash his hands. The young man slipped off the sofa and stood behind him. 'I've sold twenty today, Men.'

Stokes splashed water over his face. 'Twenty what?' He snapped his fingers. 'Towel, towel.'

Zy passed it to him. 'Twenty copies of that piece I finished off last week.'

Stokes's brow furrowed. He dabbed at his glistening moon face with the edges of the towel. 'What, that purple aberration? You jest.'

Zy grinned and produced a thick wad of notes from a pocket. 'Sold twenty down the line to Five. Six hundred credits apiece.'

Stokes coughed. 'Six hundred? For that tasteless muck? And each worth about six halfcredits.' He shook his head and one of his fingers. 'People will snap up anything on the commercial market. Don't let yourself succumb to visions of greatness, boy. I'll tell you frankly, you stand little chance of making any sale beyond the confines of that tawdry bracket.'

He leaned closer to his apprentice. 'Not, of course, that sales are the important factor in the creation of art.'

Zy looked around the gallery. 'Just as well.'

Stokes picked up his covered canvas and set it on an easel. 'Remind me. How much longer have the authorities condemned me to suffer your presence in my life?'

'Two months.'

'Yes, well.' He removed the cover and scrutinized his portrait of Mrs Blakemore. 'Make yourself useful and vamoose. There's a bar up on level three, you know.'

'For zombies.' Zy slipped back onto the sofa and lit a cigarette. Stokes grunted and continued with his work. He knew he'd have to finish the job tonight while the memory of his subject remained fresh.

'Mr Spiggot,' Pyerpoint said, 'I must ask you once again to leave this station. I have made my position more than clear. I cannot grant your request without an upgraded warrant.'

Spiggot pushed a stray lock of hair from his eyes. 'Then I may have to take my own way.' It was nearly always the same, he'd found. Doors slammed shut in his face. But where his colleagues, with their incident forms and desk reports, might have given up and turned back, he was prepared to strike out alone.

'What exactly are you threatening?' asked Pyerpoint. 'Your impertinence could land you in trouble. I —'

A high pitched tone came from a unit sewn onto the breast of Pyerpoint's tabard. He frowned and put his hand to it. 'Yes?'

'An incident, sir,' said a woman's voice. Right, thought Spiggot, that'd be the chief of security. 'Please come to the detention area. Cell forty.'

'What is the nature of this incident, Margo?'

'I cannot discuss the matter on open channel, sir.'

'Very well.' Pyerpoint stood and indicated the door. 'I have to leave now. I do not want to see you again, Mr Spiggot. If you choose to interfere with the workings of this station, it is within my power to impose severe penalties.'

Spiggot grinned. 'I've heard everything you've said, sir.'

Margo examined the items spread across the table in cell forty. An orange, a mirror, a ball of string, a yo-yo, a child's picture book, an egg timer, a slender silver object and a paper bag that contained confectionery. She picked up this item and addressed the male prisoner, who called himself the Doctor. 'What are these?'

'They're jelly babies. Sweets.'

The female prisoner said, 'Why not try one?'

Margo put the bag down. 'High sugar foods are prohibited here.'

The Doctor was aghast. 'What, no tuck shop?'

'Such items impede efficiency. Suitable relaxants are supplied in the refreshment zone.'

She studied the intruders again. A thorough search had revealed no trace of identification on either of them. Although they were carrying no weapons, their unexplained arrival remained an irritation.

'I'll ask you again,' she said. 'How did you arrive here on the Rock?'

'I keep telling you,' said the male prisoner, 'I'm the Doctor, this is Romana, we're travellers, and we arrived here by accident, and there's really no need to clap us in

31

irons. We're quite the friendliest and most inoffensive of people, aren't we, Romana?'

'Oh yes. Let us leave and you needn't worry about us again.'

Margo signalled to one of the officers standing guard on the cell door. 'Fetch the truth serum from stores. Use my authorization.'

'Yes, ma'am.' The guard saluted and left the cell.

The Doctor did not seem to be impressed. 'Truth serum? You really are wasting a lot of time.'

'We've been telling the truth for the last half hour,' put in Romana.

Margo pulled herself up to her full height. 'Your presence here is unauthorized. This station is top security. All transmat communications, arrivals and departures, are approved by myself and logged by the security computer. Your arrival was not registered.'

'Perhaps we didn't arrive by transmat,' said the female prisoner. The Doctor muttered a curse.

Margo seized on her error. 'So, as I thought, you travelled here by spacecraft and cut your way in. Who is your contact? What was your purpose in coming here? How did you locate this station?'

The Doctor held up his hand. 'Please, please, so many questions.'

The cell door swung open and Pyerpoint entered. His eyebrows shot up in surprise as he caught sight of the strangers and their eccentric dress. 'Who are you?'

The Doctor's face fell. 'And there's another one.'

'What are these people doing here?' Pyerpoint asked Margo. 'Why are they wearing disruptive clothing?'

She struggled to explain. 'They are not detainees, sir. They were first seen earlier this evening in the refreshment zone.'

Pyerpoint turned to the intruders. The Doctor gave him a toothy grin and a cheery wave. 'Hello, there. You must be in charge.'

'Do not address me in such familiar terms,' snapped

Pyerpoint. 'I am a High Archon and the station administrator.'

'Are you really?' The Doctor took Pyerpoint's hand and shook it vigorously. 'That must be very interesting.' He gestured about vaguely. 'Do you administrate all of this? How clever.'

Pyerpoint pulled his hand away. He stared at the Doctor suspiciously. 'Are you a lunatic?'

Spiggot emerged from a lift on level seven of the Rock and checked the time. At this time of night there'd be only minimum security on duty at computer control. Artificial night had already fallen. A softer light shone from the lamps positioned at intervals along the stone-flagged walkways.

The call to Pyerpoint had come at exactly the right moment. Spiggot couldn't have prayed for a better distraction. With the station administrator off his back, he was free to roam the corridors unchallenged. He liked it that way. The people he passed didn't know him and he didn't know them. He enjoyed the feeling of freedom that brought him. It was so different back on Five, where he was always being recognized and pestered for his autograph. But then, that was the price he had to pay for being so successful at his job.

The station's computer control centre was up ahead, at the end of this long corridor. He watched from a shadowy corner as an overalled worker emerged from the huge oak doors and signed himself off by running a card through a reader built into the decorative stonework of the wall. The worker nodded to him as he passed. That was the trouble with this place, thought Spiggot. They were complacent, couldn't imagine anyone trying it on. He'd seen this sort of thing before. It was a disaster waiting to happen. And it was his job to prevent that, because someone had to.

He reached into his inside pocket and pulled out a black plastic scrambler card. He'd bought it from an informer from the lower north capital, his old neighbourhood. Sure, it wasn't standard police equipment, and sure, if headquarters ever found out he was using it they'd haul his ass over the coals. But hell, they knew the way he worked by now.

He ran the card through the reader and sneaked through the big doors into computer control.

'Now, let me see if I've got this right,' said the Doctor, who was getting rather tired. 'You're accusing us of being spies and saboteurs?'

Pyerpoint nodded. 'That is correct.'

On the other side of the cell, Margo was preparing the truth serum. She broke open two phials of green liquid and poured them into hypodermics that had thin, glistening needles. The Doctor noted that Margo was breathing deeply, as if she was trying to hold down her temper.

'Well, pardon me for saying so,' he went on, quite unmoved by this gruesome display, 'but I don't think Romana and I would make very good spies, do you? I mean, look at us.' He twirled the ends of his scarf. 'If I was the leader of some subversive organization and one of my operatives walked about dressed like this, I wouldn't send him on a high risk mission to a top security area, I'd sack him.'

Margo edged closer to Romana. She prepared the hypodermic, squirting a few drops of the serum from its tip. 'Roll up your sleeve,' she ordered. Her voice was less confident than it had been earlier, thought the Doctor, as if the presence of her superior made her nervous.

Romana sighed and did as she was instructed. 'I don't suppose it will make any difference. This situation is absurd enough already.'

Margo readied the needle. The Doctor leant closer to Romana. 'Do you know, this is going to hurt you more than it's going to hurt me,' he whispered.

Before Margo could inject the fluid, her communicator bleeped. She looked to Pyerpoint for instructions. He nodded. She flicked open the channel.

'Ma'am,' said a voice from the communicator, 'Shom here. The security net registers an intrusion.'

Margo frowned. 'Not again. Where?'

'At computer control itself, ma'am,' Shom replied. 'Your orders?'

To the Doctor's surprise, it was Pyerpoint who reacted most noticeably to this news. 'Damn him!' he snarled. He flicked open his own communicator. 'This is Pyerpoint. Send a squad to computer control immediately. I want the intruder brought to the detention area, cell forty!'

'Right away, sir.'

Margo looked anxiously at Pyerpoint. She lowered the hypodermic needle. 'What is going on, sir?' she demanded. Her thick eyebrows knotted in a frown. 'Two security alerts in under an hour. Are these incidents connected?'

Pyerpoint stared at the Doctor. 'Oh yes. Your role as a decoy suddenly becomes very clear.'

The Doctor smiled at him innocently. 'Not to me, it doesn't.'

Spiggot looked around the large control centre. It was different in design from the rest of the station. More modern. A cluster of consoles faced a wide screen that displayed a constantly shifting pattern of data. The walls were lined with gadgetry and computer banks. The night watch consisted of only five officers, relaxing in their padded chairs. Some were drinking coffee, others were playing games. The atmosphere was relaxed and comfortable.

Yeah, thought Spiggot. Wide open. He sauntered over to a line of consoles ranged against a wall. He sat down and started to work on the entry codes he would need to access information from the security net. As he'd expected, the codes were triple variant, the toughest of the lot. If somebody had the skills to enter a system like this and play about with it, they'd have to be a genius. He let his fingers dance over the keyboard, and waited for the inevitable outcome.

'There!' a voice shouted behind him. He spun round in his chair. Three uniformed guards had entered the control centre, blasters raised. 'Get away from that console!' their leader shouted nervously.

Spiggot grinned and stood up. 'All right, sonny. Don't worry yourself.' He tapped the console. 'It's all in one piece, you know.'

He raised his hands. 'Back to see Mr Pyerpoint, then, is it?'

'You are agents of Planet Five police,' Pyerpoint said. 'Confess your involvement with Spiggot.'

The Doctor was confused. 'Hold on, hold on. A minute ago, we were spies. Now you think we're police. I wish you'd make up your mind.' He looked around the bare metal cell. 'I'm feeling rather tired. How long have we been standing up, Romana?'

'Forty-nine minutes and twenty-one seconds.'

'You can drop this façade,' Pyerpoint continued. 'Stop attempting to confuse the issue.'

'Me, confuse the issue?' the Doctor spluttered. 'My dear fellow, you're doing a very good job yourself. I mean, I'm not even sure what the issue is any more, and even if I did, the last thing I'd do would be to attempt to confuse it.'

'Stop talking,' Pyerpoint ordered.

He stalked over to the corner where Margo was standing. She was staring at the floor and breathing deeply. The Doctor strained his ears to pick up their conversation. They were an odd couple.

'You've been on duty for twenty hours, Margo,' Pyerpoint told her quietly. 'Return to your cabin. I will deal with this matter.'

Her head jerked up sharply. 'Are you questioning my competence as chief of security?' Her lower lip juddered.

'Of course not.' He lowered his voice. 'However, I

36

now understand the situation. These two were acting as decoys for that police officer from Five.' His face twisted with anger. 'The police treat us like fools.'

Margo frowned. 'That does not explain how they came to be aboard, sir.'

'I will discover that,' he reassured her. 'Now, please, Margo, return to your cabin.' He laid one of his wrinkled hands on her shoulder in a protective gesture. 'I don't want to have to order you.'

Margo brushed him off and left the cell. He stared after her, his expression unreadable.

The Doctor exchanged a glance with Romana. 'She's very uptight,' Romana observed.

'They both are,' said the Doctor. 'But she seems to be heading for a nervous breakdown.'

'Hmm. Hypertension? The result of a lifestyle of constant self-denial. Could an incident like this be enough to set it off?'

'Well, I hope not. I should feel terribly guilty.'

'Don't worry, Doctor. I imagine you've set off quite a few nervous breakdowns in your time.'

'Really? How kind of you to say.'

Spiggot shook off the restraining arms of the guards as they escorted him into the detention area. 'All right, sonny. I'm a big boy now. I can look after myself.'

He looked at the rows of cells. Even millions of miles out in space, in the middle of an asteroid, a prison still smelt like a prison. They could scrub up and slop out as much as they liked, but it was still there. The stench of too many hard luck stories.

The woman he'd seen earlier, outside Pyerpoint's office, was hurrying past. He raised a hand in greeting, but she'd already pushed past him. Her expression told him all that he needed to know. Intriguing. She was losing it, cracking up under the strain. He'd seen it too often to mistake the signs. And she was the chief of security. He'd found another weakness up here.

He was pushed into cell forty. As he'd expected, Pyerpoint was standing there, rouged cheeks stretched in indignation. But standing nearby were two real freakos. There was a guy who looked, well, big. He was tall and had a weird, intense expression. His big blue eyes looked as if they were about to pop out of his head. He'd probably been at the happy pills, whoever he was. His hair exploded from his head in wild curls and he had huge white teeth. He was wearing clothes that had gone out of fashion, if they'd ever been in, hundreds of years ago.

The girl with him was equally striking, but for very different reasons. She was a stunner. Long blonde hair, knowing smile. There was something about her that intrigued Spiggot. He thought he knew everything about women, but this one was something special. She had a kind of haughty, untouchable air about her.

'Mr Spiggot,' Pyerpoint said, 'it is within my authority to arrest you and your colleagues on counts of unlawful entry, trespass and causing an affray. What do you say?'

Spiggot thought quickly. Colleagues, old Pyerpoint had said. He took a quick look at the freaks. Who in starfire were they? They looked like Romanies. 'Colleagues?'

Pyerpoint became even angrier. 'It's obvious that you sent them here to distract us from your activities.'

Spiggot considered his options. It was the kind of quick-fire thinking under pressure that made him the man he was. Perhaps this was just what was needed. A handy distraction. And it couldn't do him any harm to keep in with this pair and find out what they were up to. They didn't look like crims, but how had they got aboard?

The tall man spoke. His voice was unlike anything Spiggot had heard before. It was deep and resonant, with an air of authority to it, cultured, but its origins were unplaceable. As if the guy had sprung out of some strange nowhere. 'Er, Administrator,' he said to Pyerpoint. 'I'm afraid that I've never met this gentleman before.'

38

Spiggot stepped forward and sighed theatrically. 'It's all right. Don't bother.' He turned to Pyerpoint. 'They are with me.'

'I knew it,' said the High Archon. 'On this occasion, the police have gone too far.'

The tall man held up a finger. 'Excuse me, but, as I seem to keep saying, I have no idea what's going on —'

He was interrrupted by a bleep from Pyerpoint's communicator. A voice said, 'Shom, sir. We've just received a coded instruction from Planet Five police. Message reads: Accord every access to Detective Inspector Frank Spiggot.'

Yeah, thought Spiggot. Right on time.

Pyerpoint bristled. 'On what authority?'

'The order was countercoded with the ministerial seal, sir. Top priority.'

'Yes, thank you, I do understand what that means.' Pyerpoint clicked the channel off and raised a hand to his head. A pulse was throbbing on his left temple. Well rattled, thought Spiggot.

'It appears the situation has changed somewhat,' he said, as calmly as he could.

Spiggot grinned and tried to restrain himself from looking too pleased. 'That's quite all right, sir. All charges against me dropped?'

Pyerpoint nodded. 'Of course. I shall be lodging a formal complaint with the police authority regarding your methods.'

'Think nothing of it,' the tall stranger said graciously. 'This kind of thing happens to us all the time, doesn't it, Romana?'

The girl nodded. 'Almost too often. Er, shall we be going, then, Doctor?'

Spiggot was surprised when the tall freak walked over and slapped a hearty hand on his shoulder. The weirdo had caught on quicker than the girl, but he was taking things too far. Who the hell was he?

'Oh no,' he boomed. 'We've got to help our old friend

Frank out with his latest case, haven't we?'

Spiggot decided to make the best he could out of the situation he'd landed himself in. 'Of course,' he said, smiling. 'We make the perfect team, don't we, er, Doctor?'

Pyerpoint signalled for the cell door to be opened and ushered them out. 'I'll assign you rooms for the night. There are some workers' quarters unoccupied on level five.'

'Hold up, mate,' said Spiggot. 'What about the guest suites on level six?'

'They are reserved for Archons on circuit duty,' said Pyerpoint.

'Well, unreserve them,' said Spiggot. He strode off down the corridor.

As they followed Spiggot, Romana coughed to gain the Doctor's attention. 'Yes?'

'Do we know what we're doing?'

He thought for a moment. 'Well, I know what we're doing,' he said emphatically, and hurried off down the corridor after their rescuer.

Margo felt hot tears gathering as she stumbled from the lift and slammed the shutter behind her. She collapsed against a wall and pressed her fingers to her eyes. There was a slight alteration in the rumble of the asteroid's engines as it ploughed away on its newly authorized course. The artificial gravity field adjusted to compensate and she was thrown forward.

She looked up. She didn't recognize her surroundings. This wasn't the staff residential wing on level five. This was the basement. She was sure she'd pressed the correct button in the lift. Or had she? She remembered tumbling into the lift and reaching for the control panel, her hand reaching automatically for the button marked 5. There must have been an error in the lift's programming.

She picked herself up and straightened her uniform.

This behaviour was unacceptable. She had to control herself, concentrate, and relax. She had to find her way back to her cabin.

The lift had been summoned away. She wiped her eyes with the sleeve of her tunic and thanked fortune that there was nobody around to see her in this state. This attack had been the worst. Most importantly, Pyerpoint had noticed something was wrong.

Their partnership went back eighteen years, back to his appointment as administrator. They had worked together closely. He was the nearest she had to a friend, and they dined together occasionally. They talked about politics between courses. Their opinions were always the same.

The first attacks had come about a year ago. Sudden panics, worries, nervous twitches. Now the slightest disruption of her routine could bring about the nausea. She knew she should report herself to the station medic, but the prospect of humiliation deterred her. Events of the last few months were jumbled up, dates were unclear in her mind.

And then there were the things that she was writing in her room. It was as if she was losing her grip on her personality.

It was inevitable that there would be a major security breach with her in this condition. Tonight's events shouldn't have come as a surprise, but she was shaken. She'd only sunk this deep once before, and on that occasion at least she'd been locked in her room, in private.

She heard a muffled shout from the end of the corridor. It had come from behind a large wooden door. Something urged her to investigate. She walked towards the door and suddenly realized where she was. Stokes's gallery. She'd only been here once before, when she'd been giving a group of ministers a tour of the station. Both she and Pyerpoint considered Stokes an irritation. He was another example of the government's idiocy. Why had they ever allowed him to take up residence on the Rock? He was loud and offensive, like his work, always emerging from unlikely corners at the worst of times.

She put her hand to the doorknob of the gallery. Something made her twist it. To her surprise, it opened. There was no reason why she should go in. She decided to pull herself together and turn back.

She found she couldn't. Something was calling her, pulling her forward. Her stomach knotted as she turned to leave. Unable to resist, she pushed open the door and entered the gallery.

The large hall was in darkness. Distorted images of the criminal dead stared at her from all sides. She passed a jar that contained what looked like pickled intestines and a mask cast in helicon that seemed to smile as she passed it. She shuddered. What was she doing here?

There was something moving in the darkness up ahead. She crept behind one of the pillars as a figure emerged into the light. It was Stokes. He was dressed in an ancient pair of striped pyjamas and was tying up the cord of a paint-splattered dressing gown.

'Damned insomnia,' he was muttering. 'Wretched pills have no effect.' She watched as he picked up a framed purple print and sneered at it. 'Twenty sales. Six hundred apiece. For the work of a gossoon from the Irontown slums. It defies all sense.'

He crossed to where a canvas rested on an easel and snapped on a small lamp that gave out a strong green light. His broad bald head and contemptuously curled lips took on a ghoulish aspect. He fished out some brushes that had been resting in a jar of water and sorted through some paints.

Margo squinted to make out the picture on the canvas. She recognized Stokes's subject as Naomi Blakemore, the murderess terminated that evening. The old woman's gnarled hands were crossed on her lap. Her face wore a smile that might have looked kindly in life. But Stokes had twisted it, and in his work, she had become a vicious skeleton.

Stokes settled himself before the canvas. Margo contemplated his big green head from behind. How easy it would be to smash it in. To crack him open like the egg he resembled. Or to watch his bones dissolve, to flatten him somehow, scramble him, crush him into a bundle of flesh and bone and blood. She licked her lips. A feeling of power ran through her body. Her muscles felt stronger. It was a good way to feel.

'Ridiculous,' said Stokes. 'How can I compose myself in this light?' He sat up and unconsciously flicked on a monitor. Text filled the screen, offering the options of the station's entertainment service. Stokes thought for a second, picked up a remote control, and requested information from the courtrooms.

Margo flinched. She blinked and her murderous visions faded. Why was she here, creeping about like this?

Stokes was reading aloud from the screen. 'Termination orders, April 21st. Yes, yes, know all that. Naomi Blakemore, poor darling. What a subject. One of the old school, indeed.' He patted his canvas with genuine affection. 'Seldin Vranch, yes, the fraudster, boring, boring. Jarrigan Voltt. Which was he? Oh, yes, that phlegmatic idiot they brought down this evening. They must have been very keen to get rid of him, haven't had one jump the queue that quickly in years. Poor blighter.'

He yawned, stretched, and turned off the screen. 'I'm sure,' he said as he stood, 'that as soon as my poor head touches the pillow I shall find myself alert once more to the dance of the muse.' He disappeared into the darkness.

Margo felt sick and dizzy. She forced herself away from the pillar and staggered towards the exit. In the darkness it was difficult to orientate. She stopped and tried to get her bearings.

She heard breathing nearby. She moved towards the exit, and a hand was clapped on her shoulder. Her attacker shone a small torch in her face. It illuminated his own. She recognized him as Zy, the young student assigned by the educational authorities as Stokes's apprentice.

'What are you doing here?' he demanded. Margo noted that he was wearing his day clothes, as if he was going out.

'I – I came to see Mr Stokes,' she stammered. She pulled away from him and straightened up. She couldn't bear to let anyone see her like this.

'Mr Stokes'll be asleep,' Zy told her. 'Along with everyone else.' He eyed her suspiciously. 'Don't you trust me, is that it? Coming to check up on me?'

Margo barely heard him. She tried to reply, but her head suddenly felt as if it was being drawn away from her body. She felt that something was trying to consume her, something that she couldn't name. She reeled back. When she next looked at Zy, she saw him as an insignificant obstruction. Something that could be brushed away with ease, crushed out of existence in a moment. He was, after all, a Normal.

And all Normals must die.

She cried out and fell to the ground, wailing and clutching at her head. Where had that thought originated? What did it mean? What was happening to her?

Zy, confused, backed away from her. 'I don't know what you're playing at,' she heard him say, 'but it's nothing to do with me.'

He left.

Moments later, she pulled herself up from the floor and followed him out. The pain had returned, coursing through her bones.

She reached her bare cabin after an hour of confused staggering through the empty, darkened corridors of the station. She threw herself onto her small single bed and closed her eyes. She knew she would not sleep tonight.

Her eyes opened wide. A spasm rippled through her left hand. She watched as it jerked up, clenched and unclenched, out of her control.

The writing was about to happen again.

Margo's hand led her from the bed and over to a set of

44

drawers. It unlocked the top drawer and searched through a jumble of computer manuals, maps and crumpled sheets of paper. In one corner a tiny device winked with a steady green light.

The hand pulled out a notepad. It found a clean sheet of paper and a pen, and started to write.

Margo watched as the hand produced a stream of symbols. The clean page filled up rapidly with equations solved in an unfamiliar algebra.

4

The Investigators

The Rock of Judgement ploughed past a shower of bright-tailed comets that were whizzing through the system on a course equally erratic to its own. The feeble electric light that broached the plastiglass of its many windows grew stronger as artificial morning commenced.

Lights throughout the high hallways, courtrooms, kitchens, computer rooms, cells and offices of the station brightened. Soft music tinkled from concealed speakers. A recorded voice announced softly, 'Wake up everybody. It is time to begin work. Today is April the twenty-second. There's plenty of work to do. So please, everybody, wake up.'

Romana walked briskly along the deep carpeted corridor of level six. She tapped on the door of the Doctor's suite. There was no reply. She might have known he wouldn't stay put for the night. He had probably been out causing all sorts of mischief.

She pushed open the door and walked in to the luxury apartment. As she'd expected, the silver sheets on the four poster had not been disturbed. She was about to leave when a snore came from the other side of the room. It issued from a high-backed chair that had been moved to face the cabin's porthole. The Doctor's coat was draped over its back. 'Doctor?' she called. 'Doctor?'

He leapt startled from the chair, put up his arms and took on a fighting stance, then relaxed as he recognized her. 'Oh, it's only you.'

'What have you been doing all night?'

He beckoned her forward and pointed to a table, upon which a collection of large books with yellowing pages crammed with small print had been upended. 'Romana,' he said gravely. 'I know everything.'

'I already knew that, Doctor.'

'No, I don't mean everything, I mean everything.' He indicated the books again. 'These belong to the usual occupant of this room, some judge person. Probably away hanging people, somewhere.'

Romana picked up a few of the books and inspected their spines. '*The Law, the State, the People . . . Legal Procedures in the Ultimate Court . . .*' She grimaced. '*Jokes Cracked by Archon Tablor.*'

'I know where we are and what goes on here,' the Doctor said. 'I've read most of that lot.'

'It can't have been that interesting, you fell asleep.'

'Well, I had a long day. Romana, what does Uva Beta Uva mean to you?'

She thought back to her Academy studies. 'It's near the centre of the Earth's galaxy. The star's a torroidal elliptic with fourteen planets. Colonized in earth year 2230.'

The Doctor looked somewhat taken aback. 'Spot on, spot on.' He moved to the automatic food unit and took out a slice of toast. With his free hand he put on his coat, hat and scarf. 'Now, this place is not only a court. It's also where they mete out punishment to all of their worst criminals. Murderers, mostly. A lot of the people in custody here are very dangerous, and many of them would like a chance to get out, or get rescued.' He looked out at the stars. 'A few million miles of vacuum makes a pretty good prison wall. Difficult to spoon your way through that. The place opened for business over forty years ago. What's more, the course is constantly shifting. Nobody outside can be quite sure exactly where it is.'

They watched as a green planet of middling size passed by slowly.

'A bit like us and the Black Guardian,' Romana said ruefully.

'Hmm. Now, eighty per cent of those on murder charges are convicted, and ninety-five per cent of that number end up in a particle reversal chamber. Gruesome, but what you'd expect from the human race, more or less. The few that escape that fate are transmatted back to Five and prison.' He ate the last corner of his toast. 'By this time they'll be feeling a bit jaded in these parts. Their mineral wealth dried up a long time ago.'

Romana thought back to the events of the previous night. 'I suppose it explains the drugs in the bar. The people who work here must require suppressants to keep them happy for such long spells of duty off planet.'

The Doctor nodded. 'Yes, although I doubt whether the station administrator and his chums partake of that stuff.' He wiped his fingers on a napkin. 'Let's go and find Spiggot, shall we?'

Romana nodded. 'And when his friends turn up? The people we're supposed to be?'

The Doctor grinned, pleased to be several steps ahead for once. 'Spiggot is a trained investigator, a high-ranking officer, right?'

'Right.'

'And he goes blundering in to their computer control centre, which he must know to be bristling with detection devices,' the Doctor said. 'Then greets two total strangers as trusted colleagues.'

'Perhaps he's just stupid,' Romana pointed out.

The Doctor shook his head. 'Perhaps he's just too clever by half.'

In the duty room, Shom took a deep breath. He looked again at his wristwatch. There was no choice. Procedure was procedure. He had to refer staff problems to the administrator, whoever they involved.

He called Pyerpoint's office. 'Sir. The chief hasn't reported for duty this morning.'

A brief silence. 'Strange. Have you tried her quarters?'

'There's no answer, sir,' Shom said, almost apologetically. 'She seems to have removed her communicator. Nobody on staff's seen her since last night.'

'Hold.' Pyerpoint went off line. Shom wondered how the old man was going to handle the matter. Shom had noticed something odd about Margo in the last few months, but never thought she would disappear like this.

Pyerpoint came back on line, his voice more confident. 'Shom,' he ordered. 'I intend to take full responsibility for the chief of security. You are to take on her duties for the present. I want no mention of the matter in any official report and there is to be no discussion of it within ranks, or outside. You understand this?'

'Yes, sir.'

'Furthermore, you are not to attempt to locate or contact the chief. I have known her for many years and I feel it will be better for me to deal with this, privately.'

'Yes, sir.'

Pyerpoint paused, then added, 'I hope I have done well to place my trust in you, Shom. Trust is an invaluable commodity. One ounce is worth a ton of belzite.'

Shom said nervously, 'I understand, sir. Your confidence is appreciated.'

Pyerpoint broke the link and sat back in his chair. The fingers of his left hand drummed anxiously on the desk.

A bleeper sounded from inside the desk. Pyerpoint pulled open a drawer and produced a small rectangular device that had a speaker built into the side. He pressed a button and a familiar voice came from the speaker.

'Ah, Mr Spiggot. It's a lovely morning.'

Spiggot's hand was being shaken vigorously. Three seconds earlier he had been asleep, lying with his face immersed in the folds of the bounciest pillow that the station's launderers could provide. It took another few moments to identify the grinning loon that had shaken him awake. 'Er, good morning, Doctor.'

He sat up and pulled the silver sheets close to his naked form as he saw that the girl had also entered the room. Not that he had anything to hide from a woman.

'Hey,' he croaked, 'what time is this? I feel like a . . . like a . . .' He floundered for a simile as his hand stretched out, also searching.

Romana threw him a pair of briefs from a pile of clothes stacked at the other side of the room. 'Are you looking for these?'

The Doctor snatched them away. He shook his head at the blue spotted pattern and handed them to Spiggot. 'I thought you were supposed to be in plain clothes.'

Spiggot covered his embarrassment quickly and emerged from the bed. 'You two are the craziest pair I've ever seen Central put together,' he told them as he reached for more clothes.

Romana spoke. 'Perhaps we ought to explain. We're not from Cent—'

The Doctor interrupted her, furiously gesturing for her to pipe down. 'Yes, well, what Romana means to say is that we didn't come directly from Central.' He leant conspiratorially close to Spiggot and whispered, 'Do you know, they didn't even give us a proper briefing.'

Spiggot raised an eyebrow. Held his gaze. 'They didn't?'

'No. Very irregular, I thought. So perhaps you'd like to give us details of our mission.'

Spiggot pulled his black sweater over his head and crossed to his cabin's food unit. He took a plastic cup and filled it with coffee, sighed a few times, took a few sips of the scalding fluid, walked back and forth, and then turned to face them.

'It started about two months back,' he began. 'Down on Five, one of the smart boys in the tech div labs picked something up.' He grinned. 'And that's pretty rare, I can tell you.' He waited for the Doctor and Romana to respond to his witticism but they only stared at him as if he had released a bad smell into the air and they were too polite to mention it. 'They were running a comparative systems check on their security computers using the system here. Nothing odd in that. Except that it registered minor faults in the data core that backs up the Rock's security net.'

'What sort of minor faults?' the Doctor asked.

Spiggot sipped at his coffee again. 'Big ones. About as big as a minor fault can get before it becomes a major fault. In a nutshell, the security system at this place is cracking up. So far the damage hasn't advanced, but it could get a lot worse.'

Romana settled herself on a couch. 'Why didn't you just tell them and allow them to repair it?'

Spiggot pointed a long finger at her. 'There's the rub,' he said. 'I've got a contact down in the big smoke, worked in computers years back. He's pulled off a few frauds, but nothing too big. Deal is, I ignore him, he helps me when I need him.' He finished the coffee and crushed the cup. 'I guess we're both outsiders in a way.'

'Get on with it,' the Doctor urged. 'The computers.'

Spiggot decided to ignore the Doctor's rudeness. He probably couldn't handle the idea of a loner getting results by twisting the rules. 'Yeah, well, my contact is sharper than anyone in tech div. He can hack his way into deep compu-space as easy as that.' To emphasize his point, Spiggot attempted to click his fingers but failed. Undaunted he continued.

'He took a look at the print-outs I smuggled out to him and said there was no way it was an internal fault. Someone was degrading the system. Someone clever. Someone more than clever.' He poured himself another coffee into another plastic cup. 'A genius.'

'Did you check up on the people here?' the Doctor queried.

Spiggot nodded. 'Every last one. None of them have form, but you'd expect that. Thing is, not one of the creeps has the nous to crash the system open. Whoever it is, we can't let 'em know we're on to them.' He took a huge gulp of the coffee. 'So I decided to come up here, to take a look about, on the quiet. But nothing seems to add up.'

'No, it doesn't,' the Doctor agreed. Suddenly he stood up and made for the door. 'Well, come on, Romana.'

The girl looked confused. 'Where exactly are we going?'

He stared at her as if she was a fool. 'To begin our investigations, of course. There's not a moment to lose.'

Spiggot stepped forward, worried. That wasn't the way he'd planned to use them. 'I wouldn't try computer control again, Doctor. Leave that side of things to me. I reckon you should just hang about, find out what you can.'

The Doctor fixed him with a manic stare. 'What, fade into the background, keep a low profile, listen out for vital clues, that sort of thing?'

Spiggot nodded. 'That'll do for the moment.'

'Good. We do that sort of thing very well, don't we, Romana?'

'Yes, I do, Doctor,' she said and led the way out.

Spiggot watched them depart thankfully. Things were going well. That pair of Romany crazies were fitting into his plan like they'd been part of it from the start. It was time to get on with the job.

He drained his coffee, crushed the plastic cup, checked his blaster, tucked it away in his jacket, and hurried out.

Pyerpoint switched off the listening device and replaced it in his desk drawer. He waited a moment, then snapped open a communicator channel.

'Computer control? This is High Archon Pyerpoint. I want you to carry out a deep systems check on the data core of the security net. Yes, you heard correctly.'

The Doctor and Romana entered the lift. As soon as the shutter was closed, the Doctor reached out and pressed a button at random.

'Spiggot's playing some sort of game,' Romana

observed. 'There must be a bugging device in that cabin. He wasn't talking to us but to Pyerpoint.'

The Doctor was lost in thought. 'Yes.'

'But we're playing along with him?'

'For a while.' The Doctor's huge blue eyes stared at the wall of the lift as if it was the most significant thing in the universe.

'We could always just go and have a look at the computer,' Romana suggested.

The Doctor licked his lips. 'The computer?' he said gravely. 'Oh, I think there's considerably more at stake here than a machine on the blink.'

'Is there?'

The Doctor's mood switched suddenly. 'Yes!' he cried almost manically. 'Never overlook the elementary details, Romana.'

She groaned. 'Which elementary details?'

'Never theorize ahead of the facts, either,' he told her. 'First rule of detection. Besides, you're a bright girl, I'm sure you can work it out for yourself.'

The lift came to a halt and the Doctor breezed out. Romana directed her most venomous glance at his back and followed.

Spiggot pushed open the doors of computer control. Pyerpoint stood in the centre of the room, surrounded by a team of technicians. An animated display of the security net's data core, a twisting red cylinder, cartwheeled on the main screen. It looked to be in perfect health. Spiggot nodded. A full inspection of each of the data core's four hundred and seventy-seven functions would busy the technicians for a tedious fortnight of processor checks and foreign program search and sweeps. His plan had worked out a treat. They were going to do this part of the job for him.

Still, he had to make sure he didn't let on. He put on his best look of surprise and disappointment. 'What's going on here?' he asked Pyerpoint.

Pyerpoint turned to him and said, 'A routine investigation. It is standard procedure for the security net to be subjected to random examination, at the discretion of the station administrator.'

'Oh yeah?' Spiggot's eyes flicked over to the console where he had been apprehended last night. The keyboard was in pieces and a couple of technicians had their heads inside it. He tried to look more upset.

'Is there any information you require from the net?' Pyerpoint asked with a self-satisfied smile. 'I'm sure one of our people can retrieve it for you. Now that you possess full clearance, you have only to ask.'

Spiggot glared at him. 'That's all right,' he said bitterly. 'Don't trouble yourself.' He turned his back on Pyerpoint and left the control centre.

Great stuff.

The observation dome was built into the roof of the station's highest level. An upturned bowl of clear plastiglass with a circumference of a hundred metres, it overlooked the stars. Each worker was allowed four hours' rest time in the observation dome per week, at periods allocated on the staff rota.

Margo had visited the observation dome only when a routine patrol took her there. The spectacle it offered did not inspire her. She took her satisfaction in writing reports and giving orders, and if her eyes ever did turn to the stars it was only to check that the asteroid's speed was as projected.

The dome's supervisor was therefore understandably surprised when she walked in alone wearing her plain white nightgown. He stopped himself from going to greet her. It was unwise to question the behaviour of an officer of senior rank, however strange.

He watched as she went calmly, in her bare feet, to the edge of the dome, put her hands to its side, and gazed out into space.

* * *

Yes, there is Copralis, winking through the swirling dusts of the Vyl nebula; the reference point, at relative galactic coordinates eight five four nine south west by four six nine one north by north east. Planet Two is visible at a distance of about sixty-five million miles. It will be a simple task to confirm the station's relative position and speed and align the homing signal.

Margo shook her head and the inner voice faded. A jumbled group of algebraic figures were equating in long disused sections of her mind. But she knew nothing of advanced mathematics and possessed only rudimentary skills in applied astrophysics.

Her legs were quaking. She leant her head against the glass and tried to steady herself. Trickles of sweat were collecting in her eyebrows. The tips of her fingers felt hot.

Something made her raise her head. An impatience that seemed to come from inside, from the owner of the voice. It directed her eyes back to the star it called Copralis.

'Vectors at standard cruising speed,' it whispered through her lips. 'Correlated to the adjacent angle of velocity and accountable factors of stellar drift . . .'

The dome supervisor had left his desk. 'Chief, is there anything I can do for you?' he asked nervously. 'Chief?'

She snapped her head up. 'Fool!' she spat, a line of saliva dribbling over her chin. 'They are . . .' She put a hand to her head and howled at the stars.

'What's . . . happening . . . to me?' she wailed. She reached for her communicator. She had left it attached to her uniform, back in her cabin. 'Where . . . where . . .'

The supervisor flicked on his own communicator. 'Mr Shom,' he called, 'please come to the observation dome. The chief is here, I think she's ill.'

The door of the observation dome slid open and the Doctor and Romana walked in. They stopped as they caught sight of the situation.

* * *

55

Shom looked nervously around computer control, but the technicians were too busy with their checks to have heard the call. Before he could reply, Pyerpoint put up a hand. He broke into the call. 'What's going on there?' he demanded, concerned.

'It's the chief,' the dome supervisor started to say, 'she's – '

Margo's voice came from Pyerpoint's communicator. 'Pyer . . . point . . .' she said slowly.

'Isolate her,' Pyerpoint ordered. Shom noted the lines of concern on his face. 'Take her back to her cabin. I will join you there.'

'I am coming, Pyerpoint!' Margo screamed. Her voice was suddenly powerful. 'I am coming for you!'

Pyerpoint shook his head pityingly. 'This situation is tragic, tragic,' he told Shom. He spoke into his communicator. 'Supervisor, restrain the chief.'

Margo struggled from the grip of the supervisor. 'No!' she cried. 'Leave me alone . . . you are . . .' Her face contorted as she bit at her tongue, as if trying to stop herself from speaking.

The Doctor took a step forward, He held her jaw in his hands and looked into her eyes. Something he saw there troubled him. 'Night starvation. You need a good lie down and a dose of salts,' he advised her.

She snarled. Her face was filled with hatred. She pushed the Doctor aside and ran from the dome. The supervisor halted only to register the bizarre attire of the Doctor and Romana and bolted after her.

Romana, perturbed, pushed a stray lock of hair back under her cap. 'She looked almost rabid.'

'Yes, there's something very wrong there,' the Doctor said. 'The breakdown's happened incredibly quickly. Probably been building up for months.'

'Still, I suppose it's none of our concern.' Romana looked through some papers on the vacated desk of the dome supervisor. She held up a sheet of paper

56

triumphantly. 'Oh, look, a map.'

The Doctor looked out at the stars.

Romana examined the map, committing several important locations, including that of the TARDIS, to her memory. 'If the security officer's cracking up, this station really is coming unstuck. Could there be a connection with Spiggot's mission, do you think?'

'Well, everything's connected in some way,' the Doctor replied, nodding to the stars. 'It's the nature of the connection that's important.'

'Don't be so pompous.'

He turned abruptly. 'Is that a map you've got there?'

'Yes.'

'Tell me what's on it.' He made for the exit.

She followed. 'Hmm. Courtrooms.'

'No, no. Tried one, tried 'em all.'

'Dungeons?'

'Absolutely not, I can do that any day of the week.'

'How about the gallery?'

'Ah! Now that sounds more interesting.'

'I've lost her,' the voice of the dome supervisor reported over the communicator. 'Somewhere on level ten, she slipped away from me.'

Pyerpoint switched off the channel. He turned to Shom and whispered, 'Shom, we will locate the chief ourselves. She may return to her cabin.'

Shom nodded. 'Yes, sir.'

Spiggot had returned to his luxury suite and was enjoying his midday meal, provided by the dispenser with its customary lack of culinary aplomb. He finished off the food and sighed. He longed for the simple, plain, traditional cooking of his own folk. Pies, mash and plenty of gravy. Out here in space the grub was flash but tasteless.

Still, he couldn't complain. Everything was going his way, every element falling into place perfectly. His methods had worked again. It looked like he was going to succeed once more. In a way, he thought, it was all so inevitable. Yeah, cracking crimes was the easy part of his life. But what about Angie and the kids? He'd messed up there, and badly.

He stood up. He'd given Pyerpoint enough to worry about, with the security check and the two crazies. The old goat had fallen for it all.

It was time to start the real work.

Shom and Pyerpoint found Margo as she emerged from a lift on level five of the station. Her hair was dishevelled and her eyes stared straight ahead. Her lower lip trembled.

'Margo, you need a rest,' Pyerpoint said gently. He came towards her and placed one of his gnarled hands on her shoulder. 'Let us help you.'

Her face jerked into life as she caught sight of him. 'Yes, rest,' she said oddly, slurring the words. 'I must rest. There is much to be done.'

Shom leapt back as her back straightened and she knocked Pyerpoint's hand away. She shouted, 'I cannot rest! I must have control! The time is close, Pyerpoint!'

Pyerpoint appeared perturbed by her words. 'Sedate her,' he ordered.

Shom unclipped a small stunner from his belt. He leapt forward and pressed it to Margo's neck. She lunged for him, growling ferociously. The sharpened tips of her fingernails scratched his cheek.

'I will . . . have control,' she snarled. Her legs buckled as the drug took effect. 'The time . . . is near . . .' Her eyes rolled under fluttering lids and she collapsed.

Shom rubbed his wounded cheek. The scratch had drawn blood. 'I've never seen the like of it, sir,' he said. 'What's happened to the chief? She's the last person I'd have thought —'

Pyerpoint regained his composure. 'This is not the time to speculate,' he said evenly. 'Margo is very ill. I will take her back to her cabin myself.' His face was filled with what Shom took to be confusion and pity.

Shom nodded uncertainly. He hadn't realized how much Margo meant to the old man. Pyerpoint obviously cared enough to break the rules that he was employed to uphold in order to protect her. It was touching, in a way. 'Right away, sir. Shall I call a medic?'

Pyerpoint shook his head impatiently. 'I will handle this matter. Now, return to your duties and say nothing of this.'

'Splendid!' cried the artist as he stepped back from the completed canvas. He waved his paintbrush about in glee. 'One of my very best. I astound myself! The subject, the materials, the . . .' He appeared to search his extensive vocabulary for the best way to describe the latest pinnacle of his invention. 'The . . . the piquancy! Yes, the piquancy of the whole!'

'Your brushwork is awfully broad,' said the Doctor, who was looking over his shoulder.

'Naturally,' the artist replied. 'It's a very broad work, conceptually speaking.' He broke off and stared at the Doctor. 'And who in the halls of Hades might you be?'

The Doctor bowed. 'Well, I'm the Doctor, this is Romana, and we're travellers, and we thought we'd take a look at your gallery, and . . .' He trailed off as he realized that the artist was not listening.

The fellow was frantically smoothing at his bald head with one hand, attending to hair that had disappeared long ago. The other hand was extended towards Romana. His large rolling eyes were occupied in an active appraisal of her. The Doctor huffed. Romana tended to bring this reaction out in people. It was most irritating.

'Ramona,' the artist said slowly.

'Romana,' she corrected him.

'Romana.' His slippery tongue relished every syllable. He took her hand and planted a small kiss upon it. 'An enchanting name for an enchanting young woman. Where did you come by it?'

'Prydon Academy,' she told him. 'And I'm actually a lady.'

He took a step back and emitted a seedy chuckle from the deepest point of his larynx. 'A lady, oh, of course, yes, I should have realized! A regal vision! The noble brow, the milk white skin, those pert lips.'

The Doctor coughed. 'Er, excuse me?'

The artist ignored him. He led Romana forward until she was standing directly within a pool of light that shone from one of the gallery's hanging lamps. 'Yes, yes!' he enthused. 'You, my dear, will make a scintillating subject.' He leant closer and slipped a long arm around her shoulder. 'Tell me, sweet child, have you ever posed for life classes?'

Romana was untroubled by his attentions. 'Suppose I don't want to be your subject?'

The artist waved a hand dismissively. 'Oh, but my dear, you are so clearly suited to my methods.'

The Doctor tapped him on the shoulder. 'Listen, I –'

'Do you mind, sir? I am conducting business.' He broke off and stared at the Doctor, then at his clothes. His expression altered to one of cautious welcome. 'Don't I know you?'

The Doctor thought for a moment. 'I hope not.'

'You're nothing to do with the old scratcher?'

'Mr Pyerpoint?' the Doctor guessed correctly. 'No.'

'I have it, you're from the arts committee, another of their wretched inspections. Oddstock, is it? No, no, he's dead, isn't he, though how anybody could tell I don't know. You're not that fool Mellenger, and you're certainly not Sybilla Strang, as she's a woman, just about, so . . .' He clicked his fingers. 'I've hit upon it! You're Fenton Breedley, aren't you?'

The Doctor attempted to say no, but the artist was in full flow. 'Caught the teensiest glimpse of your exhibition at the Regional back in '19. Rather unaccomplished. What are you doing here, then?'

'I'm the Doctor and I've never exhibited anything,'

the Doctor gasped.

'We're not inspectors, just visitors,' said Romana.

The artist took a step back. 'Visitors? To the gallery?' He took another look at them. 'I say, you're not *lawyers* or anything?'

The Doctor wandered over to a grotesque sculpture that was mounted on a nearby plinth. Its fierce eyes seemed to stare back at him. 'No. Just visitors. Mr, er . . .'

The artist bowed. 'Stokes, Menlove Ereward Stokes.'

The Doctor nodded an acknowledgement. 'Mr Stokes. What is the point of this collection? It does seem somewhat irregular, having an art gallery at the bottom of a courtroom.'

Stokes raised an affronted eyebrow. 'Does it so? Yes, I suppose to the nescient mind that is how it might appear. The endeavour is entirely mine. I established myself here on this miserable blasted rock seven years ago, on the death of my father. He was a planetary councillor, you know.'

'Oh, really?' the Doctor mumbled, thoroughly unimpressed.

'Yes. But the half-life of public service was not for me. His unfortunate demise provided me with the funds necessary to create this modest snuggery. I am official artist in residence.'

Romana read from a plaque attached to a representation of a deformed creature that was covered in blood. '*Ventol, the three-headed killer of the lower city.* Nasty.'

'Are all your pictures of criminals?' the Doctor asked.

'Yes,' Stokes replied. 'I have employed as my subjects many of the murderous souls to have met their deaths here over the last seven years. Most are happy to trust themselves to me.'

The Doctor shook his head as he examined more of Stokes's work. 'Why can't you paint nice things, like sunflowers?'

'Oh, Doctor. Our society needs a fearless artist to delve into the criminal psyche.'

'Hmm,' the Doctor said doubtfully. 'It'd help if you could do it better.'

Stokes snapped upright. 'What did you say?' He wagged an aggressive finger at the Doctor. 'I suppose those ageing cretins at Gelheissen sent you to check up on me, did they? I'll show them. My genius is before its time. And when I return, I'll show them!'

'I don't like people pointing an aggressive finger at me,' the Doctor told him. 'And I'm afraid I really have no idea what you're talking about.'

Stokes jeered, 'I've faced tougher men than you, Doctor. I have encountered villains worse than you could possibly imagine!'

'Oh, really?'

'Yes. The Zinctown Basher, Strapping Jack, all have passed through my studio. I dared to take a mask of Xais herself! And so your ignorant ramblings are unlikely to impress me!'

A promising argument was interrupted by a polite request from Romana. 'Mr Stokes?'

He smiled. 'Yes, my dear?'

'I was wondering what this piece signifies?' She pointed to a frame that contained a letter.

'That is not my own creation,' Stokes explained, 'but it remains a fascinating item of criminal memorabilia. It's a copy of a letter received by the police authorities shortly after the arrest of the Nisbett firm. Must be, what, five, six, years ago now. Although, of course, they never caught up with the Nisbett brothers themselves. They're still out there somewhere.' He shuddered.

The Doctor squinted up at the letter.

Dear Boss

We have got it in for your sort, after they nicked our lads. We are right down on coppers. We are respectable buisnessmen and we were provoked. You cant pin anything on us. We'll be back,

Charles and Edward Nisbett

'Appalling grammar and spelling,' the Doctor observed. 'And I don't think much of the tone.'

'Not a sentiment to express in their company, Doctor,' said Stokes. 'The kind of business they were involved in was anything but respectable. Extortion, fraud, smuggling, arms dealing, torture, multiple murder. And that was just for openers.'

Romana picked up another exhibit, a purple print that had been leant against a wall. 'Now, I prefer this.'

The Doctor joined her. 'Yes, that's much better. Easy on the eye.'

Stokes snatched the print away. 'You can't be serious, surely.'

'I think it's your best work,' Romana complimented him.

'Perhaps because it's not his,' a voice said from behind them. A young man had entered the gallery. He was smiling broadly. 'It's mine.'

Stokes threw the picture at him. 'And you can have it.' He gestured to the Doctor and Romana. 'Don't imagine that these people have any critical skills, Zy. I mean, just look at them.'

Zy sneered at him. 'You know, Men, there are two things I have to tell you.'

Stokes sneered back. 'Oh, really? My ears await.'

'First is, I've made another sale today and upped the price. Second is,' he paused for effect, his clear blue eyes glistening with malice, 'I'm putting in a bid to take this place over when your lease runs out. End of July, isn't it?'

Stokes flushed as purple as Zy's picture. 'You! An Irontown upstart barely out of his creche! I have to laugh! And how do you intend to raise the funds?'

'The government have agreed to grant me an award,' Zy said smoothly. 'I spoke to the arts committee last night over vidi-link. And I can get the rest through my sales.'

Stokes's arms flapped furiously. 'Ludicrous! It's my duty to warn you, I suppose. Your talent stretches no further than your own deluded imagination!'

The Doctor nudged Romana and they slipped out of the gallery, leaving the artists to their argument. The raised voices echoed out of the gallery and along the corridor leading to the lift.

'Oh yes?' Zy was saying. 'And when was your last sale? What do you really think you're doing here with all this junk? It's so much garbage.'

Stokes screamed, 'Cretin! Out! Out!'

The shelves of the station's library creaked with books, thick volumes crammed with judgements, rulings, transcripts and statutes. Staircases curled from shadowy corners, tempting the browser up or down to specialized sections on agricultural policy, reports on remand reform, successfully contested libel actions. Pale librarians shuffled along the aisles, arranging and re-arranging the texts. Barristers and their clerks spoke in loud, bluff voices and stood importantly on step ladders, reaching for obscure sources as if they were pioneers planting flags on towering summits.

Spiggot made his way to the far end of the library, and a section of shelving devoted to what were known as dead files. It was here that papers pertaining to matters dealt with by the courts of the Rock found their final resting place, finished cases that waited five years for public interest to fade before being fed to the shredder. Spiggot coughed at the dust released as he tugged one of the crumbling cardboard files from its position. He couldn't believe that this stuff hadn't been transferred to computer. The legal profession's centuries-old distrust of technology was scarcely credible. Another area of weakness.

He peered at the faded writing on the edges of each bulging file. The cases were ordered by a complicated numbering system that made no sense. He gritted his teeth. He wasn't used to grubbing about with damp old files. There were rows and rows of the things. It might take him hours to find what he was looking for.

And all the while, valuable time was passing.

* * *

Pyerpoint led the dazed Margo into her cabin and settled her on to her bed. Her head turned from side to side on her starched pillow. 'I . . .' she started to say. 'I . . .'

'Ssh now,' Pyerpoint told her. His attention was taken by the open pad on her desk drawer. He picked it up and stared at the rows of equations.

'Margo,' he told her. 'You must stay here and relax.' He sat on the bed and took one of her hands. 'Do you understand me? You must stay here. Relax. Don't trouble yourself. Everything will come right soon. I will protect you, old friend.' He gave the hand a slight squeeze of reassurance.

She smiled up at him and nodded. 'Yes, relax,' she whispered. 'I must relax.' Her eyes closed and her head fell back on the pillow.

Pyerpoint waited a moment. He carefully removed his hand from hers and stood up. He looked down at the mathematical symbols on the page in his hand and frowned. 'What is she doing? I've done all I can for her. What is this?'

He replaced the sheet of paper and left the cabin, locking the door behind him.

Margo's eyes opened.

Pyerpoint took a lift up to the courtrooms. He walked with a heavy step along the crowded corridors, his grim presence enough to startle into silence an excited huddle of lawyers noisily engaged in arguing a technical point at the end of the working week.

He was about to return to his office when a call came through from Shom. 'Sir, Spiggot has gone to the library. Do you want us to find out what he's up to?'

Pyerpoint thought. 'No, Shom,' he said. 'I understand the way his mind works. He is attempting to confuse and divert us. Leave him to it.'

The Doctor and Romana watched Pyerpoint from a nearby alcove. He straightened his tunic and entered the suite that contained his office.

The Doctor was puzzled. 'What's old Spiggot doing in the library, then?' he wondered aloud. 'Unless – ah!' He held up a finger. 'Yes, of course!'

'He's probably gone there to check files about whatever it is he's not telling us,' Romana said casually.

'Why do you always have to spoil it for me?' asked the Doctor. 'You're not supposed to have worked that out yet.' He chewed his bottom lip. 'There is something you can do for me, though.'

'What, check up on Spiggot?'

'No, no. Just stay here and keep an eye on things. I won't be long.' He fumbled in his pockets, produced a small tin whistle and blew into it. 'We need K9. I thought I'd meet him on the way.'

He started to walk away. Romana grabbed his arm. 'Doctor. Why do we need K9?'

He grinned back at her. 'Because K9 can carry out instant checks on computers.'

'You said the computer wasn't important.'

The Doctor nodded. 'Yes, I did. But perhaps its apparent lack of importance is in itself important, eh?'

He tried to leave again. Again Romana stopped him. 'Doctor?'

'Yes, what now?'

'You're very irritating.'

He smiled. 'I suppose I am. But it's ages since I got the chance to do some good old-fashioned criminal investigation.' His tone suddenly became very serious. 'There's a crime behind a crime here, Romana. And Spiggot isn't telling us, or Pyerpoint, or anybody else, half of what he knows.' He strode off down the corridor.

Stokes was alone in the gallery. He had gathered Zy's materials and cases and tipped them into a heap. He wiped away a trail of dribble that slid from his mouth at the prospect of losing the project he had originated to that young fool. 'He wouldn't dare. The arts committee will laugh him out of their office after one glance at his derivative doodlings. The scheming little devil, I'll —'

A click came from the darkness that shrouded the huge door of the gallery. Stokes called out, 'Who's that? Who is there?'

He walked forward. There was no response.

'I said, who is there? Zy?' The miserable runt was afraid to show himself. 'Don't hide in the shadows, boy, I know you're there. What are you —'

Blackness.

The butt of a standard issue blaster came down across the back of Stokes's head. All sixteen flabby stone of him slid heavily to the marble floor in much the same fashion as a badly designed building slips off a cliff edge.

Margo returned the blaster to its place on her belt. She looked around at the gallery and laughed. What nonsense!

It had been easy to escape from the cabin. That idiot Pyerpoint had thought to imprison her behind a simple door-lock! She had put on her uniform, crept to the emergency stairs and made her way down to the gallery unobserved.

She picked up the sculpture of Ventol, the three-headed killer of the lower city, and threw it across the room. It smashed into serrated chunks and threw out a cloud of dust.

'I have returned!' she said exultantly. 'The time has come at last! The process has worked. I have full control!'

She reached for another of the exhibits.

The ultrasonic signal of the Doctor's whistle penetrated the transdimensional envelope of the TARDIS and made itself known to the small section of awareness K9 had left on line as he recharged his energy banks. The head of the robot dog tilted upward and his eyescreen glowed a healthy red.

'Coming, Master,' he said. 'This unit is fully recharged and functioning at ninety-six point eight seven per cent of full capacity.'

He sent a signal to the console that tripped the door control and whirred through.

The woman that had been Margo surveyed the ruins of the gallery and nodded approvingly. A beastly hiss issued from her lips. It would be good to kill, she thought. Just one Normal, now, as an appetizer. She would relish the taste of a death. The hefty weight of Stokes lay temptingly sprawled before her, but she dismissed him. She wanted to look into the eyes of her victim, to witness the terror that her gaze could bring. She had to kill.

She left the gallery and returned to the stairway. A Normal was sure to pass by eventually.

Romana sat on one of the leather buttoned couches that lined the corridors outside the courtrooms. The large and loud clock above the main courtroom had just struck six. Most of the lawyers and staff had returned to their quarters. She was reviewing the events of the last few hours in an attempt to follow the Doctor's reasoning. She was by now more than accustomed to his arbitrary behaviour and leaps of logic, but her examination of the facts could not clarify why he should have become so concerned over a sabotaged computer and a lying policeman. She suspected he was looking for complications that weren't there. She was also becoming bored.

Her boredom disappeared in an instant as she saw Zy walking along the corridor. His eyes were fixed ahead and he walked past without noticing her.

Curious, she climbed from the couch and followed him from the court area, taking care to keep her distance. He led her to a large metal door at the far end of the corridor. He stopped and glanced about nervously. She hid behind a pillar and watched as he slid the metal door open and walked through. Romana waited thirty seconds and pursued him. She knew from the map she'd memorized earlier that the door led to the emergency stairway, a network of steps that hugged the side of the station's buildings and led not only to the other floors but also to the Rock's emergency escape capsules.

Beyond was a narrow staircase that tapered spirally downwards into darkness. Old electric lamps shone up through the latticed metalwork of the steps. A chequered pattern of shadow fell over Romana's face.

The clatter of Zy's hurrying footsteps echoed up the shaft of the stair-well. Careful not to alert him to her presence, she slipped off her boots and tiptoed after him.

Spiggot checked another file. His eyes widened as he saw the name of the case. At last! He tugged it from the shelving and took it to the nearest desk for closer examination.

It had been stuffed with bundles of reports and notes and tied with rotting green string. He unpicked the knot and delved inside. It contained a lengthy summary of the case and relevant points of law, copies of the sentencing certificate, and a set of photographs sandwiched between squares of brown card secured in a plastic binder. Spiggot flipped the binder open.

It was much as the system had been told by the eager media three years before. The victims had been squashed flat, compressed into bundles of blood-drenched skin and bone. Spiggot had seen death in many forms. It was part of the job and he was accustomed to it. But he'd never seen it like this. He swallowed to calm his stomach and, recalling his rookie training, thought of ordinary, better things. His goldfish, his house, Angie and the kids.

He found the death certificate pressed beneath the book of photographs. It stated clearly that Xais, self-proclaimed princess of the Guaal Territories, last of the Ugly Mutants, genius, terrorist and killer of at least two thousand humans, had been terminated by particle reversal almost three years ago. The certificate had been signed by Margo and was countersigned by Pyerpoint.

He closed the file and tapped a finger against his teeth. 'Then who,' he wondered, 'killed the miners on Planet Eleven?'

Zy had led Romana on an exhausting climb down eight flights of stairs and had now reached the junction of the stairway with the basement. Romana watched from what she considered to be a safe distance.

'The old coot,' she heard Zy mumble as he turned for the exit that would take him back to the gallery. 'He's finally going to get what's been coming to him.'

A step creaked under Romana's foot and Zy's head turned. She knew there was nowhere to hide so she stepped from cover. 'Hello,' she said, returning her boots to her feet.

He jumped. 'What are you doing here?'

'I've just been having a look around,' she said. 'I'm free to. This is a public area, isn't it?'

Zy stared up at her, trying to judge the situation. She could see that he was considering what action to take. 'What are you? An investigator? Or one of Stokes's mates?'

'Neither,' she replied.

Zy sprinted for the staircase. He pushed past her and clattered up the steps. Romana pulled herself up and hurried after him. He couldn't be more than ten seconds in front of her. She followed him around the corkscrew staircase without pausing to take a breath.

'Wait! I only want to talk with you!'

The rattle of Zy's footsteps stopped abruptly. She imagined that he must have passed through a doorway and returned to the main building. She vaulted the next steps three at a time, wishing for once that her legs could be as long as the Doctor's. But there was no sign of a doorway.

She stopped and looked about, confused. Her lungs panted like bellows as she drew short breaths. Zy had

70

disappeared. Perhaps into a secret passage or something? It would be only natural for a building like this to contain several.

Another sound came from the steps above her. A gentle percussion on the edge of her hearing. A dripping noise.

The lights went out, above and below.

Romana gathered her wits and turned the corner. 'Zy?' she called.

No response.

The dripping continued. She climbed another few steps slowly. The toe of her boot nudged something sticky. She knelt down and dabbed at the glutinous patch with a finger. She let out a cry.

Human blood.

Somebody started to walk down the steps in front of her. In panic, she tried to retrace her route but lost her footing. She tumbled down the staircase. Her head banged painfully against a strut on the landing below and she lost consciousness.

The lights flickered back on.

Standing over the body of Romana was Margo. She stood proud and upright, her hands on her hips. The boots of her uniform were caked with blood.

Clamped over her face was the shining silver mask of Xais. Her eyes glinted cruelly through its slanted slits.

5

The Ghost

Stokes's consciousness creaked him awake. He blinked and rubbed away blood that had flowed into his eye from the wound on his brow. The lights of the gallery revealed devastation to his slowly focusing gaze. Pictures were torn from their hangings, sculptures smashed into dusty chunks. Spilled paints congealed in shiny multi-coloured pools.

With an effort he stood up. The muscles in his back wrenched and he immediately toppled down. His bleeding head fell back. 'This will be your undoing, son,' he muttered. 'I'll have the old scratcher throw the book at you.' He pulled himself up again and staggered over to the sink.

His feet crunched over the slashed canvas of Mrs Blakemore. He gasped and picked up the pieces of the splintered frame. 'Priceless,' he whispered. 'My greatest work in oils.' He howled and started to shudder. Patches of deep purple coloured his cheeks. 'You won't be able to walk after I've finished with you!'

The Doctor walked down one of the corridors on level three, looking for the relaxation centre. It had to be around here somewhere, and from there it was only a short distance to the TARDIS. He looked from side to side, weighing the possibilities. His sense of direction really was appalling, but then there had been a lot of corridors in his life.

A familiar whirring came from his left. He turned to see K9 trundling along with customary merriness.

'You took your time,' the Doctor said.

'Delay occasioned by variations in topology of environment, Master,' K9 reported.

'Yes, and I don't suppose all those stairs were too easy, either.' He knelt down to address the dog. 'Listen, K9. What do you know about the Uva Beta Uva system?'

'Uva Beta Uva system. Fourteen planets around torroidal ellipt—'

The Doctor put a hand over K9's muzzle. 'Yes, yes, I know all that.'

'Thus request for information illogical, Master.'

The Doctor stood up. 'Let's go and find Romana.' He set off along the corridor.

K9's sensors swivelled and he set off the other way. 'Mistress located in this direction, Master.' He paused before adding, 'Suggest error in your cartographical analysis.'

The Doctor shook his head impatiently. 'No, no. She's on the move. That girl just can't stay still for a moment.'

K9's tinny voice stepped up in pitch. 'Master, alert. Further analysis indicates local release of,' he clicked and ticked, 'radiation in vicinity of the Mistress.'

'What kind of radiation?'

'Spectrum not in my memory. Mistress may be in danger.' K9 sped off down the corridor. The Doctor hurried after him.

Margo opened her eyes. She felt better than she had for months. Her head was clear of the worries and doubts that had been whispering through it. She was in her bed, in her cabin. The clock on her bedside table told her that it was 1840 hours.

What was she doing in bed? She swung her sheets aside and saw that she was wearing her uniform. The single-breasted lapel was stained with blood.

She screamed and leapt from the bed. The whispering voice returned. A ghost in her head. *The time has come. Surrender yourself to me.*

73

'No,' Margo whimpered. 'No, leave me alone.' She pushed her knuckles to her mouth to stop herself screaming again.

You cannot resist, the voice said. *You must die eventually, like all Normals. Why prolong your existence?*

Margo put her hands to her head. It was filled suddenly by memories that she knew were not her own. An image was being fed to her, assembling itself segment by segment.

She saw a cluster of tents pitched on cold grey soil, around which were gathered people dressed in simple sacking garments. Huge umber clouds filled a reddish sky. A hand was grasped tightly in her own. She looked up and saw a tall woman, dignified and beautiful. Somehow she knew this was her mother. The memories were those of a child.

Three horses were galloping into sight through a split in a nearby formation of rock. The riders wore suits of silver fabric and carried long rifles, their faces, angry and excited, visible through the clear plastic panels of their hoods.

'Ceerads!' their leader shouted, reining in his horse. 'More here!'

The child felt her mother's hand leave her own. The space it left felt big and empty. She watched as her mother walked slowly towards the men. Her own people, who were backing from the newcomers in fear, parted to allow her through.

'Get back!' the leader of the riders shouted at her. He raised his rifle. The child thought he looked very young. Not much older than herself. 'Get back, Ceerad!'

The child hated that word.

'Put down the weapon,' her mother called out. 'Leave this place. This settlement is protected under the Mutants Rights Act 2278.'

The leading horseman laughed and some of his men joined in. It didn't sound like a laugh, the child thought. Not the kind of laugh she liked. It sounded dirty. 'You're

Ceerads,' he said. 'You don't —'

One of the men of the settlement rushed forward, an old man with hunched shoulders and a growth between his eyes. A cudgel was grasped in his hand. He was terrified. He did nothing but shiver and wave the rusty weapon up at the riders.

The leader put a bullet through his head. The child watched as the old man's face exploded in a red blur. Everybody started to scream. She tried to find her mother. Her heart was beating faster and faster until she thought it might burst from her chest. There was lots of shooting and screaming, and people were falling, covered in blood. She knew it was right to pretend to be dead, that's what she'd been told, so she flung herself down into the dirt and tried really hard not to move or make any kind of noise. Her insides felt mixed up and she wanted to cry and cry.

The noises stopped after a while, but she knew she had to keep still. She heard the horses coming closer. One of them stepped over her. She could tell it was frightened too from the smell it was making. She heard the voice of the leading rider, not far away.

'They're finished. Cleaned up, it's the last site.' He was trying to sound pleased.

'What do we put on the report, sir?' said one of the others.

'Ritual suicide,' said the leader. 'Ceerads at site AKB found dead. Cause of deaths suspected internal poisons.' He paused and then ordered, 'Burn them.'

'Yes, sir.'

The child understood every word. Her people had been slain by the Normals. Everyone she had ever known had died in the last few minutes, taken suddenly, for no reason. The Normals were going to say her people had killed themselves because they were unhappy and diseased.

A funny feeling started in the small of her back. It was more than anger. She had felt that many times before when she thought of Normals. It was even more than hate. It made the skin at her temples feel stretchy, as if her head was getting bigger and bigger. She knew she would have to open her eyes to let the feeling out, even though that was the stupidest thing she could do.

She rolled over. One of the men noticed her and called, 'Sir, there's one left, a kid.' He sounded nervous.

Her eyes opened. There were bodies all around, twisted and broken, covered in dirt and blood. One of the men was preparing to throw something from a can over the pile of dead. Another held a flaming brand.

The leader said, 'Kill it.'

'But it's a kid, sir,' said the man who had seen her moving.

'It's a Ceerad spawn,' the leader said. He raised his rifle and pointed it at her face.

The child felt the hate feeling leave her eyes before he could pull the trigger. It shot across the space between them. She blinked and looked again. Where the leader had been standing there was a bundle of bloody rags and scorched metal.

One of the other men shouted, 'Get back, it's a psi-killer!'

The hate feeling came back. Ceerad, psi-killer, mutant. Words that she would never have chosen for herself. Words that were a trap. Hate words.

The men died as she looked at them. This time she looked as she did it and it felt really good. They just had time to scream before they burst. It pleased her. With the last one, she actually caught a glimpse of his bones coming through his skin as it happened.

Then there were no sounds at all. She stared at the heaps of death that surrounded her. The Normals had caused it all. They had to die. And not just these. All of them. There would be a ship somewhere. She could learn how to use it, she was very clever, she knew. And then she could leave Guaal and go into space. There would be so much hate for her there.

Do you see? Do you feel my pain?

Margo's mind struggled to reassert itself. 'I had nothing to do with that . . . please, leave me . . .'

Your species are all alike. You are all guilty. Inferior creatures. You are all to die. I will cleanse the universe of homo sapiens. You will be the instrument of my revenge.

Margo's hand jerked forward. It opened her dresser. The silver mask lay on top of the neatly folded clothing.

Take it. Wear my face. You will submit.

An inspection hatch on the stair-well creaked open and the Doctor's head poked through. 'More stairs, worse luck, K9,' he said. He hoisted the computer into his arms and carried him into the semi-darkness of the stairway. 'How's that radiation?' he asked.

'My sensors indicate that it is clear, Master,' K9 reported. 'Mistress Romana is approximately ten metres down and to your right.'

The Doctor hurried down the steps. 'Romana!' he called. He caught sight of her body, put K9 down, and rushed over. He felt for her pulses and opened one of her eyes. The pupil was unseeing.

'Concussion,' he diagnosed. He checked the back of her head where it had hit the stair rail. 'A nasty bump, but she'll be fine.'

K9 trundled forward to examine a liquid that was trickling down the upper steps. His head lowered as he carried out a swift analysis. It was almost as if he was sniffing. 'Master. I have detected traces of human blood.'

The Doctor was shocked. 'What?'

'Human blood, group O, plasma in a solution of –'

'Shut up, shut up.' He took a torch from his pocket and shone the beam up the stairs. His face blanched and he licked lips that were suddenly dry.

K9 moved forward to investigate. The Doctor covered the dog's eyescreen. 'No, K9. It's not a very pleasant sight.'

K9's sensors ticked. 'Human body, male. Cause of

77

death: disruption of internal and external organs.' His head pricked up and his blaster emerged from his nose. 'Danger, Master. Hostiles approaching.'

A clattering noise came from above. A small group of guards appeared. They were led by Shom. He stopped at the sight of the Doctor. 'Hello, sir.'

'Hello,' the Doctor said grimly.

'We saw you entering the stairway, sir,' Shom explained. 'Thought you might be lost and need our assistance.'

The Doctor regarded him with contempt. 'You're responsible for security here, am I correct?'

'Yes, sir.'

'Yes, well while you've been spying on me, somebody has committed a murder.' He pointed past them in the direction of the human remains. The guards rushed up the stairs to investigate.

Shom looked at K9. 'What's that, sir?'

'That's my dog,' the Doctor said simply.

'Oh,' said Shom.

The Doctor stared after him as he joined his men. He heard Romana groan as she regained consciousness and knelt to face her. 'Well done, old thing,' he said, patting her hand. 'How do you feel?'

She forced a smile. 'The way I usually feel after I've been bumped on the head.' She reached over and patted the robot dog. 'Hello, K9.'

K9 gave a pleased burble.

'Did you get a clear look at him?' the Doctor asked anxiously.

'Who?'

'The murderer.'

Romana groaned again. 'Can't we discuss this in more civilized surroundings?'

An anti-bruising bandage and a glass of fruit cordial from the mini-bar of her suite were enough to restore Romana's wits. She was now pacing up and down the room and attempting to explain recent events to the Doctor and K9.

'Then I must have blacked out,' she concluded. 'I think whoever it was assumed I was dead.'

The Doctor rubbed at his chin. 'Hmm. What was that Zy fellow doing there in the first place, I wonder? Going for an escape capsule?'

Romana shrugged. 'I think he'd just gone for a walk, to cool off.'

'It's not important,' said the Doctor. 'He just happened to be in the wrong place at the wrong time.'

'I know the feeling.' Romana finished her drink and put the glass aside. 'And this place is full of security cameras. Whoever killed him won't be at liberty for very long.'

K9 spoke. 'Negative, Mistress. I have been studying this station's security system.' The map had been propped up before him. 'The stairway does not contain monitor devices.'

'What's more, the corridors around that area would be near enough empty at that time of the evening,' the Doctor put in. 'They'll all be at their recreation centre. So the murderer could quite easily have gone about his dastardly business without being spotted.' He stood up and whispered to Romana, 'I'm more interested in the radiation K9's sensors picked up at about the time that fellow met his end.'

Romana frowned. 'Radiation couldn't cause such a localized effect, it's impossible.'

The Doctor wagged a finger. 'Improbable, shall we say?'

'No, Doctor. Impossible.'

'Master,' K9 piped up. 'This unit is keen to clarify earlier statement. Energy released in the vicinity of Mistress Romana was identified as radiation by vocabulary bank. I cannot say if this diagnosis is correct.'

The Doctor knelt down. 'Did you take a profile of the readings for full analysis?'

K9's head drooped. 'Negative, Master. Such an action relegated by concern for the Mistress.'

The Doctor patted his tin head. 'Good dog, K9, don't worry yourself about it.' He looked up at Romana, his expression grim. 'I have a terrible feeling that we've been wasting time.'

'What do you mean?'

He stood up. 'Whatever's going on here is far more serious than I imagined. The power to kill like that could be the least of this person's abilities.' He gave another of his sudden smiles. 'I think it's time we had another little chat with friend Spiggot.'

'You think the murder is connected to the computer sabotage?'

'I think it's more than likely.'

Shom looked around the stair-well. Flashes from the camera of the security photographer lit the deeply lined face of Pyerpoint, who had joined him on the stairs.

'It's Zy, sir, Stokes's apprentice,' Shom reported. 'I don't know what hit him.' He loosened the collar of his uniform. 'There isn't much left.'

Pyerpoint shook his head. 'Murder aboard this station. It's a terrible business.' A group of men walked past carrying a stretcher. He halted them and reached for the white plastic sheet that covered the remains. 'I wish to see this.'

'There's not much left, sir,' Shom warned him.

The plastic sheet was lifted. Shom saw a look of revulsion cross Pyerpoint's face. But mixed in with it was a brief tension of muscles about the jaw that he could have taken for anger. It was the same irritated response displayed by Pyerpoint when a barrister rambled into a long and specious argument.

Pyerpoint replaced the sheet and waved the stretcher party and their grisly burden away. 'And you say the Doctor was here?'

'Yes, sir, with the young lady and some kind of

computer. He said it was his dog. Do you think they did it, sir?'

Pyerpoint gave one of his rare laughs. 'They are police officers, Shom. I think it is obvious who was responsible.' His jaw tightened. 'I argued against the government for years on this matter. Perhaps now they will see I was right.'

'You think it was Stokes, sir?'

'I do. That idiot should never have been permitted to take one step aboard this station. Find him.'

'Yes, sir.' The junior officer started to move away.

'And Shom — I want security status raised to black. No transmat communications, arrivals or departures, are to take place without personal authorization from myself.' He hesitated. 'This matter is to be kept private for the moment. I don't want to cause a panic. Tell the people there has been a technical fault.'

'We regret to inform you that a technical difficulty will delay all transmat communications for the next few hours. Please be patient while we assess the situation. Normal service will be resumed as soon as possible.'

Spiggot sneered up at the speaker. 'And the first beacon satellite has just gone into orbit. Wonder what they're trying to cover up?'

He lit another cigarette, popped it into his mouth, and opened the door of his cabin. It contained Romana, who lay on the couch. 'How did you get in here, then?'

The Doctor's head popped from the mini-bar. 'No sign of any ginger beer, Romana,' he said. He caught sight of the detective. 'Ah, Mr Spiggot. We were just about to have a drink, would you like to join us?'

'This is my room, mate,' Spiggot said threateningly. 'I think we should have a little talk about privacy.'

'Really?' the Doctor said. 'I think we ought to have a large talk about murder.'

Spiggot sighed and threw the bulging Xais file onto a table. Romana picked it up and started to examine the contents. 'Hey,' called Spiggot, 'hold it a second, lady. And what's all this about murder?'

The Doctor forced a drink into his hand. 'We were very much hoping you could tell us. Have a cherryade.'

Spiggot looked down, confused, at the soft drink. Not really his style. 'I've already explained, the computers —'

The Doctor put a hand over his mouth. 'No more flim-flam, please. The performance is over. And you needn't worry about the bugging device, either.' He removed his hand.

Spiggot shook himself. He hadn't reckoned on this. They were cleverer than they looked. 'You knew?'

Romana looked up. 'Oh, yes.'

The Doctor grinned triumphantly. 'To use an old Earth expression, Mr Spiggot, you were throwing us a line. All that stuff about the security net was designed to get Pyerpoint looking in the wrong direction, yes?' He clicked his fingers and what looked like a metal box on wheels trundled into view.

'Bugging device located and destroyed as instructed, Master,' it reported.

Spiggot jumped back, alarmed. 'What the hell is it?'

The box took this as an invitation to introduce himself. 'This unit designated K9 Mark II. Purpose: to assist and protect the Doctor Master and Mistress Romana.'

Spiggot shook his head in bewilderment. 'Where are you lot from?'

Romana smiled. 'Aren't we from Central?'

'That was all part of it, too,' Spiggot admitted uncomfortably. 'I took a gamble that paid off. I figured you were stowaways and were looking to get baled out. Decoys and distractions, see. Good tactic. Always works. With you two running about, old Pyerpoint would be kept even busier. I knew he'd order a check on the security data core after he overheard our conversation. That's just what I want, because believe it or not, I was telling you the truth. It'll take days, and I can get on with the other business which I didn't tell you about.'

'How were you to know we weren't criminals?'

Spiggot gave a wry grin. 'I can sniff a crim from the other side of a nebula, love. And I've seen characters like you before. Spaceniks, Romanies. Harmless. But useful.' He was pleased to have an opportunity to explain himself. 'Thought I'd read you right. Still, when you want results, you have to take risks.'

'Quite right,' said the Doctor. 'We work in similar lines, you see. You might say that we,' he indicated himself, Romana and K9, 'are freelancers. We saw through your deception straight away.' He sniffed. 'And your perform-ance was just too reckless to be convincing. The delay in your warrant, your ham-fisted break in, none of it made sense. Unless you weren't telling the whole truth.'

'Which had to be something very important if you were keeping it back from the High Archon.' Romana held up the file. 'I presume this is it. Makes for rather gruesome reading.'

The Doctor raised an eyebrow. 'Oh, really?'

'Committal papers, indictment and trial documents in the case of the State of Uva Beta Uva Five versus Xais of Guaal,' Romana read aloud. 'According to this, she killed at least two thousand people in the space of two years. And all before her nineteenth birthday.'

'I never liked early achievers,' the Doctor said with feeling. 'I was barely out of long socks at that age.'

Spiggot was glad of the chance to explain the situation. 'Haven't you heard of her?'

'We travel a lot,' Romana said.

'She was a Ceerad. Some say the last. She —'

The Doctor held up a hand. 'Sorry. Ceerad?'

Spiggot looked at him, confused. 'You have been away, mate. Ceerad. Stands for Cellular Remission And Decay. They were mutants, see. Escaped the purge of Vanossos and set up settlements on Six. Her particular talent was to crush people where they stood.' He pursed his lips and made a squelching sound. 'Over in a flash but very messy.'

Romana and the Doctor exchanged a glance that was deep with significance. 'Spiggot,' the Doctor said, 'I think you'd better tell us everything you know about this Xais.'

Stokes pressed a bag of ice on to his wound and winced. A couple of cups of tea, topped up with a dash of his favourite liqueur, had gone a small way toward the restoration of his spirits, along with the visions of Zy's likely humiliation and punishment that were passing through his imagination. 'Oh yes,' he said with relish, adjusting the bag to tend to his throbbing brow, 'they'll spread you out and flog you until your bones squeak, my lad.'

The door of the gallery burst open abruptly and a group of guards burst in. They brandished blasters. Their leader, a young chap Stokes recognized as Shom, took a step forward. 'Stop right there!' he shouted.

'I wasn't intending to go anywhere,' Stokes said disdainfully. 'It took you long enough to get here. But then, I have come to realize that efficiency is the last thing one may expect from you gentlemen.' His eyebrows shot up as he noted Pyerpoint pushing through the group of officers into the gallery. 'The Great Sandshaker preserve us. This is a most unaccustomed pleasure.'

Pyerpoint stared at him. 'Stokes, I warn you, do not attempt to resist arrest. You will be shot if you try.'

'Arrest?' Stokes gasped. 'You dangerous and deluded old prune, what erroneous conclusions has your ageing intelligence brought you to now?' He gestured about him. 'I think you would be better occupied locating the miscreant responsible for this vandalism!'

Pyerpoint signalled to the men. 'Take him.'

The guards moved forward and took Stokes by the arms. He stood still, almost unable to speak, his face gathering colour again. His mouth opened and closed a few times before he managed to say, 'Pyerpoint, you senile trout, I fail to see the slightest glimmer of logic in this action!'

The High Archon said gravely, 'Menlove Ereward

84

Stokes, I arrest you for the murder of Efrik Zy. Anything you say will be taken down and may be used in evidence against you. You do not have the right to remain silent.'

Stokes was now totally perplexed. 'Zy is dead?' he said incredulously. 'But surely —' He took the bag of ice from his head and revealed the wound. 'Look at this. Listen, I've been quite insensible for the last hour at least.'

Pyerpoint turned to Shom. 'Take him to the detention area.'

'When the miners went in to Six the Ceerads weren't happy. A lot of them topped themselves. Some of them formed little armies. They didn't stand a chance,' Spiggot explained.

Romana was appalled. 'You're talking about genocide. An entire genetic strain wiped out.'

Spiggot looked unmoved. 'Don't get sentimental about it, dear. They were in a pretty sorry state. Probably better off dead.'

'I doubt it. Carry on.'

'Well, Xais got away from Six somehow. Pretty soon after, there were terrorist incidents on Five. Buildings, people. Random attacks. Hundreds killed. The worst thing about it was what she left behind. Squelched stiffs.' He paused. 'The tech div boys reckoned there was something up with her genes that let her do people in just by looking at them. Some sort of impulse she could send out. An enlarged brain, and that meant she was pretty much a genius, too. Computers, bomb-making, an expert.'

'Then how was she caught?' asked Romana.

'They tricked her. Clamped a metal box around her head. Then she was powerless. Put her on trial here, about three years ago, and she goes to the particle reverser. No surprises.' He stubbed out another of his cigarettes. 'That should have been the end of it. Then, two months ago, a survey base was done in, on Planet Eleven.'

'I thought this system had been fully mined out,' said Romana.

'Not Eleven,' Spiggot explained. 'It's pretty small, and the atmosphere's too thick for a survey to be done from orbit. But with the recession on, the big mining corps can't afford to pass anything by. McConnochie Mining put down a base there at the end of last year and started to carry out a survey. Anyway, someone pretty clever waylaid their transmat beam, got in, killed their engineer and switched off the life support. Wiped their computers and transmatted out again. We thought it was pirates at first.' He grimaced and stared into the distance. 'Then we saw the body of the engineer. Squelched.'

Romana began to understand Spiggot's mission at last. 'So you were sent here to check up on the execution of Xais?'

'Uh-huh. I had to cover my tracks, 'cause the whole thing's secret. No one outside the force and the top brass at McConnochie knows about it. And, of course, in a case like this, nobody's beyond suspicion.' He picked up the file and weighed it in his hand. 'And there's no doubt about it. Xais fried three years ago.' He shook his head, looking puzzled. 'Looks like I've got a ghost on my hands.'

'It may interest you to know,' the Doctor said, 'that your ghost has struck again.' He related the story of Zy's death.

Spiggot sprang from the couch and started to pace up and down the room. Romana reflected that the carpet had probably not been paced over quite so much for many years. 'There must be a link,' the policeman said. 'Someone's found Xais's secret, I reckon. Worked out how to kill like her.' He nodded, resolute in this theory. 'And it falls to me to nail the creep.'

Romana put a sympathetic arm on his shoulder. 'I shouldn't worry, Mr Spiggot. You've got us to help you.'

He brushed her off. 'Oh no, love. I work alone.' His features took on an expression Romana recognized from portraits of martyrs the Doctor had hung in the TARDIS power room. 'I can't get too close, see. It's what gets me results. If anyone takes risks, it's going to be me.'

The Doctor seemed to have lost interest in Spiggot's aggrandisement. 'A ghost, eh?' he mused. 'What do you make of that, K9?'

The computer had been listening to the conversation attentively. 'Existence of ethereal phenomena unproven, Master. Suggest corporeal explanation for anomaly.'

'Oh really? What explanation?' Romana knew that K9's ability to see things in purely logical terms had proved useful before.

This was not to be such an occasion. 'Cannot specify. Insufficient data.'

'No, you never do know the answer when it's something important, do you?' The Doctor turned to the others. 'Let's go and find some more data, shall we?'

Spiggot's objection to their further involvement was cut short by a bleep from his communicator pad. The voice of Pyerpoint issued from the tiny speaker. 'Doctor, Romana, Spiggot. I wish to see you all in my office immediately.'

'We'll come straight away,' the Doctor replied. 'There's a lot to talk about.'

'I have already made the arrest,' Pyerpoint said. 'I require you to make a statement regarding your involvement in this matter.'

Romana was confused. 'An arrest? Who?'

'Stokes, of course,' said Pyerpoint. 'I shall expect you forthwith.' He broke the call.

Spiggot nodded slowly. 'Stokes, yeah, the artist guy, I've heard about him. And he had contact with Xais before her execution. She could have shown him a few tricks. Motive, means, opportunity. It all fits.' He appeared slightly disappointed that what had seemed only a few moments ago to be a challenging mystery had evaporated.

The Doctor stared at him incredulously. 'I wonder how you have ever succeeded in your profession,' he said. 'It doesn't fit at all. Not even slightly.'

6

Nothing but the Truth

The electronic bolts of the cell slid to and Stokes was alone. It was a cell he had visited on several occasions in the course of his artistic endeavours, and contained in common with its fellows a low bed covered by grey blankets, a small and indecently public washroom cubicle, and a table and chair. He sat on the bed and shook his big bald head. If he had been the kind of citizen that is more usually caught up in a miscarriage of justice, the sort with faith in the traditions of democracy and their application, he might have been prepared to sit and wait patiently until the facts became clearer and his release was assured. But Stokes had seen far too much of the realities of life in the judicial system, and what little regard he may have held it in had disappeared long ago. 'The illusion of freedom,' he would say to the few that still listened, 'is one of the luxuries of affluence. We are all prisoners to a greater or lesser degree, if we could but confront the fact.' In the more prosaic atmosphere of his present environment he was forced to review this pronouncement.

'The trifling fatheads,' he spat at the walls of the cell. He looked up at the monitor camera in the corner. 'I hope you can hear me, Pyerpoint,' he shouted. 'Let me say that if you believe in earnest that I was responsible for the demise of that wretched boy you must be several degrees closer to utter cretinousness than I had previously credited!'

The Doctor watched as Pyerpoint flicked off the monitor, unimpressed by the outburst. The old judge turned to face his party, who had just entered his office as instructed. 'Please be seated. I do not intend to detain you for very long.'

'Mr Stokes doesn't seem too happy,' the Doctor said as he settled himself into one of the uncomfortable straight-backed chairs.

'Mr Stokes is an immature and foolish man,' Pyerpoint said. 'Qualities that, ultimately, have led to this situation.'

The Doctor swung his booted feet up onto the desk. 'Are you sure about that? I hope you're not allowing any personal dislike to cloud your judgement.'

'Of course not, Doctor,' Pyerpoint said. 'I –' He broke off as he registered the presence of K9 for the first time. 'What is that?'

'K9 is one of Central's latest gadgets,' Romana lied. 'A police dog like no other. Fully equipped with reasoning intelligence, trillion plus strainer memory wafers and compatible sensor array.'

K9, obviously feeling rather grand, beeped importantly.

'Never mind about K9,' the Doctor said quickly, keen as ever to shine the light of attention back on himself. 'I'd like to know on what grounds you've arrested Stokes.'

'This is an internal matter, Doctor, and need not concern you,' Pyerpoint said. 'Your involvement is limited to the fact that your colleague discovered the body of the victim. I should like you,' he addressed Romana, 'to make a formal statement on this matter.'

'I'll be more than pleased to,' she said. 'But it won't alter the fact that Stokes cannot have been responsible for the murder.'

Pyerpoint frowned. 'What makes you so certain of that? The men were known to quarrel regularly. It appears that Stokes's gallery has been vandalized. I believe that Stokes followed Zy to the stairway. There, incensed with rage at the youth's destruction of his work, he bludgeoned him to death.'

Spiggot broke in. 'It comes back, sir, to my mission

here. See, it's a mite more complicated than I had you believe.'

'Oh?'

'There's something up with your computers, sure enough,' Spiggot went on. 'Now, I can't really discuss the other matter, but I —'

The Doctor swung his feet from the desk and bolted out of his chair. 'I've had enough of all this mystification,' he said angrily. 'What Spiggot is trying to say is that the murder of Zy resembles the deaths caused by Xais.'

'Xais?' Pyerpoint replied. 'Doctor, Xais is dead. I saw her die, three years ago. What can you mean?'

The Doctor leant over the desk and stared deep into Pyerpoint's eyes. 'Listen. You cannot treat this as a routine murder inquiry. Look beyond the immediate facts. What else but Xais's powers could have caused the injuries to Zy's body? Stokes wielding a length of lead piping? I hardly think so.'

Pyerpoint seemed unmoved. 'Doctor, the deceased is scarcely cold. A post mortem has been scheduled for tomorrow morning. Until the results are known, speculation on the cause of death can only prove unhelpful.'

The Doctor slammed his hands down on the desk. 'I've already carried out a post mortem, Pyerpoint. With K9.'

'That ridiculous dog thing?'

Romana sniffed. 'K9 is more sophisticated than any device your civilization will produce in the next three thousand years.'

'Never mind about that.' The Doctor punctuated the dramatic delivery of his words with precise movements of his hand. 'Pyerpoint, you must put this station on full alert.'

'I already have, Doctor. Nobody from the lowest graded lavatory attendant to my fellow Archons can transmat away without my permission.'

'Good, good,' the Doctor said, only slightly taken aback. 'Now, release Stokes and get on with the real inquiry. Find out who has learnt to use Xais's powers.'

Pyerpoint raised his voice. 'As I have told you, Doctor, Xais was executed three years ago.'

'And as I keep telling you, Pyerpoint,' said the Doctor, 'somehow, somebody has learnt to kill in the same way.'

Xais opened the bottom drawer in Margo's cabin and withdrew the small device with the blinking green light. Built into the base were two switches. She pressed one of them. The device's emission of green light became constant. Excellent. The signal had been received. All was proceeding according to her plan.

Perhaps it had not been good to kill the Normal on the stairs. The last few hours before the arrival of her partners were crucial and she could not risk drawing attention to herself. But then, the Normals believed she was dead. They would not connect her to the killing. And the temptation to kill had proved irresistible.

Soon there would be many more such deaths. She considered the prospect eagerly.

She raised a hand to her face and touched the mask. It felt cold and metallic, but the contours of her features were almost exactly how she remembered them from her first existence. The idiot artist Stokes had done well, she thought. His finest work. She might allow him to live long enough to witness the beauty of his unwitting creation.

The stars glimmered through the porthole of the cabin. The streams of equations that lay scattered about the room had proved to be correct. She had calculated the exact position of the Rock, and beamed the homing signal along a chain of pirate satellites that led out of Uva Beta Uva into other systems. Now the time had come for the next stage of her operation.

There was a problem. The computer defences of the Rock would have to be dealt with. There was a risk in removing the mask, but she had to reach the control centre unchallenged and there was no other way. And soon, she thought, there would be no need to remove it, until the host body was exhausted. Until full activation had been achieved.

She pulled the mask from her face. The slight psychic shock awakened a trace of Margo's dormant consciousness. *What's . . . what's happening to me?*

Xais suppressed it. 'You will be gone soon, woman. You will die. I control this form now. Accept your fate.'

Their interview with Pyerpoint over, the Doctor and his colleagues were talking in the long hallway outside the courtrooms and chambers. The dimmed lighting and the echo of their voices around the stonework gave the scene an eerie aspect.

'He can't see it,' Spiggot was saying, shaking his long permed locks. 'He's in charge so he thinks nothing can go wrong here. But it has to be this accomplice of Xais, who killed Zy and those miners on Eleven.'

'That's what really puts Stokes outside suspicion,' Romana remarked. 'He might murder his assistant. But why should he attack a survey base? And he surely can't have the skills that were necessary to hijack the mining company's transmat link.'

'You're right, pet,' Spiggot said enthusiastically. 'Why don't I go back and tell Pyerpoint about that, eh?'

The Doctor put out a restraining arm. 'No, no, not yet. The fewer people that know about the attack on Planet Eleven, the better. If we convince Pyerpoint of our theory, how's he going to respond?'

'All guns blazing, I imagine,' said Romana.

'Exactly. I think it's better if whoever it is doesn't get to know we're on to them.'

'What's to stop Pyerpoint spreading the word about now?' asked Romana.

'He thinks we're talking nonsense,' the Doctor said. 'I doubt if he'll repeat it. He's got a very dusty old mind. Must be the effect of sitting all those years in dusty old chambers.'

Spiggot lit another cigarette. 'Come on, man,' he said.

'We've got to do something. I think I'll take a look down in the gallery, see what I can turn up. Others may have missed something.'

'Good idea,' the Doctor said. 'I'll join you.'

Spiggot's face fell. 'Listen, mate, I'm used to working on my own. Doing things my own way.'

'I know, I know, it's how you get results,' the Doctor finished for him. 'But just for once, would you be prepared to indulge a willing amateur?'

Spiggot considered the appeal for a while and finally nodded. 'Don't suppose it'll do any harm.' Secretly, he was rather pleased that the Doctor would be accompanying him. OK, the bloke was weird, but there was something reassuring about him.

'Splendid,' said the Doctor. He turned to his companions. 'While we're doing that, Romana, why don't you go and see Stokes in the cell block? See if he can tell you anything.'

Romana nodded. 'Where shall I meet you?'

'How about back at Spiggot's cabin?'

Romana indicated her understanding of their arrangement and left to carry out her task. K9 motored forward eagerly. 'Orders, Master,' he requested, tail wagging.

'K9, I want you to go to computer control, it's on level seven. You'll have to take the lift. I want you to search the station's defence and security systems for any signs of interference. Take particular interest in the transmat system at around the time of the attack on the mine, which would have been?' He glanced at Spiggot.

'February 28th last,' said the policeman. 'You think the attacker was working from here, then. It adds up. A guy who can hack into the data core of the security net could probably divert a transmat beam as well.'

'Yes. And K9 could do with the exercise. Go on, then,' the Doctor urged the dog. K9 set off on his task.

Spiggot stared at the Doctor. 'You seem to have taken over this investigation. I'm not sure if I like that. I still don't know who you are.'

The Doctor was already striding off down the corridor. 'A little trust is all it takes,' he called back. 'Come on, Spiggot, do keep up.'

The gallery had been wrecked by a display of force that surprised even the Doctor as he and Spiggot entered and picked their way through the debris and around the security team who were dusting for geneprints. Not a corner of Stokes's hideaway had been left undisturbed. Fragments of glass glistened around their crunching feet.

'What a mess,' said Spiggot, rather unnecessarily. 'Whoever did for this little lot certainly knew their business.'

The Doctor knelt and examined a fallen statue that had been broken into several chunks. 'The strength required to destroy something like this would be phenomenal. Note also that this glass has been stamped on by the heel of a boot. And Zy was wearing soft-soled shoes.' He looked up. 'When is all this supposed to have happened?'

Spiggot consulted his notebook. 'Between about 1745 and 1800 hours. While I was in the library and you were looking for your K9.'

'Hmm. But Romana saw Zy descend the stairway at 1800 hours.'

'She believes she did,' said Spiggot. 'We only have her word for it. She might have got mistaken, with that knock on the head and all that.'

The Doctor waved his objection aside. 'Her word is enough, believe me. And she's very good on time. Almost too good.' He rubbed his chin and stared into space. 'And K9 and I found Romana at 1825. So, even if we were to believe that Zy was responsible for this vandalism, which incidentally I don't for one minute, we would have to credit him with superhuman strength and speed.'

Spiggot sidled close to the Doctor and whispered from the corner of his mouth. 'Doctor?'

'Yes?'

'Xais had superhuman strength and speed.'

'I know,' the Doctor said, with withering loudness. 'So her imitator must have come here and knocked Stokes flat, then wrecked the place, then crept up the stairs, then killed Zy. But why? What brought the murderer here, of all places?'

Spiggot shrugged. 'Perhaps he didn't like the pictures.'

The Doctor hurried out of the gallery. 'This sort of wanton devastation doesn't square with the attack on the mine, either. That was cleverly contrived and planned to the last detail.' He chewed at a thumbnail. 'I have a feeling, Spiggot, that I'm overlooking something.'

The computer technicians working in the control centre were understandably alarmed when K9 entered and sped himself grandly across to the central data unit of the array of input consoles.

Shom, who had returned to the control centre to compile his report on the murder of Zy, hurried over. 'Hey! What are you doing?'

'Please connect me to the data core. I have been instructed to inspect it.'

Shom laughed. 'K9, aren't you?' He bent over and patted the dog on the ears. 'Well, K9, I think you'd better just go back wherever you came from and leave this to the experts, all right?'

K9's eyescreen flashed briefly. 'My function is to assist. My abilities are considerably greater than yours. You will connect.'

'I don't like your tone, doggy,' said Shom. He took a screwdriver from a nearby toolkit and advanced on the metal panelling of the intruder. 'And I'd rather inspect you.'

He brought the screwdriver onto the panel and dropped it immediately, clutching his hand. 'What have you done?'

K9 seemed even more impatient. 'I am programmed to protect myself. You will do as I instruct and connect me to the data core.'

Shom jumped to attention when he noticed that Pyerpoint had entered the room. 'Sorry, sir, I didn't see you there.' He indicated the console where he had been working. 'I've been, er, making my report on the murder, sir.'

'Obviously.' The High Archon's expression was disapproving. 'Reluctantly, I must ask you to comply with this strange animal's request. It has, would you believe, full clearance from the police authorities.'

K9 burbled happily as Shom fetched a long lead and attached one end to his sensors and the other to the central unit. A low hum of power sounded as information passed between the two systems. K9's tail sensor started to wag. 'I am linked to the data core. Inspection commencing.'

'I doubt,' said Pyerpoint, 'that it will be of any use. I am becoming increasingly concerned for the mental stability of these investigators.' He looked scornfully down at K9. 'What a ridiculous contraption.'

K9's head perked up. 'I have discovered an anomaly in the programming of the security net,' he reported. 'Reconfiguring to probe deeper.'

'That's impossible,' spluttered Shom. 'The security net is impregnable. I thought the team were looking for faults in the data core?'

Pyerpoint turned away, troubled. 'Would it be possible for anybody to interfere with the core to such an extent that the net itself was corrupted?'

'Sabotage our defences without us even knowing?' Shom replied. 'Well, not unless they were a genius.'

Pyerpoint sank into one of the chairs that lined the control centre and put his head in his hands.

'A visitor for you, Mr Stokes.'

The artist refused to lift his head from the book he was reading. 'Pyerpoint,' he called up, 'wrongful arrest may not yet be classified as a crime, but allow me to remind you that I am not without influence on Five. It is within my powers to broadcast the news of your incompetence as far and as wide as I wish. You may rest assured that I —'

He was interrupted by a polite feminine cough. 'Hello, Mr Stokes.'

He looked up and put the book away. 'The fair Ramona! I have done you a great disservice, mistaking you for the wrinkled ingrate responsible for my incarceration. But I am forgetting my manners.' He stood and offered her his chair. 'Please be seated.'

'That's quite all right,' she told him. 'I prefer to stand. And it's Romana. How are they treating you?'

He slumped back in his chair. 'Miserably, my dear, as might be expected. They really have excelled themselves on this occasion. I had no love for that young chap, of course. Frankly, I will shed no tears for his passing.' He straightened his cravat and his large eyes swivelled in their sockets. 'But to accuse me of his murder is preposterous. For one thing, I was knocked out. What am I supposed to have done, crept up behind myself and cast myself down? Then walked unconscious out to the stair-well and killed the boy? Ludicrous.'

The girl knelt down beside him and raised a hand. 'Please. The Doctor and I believe you. We're working to secure your release.'

Stokes smiled, rather pleased. 'Are you, sweet? Are you really? Tell me,' he leaned closer to her, 'this Doctor friend of yours. Are you and he, er?' He waved a hand in the air to complete his query.

'We're friends,' said Romana. 'For most of the time. Now, did you see who attacked you?'

Stokes shook his head. 'I didn't catch a glimpse. The brute struck from behind. I assumed it was Zy.'

'It couldn't have been. There wasn't time. It must have been his killer.'

Stokes sat up, alert. 'A third party, eh? Intriguing. And yet, that would make more sense.' He looked at her wistfully. 'Tell me, why are you not a High Archon and administrator of this station? You are prettier and cleverer than the present incumbent.'

She seemed unswayed by his flattery. Wonderful haughty creature. 'I want to ask you about some of your work. Tell me about Xais. How did she come to model for you?'

Stokes was surprised. 'Xais? Xais of Guaal? In the usual way. I offered my services and she accepted. She had to be drugged while I took the cast, of course, to prevent her from shooting those deadly beams from her eyes. The casting process took only minutes. It was a very simple job, but the results were most impressive.'

'You cast a bust of her features?' the girl asked.

'No, no, dear, a mask. In helicon. She was most insistent about that. It had to be helicon. Criminal types are often rather particular.'

'Helicon,' said the girl. 'A soft mineral found mostly on satellites or small planets. Low conductivity, low strength. Almost valueless, isn't it?'

'Not for Xais of Guaal,' Stokes said proudly. 'She appreciated its use as a modelling material, in its cool liquid form. I had a consignment transmatted over from one of the mining corporations. For a perfect mask of shining silver, encapsulating her evil beauty for all time. The upturned sockets, the cruel lips.' He moaned. 'Now, along with all my other work, destroyed in an act of thoughtless –' He broke off abruptly. 'Wait one jolly second!'

He sprang from the chair. 'The mask! The silver mask!' he cried. 'Of course!'

'Of course?'

He turned to face her. 'I know every item in that gallery, young lady. Every piece of my work I have catalogued, up here.' He tapped the sides of his shiny head, which was now covered by droplets of perspiration. 'And I can tell you, that when I raised my head and cast my glance about, and saw the shattered remains of my life's work, the mask of Xais was not there!'

7

The Ogrons Invade

Further out in space, millions of miles from the present position of the Rock of Judgement, was a small cluster of luminous green fluid particles. A large black spaceship sat within the folds of the cloud, concealed from the prying sensors of any other craft that might pass through this remote sector of space. The ship consisted of a bulbous snout and a bulging body section. Its dented hull was marked and scarred by the countless landings and blast-offs it had accomplished in a variety of planetary atmospheres. Bolted to its side was a stubby neutron cannon.

The black ship began to turn, slowly at first. It steadied and zipped out of the cloud, its roaring rear thrusters trailing thick superheated fumes.

Spiggot crushed another plastic cup. Unfortunately, he had forgotten to drink all of the coffee that had been inside it and the scalding liquid splashed over his sweater.

'Do try and be more careful,' the Doctor advised, handing him a napkin. 'We'll get nowhere with you being so jumpy.'

They had returned to Spiggot's cabin to wait for Romana, as arranged. Spiggot had spent anxious minutes going over the facts of the case and failing to see any pattern. 'Trouble is, Doctor,' he said, mopping up the mess, 'there's no reason why this person should kill Zy, is there?'

'Should there be?' The Doctor had returned to the study of the file on Xais. He tapped the page he was reading. 'It says here that one of Xais's great weaknesses was her irrational hatred of all humans. She was extremely intelligent, yes. But sometimes she lost control and just killed the nearest human for the sake of it.'

Spiggot lit another of his cigarettes. 'But we're not looking for Xais, Doctor. Xais is dead. We know that.'

The Doctor vaulted from his chair, seemingly consumed by some revelation. 'Do we, Spiggot? Do we really? We know that she was put to the particle reverser. But do we know that she's dead? Do we even know what dead means? "How wonderful is Death, Death and his brother Sleep." ' He coughed and pointed to Spiggot's cigarette. 'Please put that out, it stops me from thinking.'

Spiggot ignored his request. 'What do you mean, do we know she's dead. Of course we do.'

'But how do you kill someone, eh? Eviscerate them, crush them, reverse their particles. But do the dead always stay dead, mm?'

Spiggot found himself almost disturbed by the Doctor's intense gaze and ominous words. But common sense prevailed. 'I thought we'd decided that there was no ghost.'

The door of the cabin opened and Romana walked in. Without any attempt at greeting, she asked urgently, 'Doctor, what do you know about helicon?'

'It's a soft mineral,' he replied. 'And not a very useful one, either. Low conductivity, low strength. Low interest. Don't they mix it with Ball's ore to line pipes?'

'Nothing else?'

Spiggot spoke up. 'It's worthless. Any schoolkid knows that.'

Romana looked between them. 'It might not be.'

The Doctor tilted his head, a sign Spiggot recognized as a portent of trouble. 'Romana, I'm glad to see you taking an interest in planetary geomorphology, but please try to keep your mind focused on one thing at a time.' He turned to Spiggot. 'This is her trouble, you see. No concentration.'

Romana went on, 'Doctor, Stokes made a mask of Xais using helicon. It was taken from the gallery this evening. The only item that was removed.' She lowered her voice. 'Do you think the mask might be connected to the killing?'

His reaction was immediate. He raced for the door of the cabin, his long legs taking him from one side of the room to the other with a couple of loping strides. 'Well, come on, then!'

Romana raced after him. 'Where are we going?'

'To find Pyerpoint. Do try to concentrate!'

Spiggot tapped Romana on the shoulder. 'Would you mind telling me what's going on?'

'I'm afraid I would,' Romana shouted back as she raced after the tasselled ends of the Doctor's scarf, which were disappearing around the corner of the corridor. 'There isn't time.'

Shom watched anxiously as K9 continued his silent communion with the security computer. The technicians, now feeling more than slightly redundant, were huddled in a bemused group on the far side of the room. The big screen of the control centre still displayed the revolving cylinder that served as graphic representation of the system. K9's investigations had revealed the full extent of the corruption of the computer and the cylinder was now cracked and chipped in several places.

Shom knelt to address K9. 'How was this done?' he asked incredulously. 'The entire system's been degraded.'

K9 was too busy to reply. 'Please do not ask questions until analysis is complete.'

'It cannot answer you,' Pyerpoint told Shom, 'because this is another of Spiggot's distractions. Such interference is impossible. This,' he pointed to the screen, 'is supposed to fool us. They've programmed the machine to falsify its findings.'

The doors of the control centre opened and Margo walked in. She was dressed in a clean white tunic. Her movements were as they had always been, calm and efficient. It was as if the disturbances of the previous days had not occurred. 'Sir.' She addressed Pyerpoint.

He hurried to her side and took her arm. 'What are you doing here?' he asked. 'I advised you to relax in your cabin.'

She stared back at him. Shom noted an unusually insolent tone in her reply. 'I wished to apologize for my behaviour, sir. And to convey my willingness to submit to your authority in person.'

Pyerpoint relaxed his grip on her arm. 'There is no need for that. Please. Return to your cabin.'

K9 spoke up. 'Warning. Danger. This station is in danger.'

Pyerpoint turned abruptly. 'What is it talking about now?' He waved Shom forward. 'Disconnect it.'

'Warning. Danger!' K9 continued. 'The security net has been blinded to signals on band 456601 of the hyper three carrier beam since February twenty-eighth. My sensors indicate that a coded signal on that frequency is now being transmitted from this location.' He whirred and clicked, his delivery speeding up. 'Furthermore, interference extends to override of the station's transmat system. Records of transmat communications on February 28th have been falsified.'

'It's talking nonsense,' Pyerpoint insisted. 'Disconnect it.'

Shom moved to comply, but then the door crashed open and the Doctor stormed in, followed by an anxious Romana and a breathless Spiggot. 'I'm afraid he isn't, Pyerpoint! K9 never talks nonsense, well hardly ever.'

The High Archon flushed. 'I've had quite enough of you and your colleagues, Doctor. I must ask you to leave immediately. I shall be making a complaint to the police authority over your con—'

The Doctor reached forward and shook him by his scrawny shoulders. 'Listen, listen! Your computer has been overridden by an expert. Xais!'

Pyerpoint knocked his hands away. 'Doctor, Xais is dead. I saw her die!'

Spiggot leapt forward. 'It sounds crazy, I know. But we think she's found a way to bring herself back to life.'

'Your behaviour is starting to bore me, Spiggot,' Pyerpoint said. 'Get off this station or I'll have you thrown off.'

So, the Normals were perhaps not all so stupid. These investigators had uncovered her presence. But it was of no consequence. They would soon be dead.

She looked around the control centre. She had to complete the task she had come here for and this argument would serve as a good cover. The control panel of the security computer was unattended. She went to it and reached a hand out to a particular panel of switches. Her fingers fluttered over the keyboard in a blur. She nodded, satisfied, as a row of green lights flicked to red and then died. And the Normals believed this was a sophisticated system!

Unnoticed by those engrossed in the argument, a wisp of smoke started to curl from the collar of the ridiculous mobile computer. Xais was pleased. It was a conceited, ugly little thing.

She walked from the control centre unnoticed, and made for the nearest lift. Safely inside, she took the silver mask from her tunic and clamped it over her face, then pressed the control that would take her down to level four.

'Helicon is a quite worthless mineral,' Pyerpoint insisted. 'As any schoolchild could tell you. It is used sometimes as part of an alloy, to line pipes, I believe.'

'It may have all kinds of properties we can't comprehend,' the Doctor went on. 'Listen, you must evacuate this station and call for help from Five.'

'Certainly not.' Pyerpoint straightened himself. 'I do not intend to evacuate on the strength of one very

103

straightforward murder and a technical fault. Now, you are going to leave. Do I have to use force?'

'Pyerpoint,' the Doctor stormed. 'This station is in terrible danger!'

The argument was interrupted by a high-pitched mechanical groan that issued from K9's voicebox. A steady stream of smoke came from the robot dog. His casing glowed red.

'K9!' cried Romana. She hurried to his side.

'Imperative disconnect, Mistress!' he was able to gasp as he was overpowered. 'Power supply to systems overloaded. Imperative – disconnect!'

Romana attempted to obey, but the heat surrounding K9 was too great and she snatched her hand back. A roar started to come from the console to which he was connected.

'January is the equivalent,' K9 rambled, his delivery speeding up. 'Harriet married a soldier planetary density varies if Otto has six marbles, who is Vlassilivich . . .'

The Doctor pulled Romana back and cried, 'Down!' He grabbed Spiggot with his other hand and flung them both to the floor. Pyerpoint, Shom, and the technicians, warned by instinct of what was to happen, covered their eyes and dropped to the ground.

The console bellowed, groaned, and erupted in a shower of dazzling green sparks. Molten blobs of what had been circuit boards and processor links spattered the occupants of the room. A second explosion tore through adjacent consoles. Palls of choking black smoke were released. The lights flickered, went out and were replaced by emergency systems that glowed feebly.

Typically, the Doctor was the first to react. Covering his mouth and nose with his scarf, he stumbled through the smoke to where he remembered the fire apparatus was located. He hefted a fire extinguisher and tossed it to Romana. She caught it and started to beat back the flames with jets of foam. The Doctor joined her and they had the blaze under control in under a minute.

The odorous smoke started to clear slowly and K9 was revealed. His personal defences had protected him from much external damage, although his shell was blackened and scarred, but his head was angled upward and his eyescreen was unlit. Romana stepped forward carefully and wiped the foam from his casing.

'His integrators have gone,' the Doctor diagnosed. 'But he's designed to shut down if something like this happens. I wonder why he didn't?'

Romana patted the nose of the deactivated dog. 'He was trying to warn us. Don't worry, K9, we'll soon have you patched up.' To her astonishment K9's eyescreen flashed briefly.

'Thank goodness,' said the Doctor. 'For a moment there, K9, I thought your goose had been cooked.'

K9's head moved slightly and he said in a small voice, 'Not understood, Master. This unit does not contain Earth water-fowl.' His voice slurred and he became inactive again.

Spiggot had picked himself up from the floor. Coughing and choking, he joined them at the burnt-out wrecks of the computer consoles. 'Flaming hell,' he said.

'Quite,' the Doctor observed.

Spiggot looked along the lines of smouldering data stores. 'Looks like they've lost it all. Did your K9 do all of that?'

'It wasn't K9,' Romana said. 'The power to the computers was stepped up. The failsafes must have been overridden.'

'And only a genius could have done it,' she and the Doctor said together.

'A genius like Xais,' the Doctor completed. He stopped abruptly and put a hand to his head. 'Of course! That woman who was here, er . . .'

Romana supplied the name. 'Margo?'

'Margo. She must have set the power to overload. It would explain her breakdown,' he rationalized. 'If —'

'If she's possessed by the mask,' Romana went on. She

picked up a cooling chunk of debris from the nearest console. 'And she's left us defenceless.'

In the grim silence that followed these words, she heard a clamour build up outside as the citizens of the Rock began to realize that something was wrong.

Pyerpoint staggered up to them. His scorched eyebrows and sooty cheeks might have amused Romana in different circumstances. It seemed that, at last, the truth was beginning to reach him.

'Doctor,' he said urgently, 'K9 said that a signal was being sent from here, on a frequency that the security net had been blinded from picking up. If that's true, somebody out there knows our position. And without control of our laser cannon, we can do nothing to repel them.'

Spiggot flung his arms wide in frustration. 'Oh, that's just great, man! So we're sat here like a barmcake waiting for the toaster!'

Pyerpoint turned to Shom. 'Get after Margo. Find her! She's gone insane.'

'Right away, sir.' Shom turned to leave.

'But you must not kill her, Shom,' Pyerpoint said firmly. 'She must not die!'

Shom hurried away.

Romana righted one of the plastic chairs that had been knocked down by the explosion and sat dispiritedly. 'If she's sent for accomplices, they could arrive at any moment.'

The Doctor waved an arm airily. 'Not necessarily. She may have done all this just to shut K9 up. I shouldn't worry if I were you, Romana.'

The asteroid lurched to one side and they were all thrown to the floor again.

Romana lifted her head and looked across at the Doctor. 'Of course,' he said, 'I could be wrong about that.'

The corridors of the administration offices on level four were silent and dark. Every step Shom took along the stone-flagged walkways retorted sharply like a book slammed shut. The emergency lights served only to increase the empty strangeness of a place that had been designed, in part, to intimidate those who entered it.

Shom stopped. Had there been a noise from the darkened alcove to his left? He unholstered his blaster, swallowed and called, 'Margo? Margo, it's Lieutenant Shom. I've come to help you.'

There was no response. He stepped closer. 'Margo?'

Something glinted silver in the pitch blackness ahead.

She was upon him in less than a second. His blaster was kicked from his grip with one upward sweep of her leg. The beautiful blank silver mask touched his face. It smelt of iron. The way blood smells of iron.

'Hello, soldier boy,' she hissed. He whimpered and tried to pull away, but her hands were tight around his waist. Her breath was hot. One of her hands reached out and brushed a lock of hair from his forehead.

'What are you doing?' he protested, more disgusted than scared.

'She always wanted to kiss you,' Margo spat. 'I know that, you see. I have looked into her mind. I know her memories, her fears, her desires. The small emotions of the Normal.'

He struggled in her grip. 'Why are you doing this?'

She clutched him closer. He caught a glimpse of her eyes through the slits of the mask. They were shiny, round and black. 'Why? You, Normal, ask me why? But then, how can you know? How could you ever know the hate I feel?' He struggled again and she threw back her head, exhilarated. 'Go on, squirm for me. I find it amusing.'

Shom found himself slammed up against a wall. The woman's strength was incredible. She grasped the collars of his uniform and lifted his feet off the ground. The long nails on her fingers caressed his cheek. He tried to pull his eyes away from hers but she held his gaze.

'The Doctor was right,' he stammered. 'You are Xais!'

'Correct,' she said proudly. 'And let your race know I have returned for my atonement!' She angled her head.

He started to scream. He felt the pain begin above his eyes, as if a long sharp blade was being driven directly into his brain. The pain spread, bursting blood vessels across his forehead. It swallowed his face, his neck, his chest.

He felt his stomach burst.

Xais took her hand away and watched with satisfaction as the remains fell to the floor with a pleasing wet sound. Then she picked up Shom's blaster and walked away.

The asteroid shook again, the vibration sending the Doctor and Romana rolling over to the door of the control centre. 'We must get back to the TARDIS!' Romana shouted. She tried to stand but a further tremor knocked her down.

Spiggot called over, 'They'll blast us to pieces!'

The Doctor shook his head. 'I think not. They haven't come all this way to blow us up. I think they're trying to dock.' The room shook once more. 'And they're making a rare old mess of it.'

The black ship turned for another attempt to connect with the docking ports built into the side of the asteroid. Its snout struck an outcrop of rock and its aged engines wheezed in protest. A few seconds passed. The ship moved again. Its thick bulk turned slowly.

The Doctor pulled Pyerpoint up. The old man was doing surprisingly well, the Doctor thought. Probably kept himself in good shape despite all those years sitting on draughty benches. 'They're trying to dock!' he called. 'How do I reach the docking port?

Pyerpoint shook his head. 'Head for the transmat, Doctor. You must evacuate, all of you!'

The Doctor gripped him tighter. 'The docking port!'

Spiggot lurched over. 'I know the way, Doctor,' he called as the room began to buck, shaking them and a variety of free-standing objects up and down. 'The docking port's down on level four. It hasn't been used for forty years!'

The Doctor clapped him on the shoulder. 'Good man. Lead the way.' He followed Spiggot to the door. 'Look after K9,' he called back to Romana.

A thick tube slid slowly on hydraulic treads from the flanks of the black ship and connected with a small hatchway that was partly concealed between jagged formations of rock. Jets of steam hissed from the far end of the tube as internal clamps unclenched automatically. The tube was secured magnetically to the hatch.

'Well, we've stopped spinning, for one thing,' Spiggot said as he and the Doctor emerged from the lift on level four.

'That may not be good news,' the Doctor pointed out. 'They've almost certainly docked.' He raced forward along the corridor, but stopped short when he caught sight of something lying in a wet bloody heap against a wall. 'She's been here.'

Spiggot shook his head. 'She's a sick girl, all right.' He pulled his blaster from his jacket. 'Looks like a bullet's going to be the only way.'

The Doctor hurried on. 'Be careful, Spiggot,' he said. 'And let me do all the talking.'

The wall at the far end of the corridor had been blasted away, presumably by Shom's gun. Chunks of metal and oak panel were scattered about the hole. Spiggot nodded in reply to the Doctor's questioning glance. 'They had no need for a docking bay after the transmat was built so they bricked it over.'

The Doctor ducked his head to enter the hole. Beyond was a long tunnel of rock that widened and opened out into an open space that formed a kind of cavern. Built into the far side of the cavern was a large, circular metal hatchway. Standing before it, hands on hips, her back to them, was Xais.

Spiggot levelled his blaster. 'Couldn't be better,' he whispered, taking aim. 'One bullet in the back. End of problem.'

'Don't be a fool,' the Doctor said fiercely. 'What happens if you miss?'

Spiggot squared his jaw. 'I've never missed.'

'Not while there's another way. Stay here and don't shoot unless I tell you to.' That said, the Doctor slipped away towards the hatch. Spiggot muttered resentfully and tightened his grip on the blaster.

As the Doctor neared the hatch, he heard sounds from the other side, a chorus of animal grunts that was almost familiar. He couldn't make out any words. The hatchway seemed to be stuck, as if the new arrivals were having trouble opening it.

He stepped forward bravely. 'Hello, Margo.'

The woman whipped round to face him. 'I am Xais!' The Doctor was unprepared for the force of her personality. He took an involuntary step back as the cruel head tilted back, as if it was about to release more terror from its eyes. Then Xais seemed to relent. The mask regarded him with interest. 'And you are the Doctor. You are unlike the other Normals.'

He shrugged. 'I'm not sure how to take that.'

Xais came closer. 'You speak casually for a man who is about to die.'

'About to die?' the Doctor said, indignant. 'I should hope not. There are a number of interesting things I haven't quite got round to yet.' He stared straight at her, daring to look into eyes that he knew could kill him in an instant. 'Hello, Margo,' he said again.

'Margo is dead,' Xais said triumphantly. 'I control this body.' She raised a hand and caressed the mask. 'The fusion will soon be complete. The long darkness will be over forever. I shall be immortal!'

'Fight her, Margo,' the Doctor said softly. 'I know you are there.'

Xais tore her gaze away from him. 'I will kill you,

Doctor.' Her voice faltered and her knees trembled. 'Help me,' she said in Margo's voice. 'I do not want to kill. Help me, Doctor.'

He let out a deep breath and ran his tongue over dry lips. The next stage of his plan was crucial. 'Margo, you must take off the mask. Remove it, that's right.'

Her hands raised slowly, reaching for the temples of the silver face. They faltered slightly. She gurgled, trying to suppress the alien voice of Xais.

'That's it, Margo,' the Doctor encouraged her. 'You can do it. Take off the mask.'

The tips of her fingers curled around the edges of the mask, where it had become joined with her skin. It started to come away.

The hatchway blew open with a blast of air that knocked them both off their feet. The Doctor was dimly aware of tramping booted feet and pig-like snorts surrounding him. He shook his head to clear it, spat out a mouthful of dust, and attempted to rise.

Standing over him was a stocky figure that was nearly seven feet tall. It wore huge black sixteen-hole boots, trousers made of a rough sacking material, and a shirt of the same covered by a jerkin of a shiny purple material. These clothes could not disguise the stooped shoulders and beast-like crouch of their owner. Gripped in one of the enormous hairy hands that dangled from its long thick arms was a dirty and very large rifle of futuristic design. The creature was dark skinned. A mass of hair hung over its collar. The large dome of its head topped a heavy brow. The features beneath were simian; thin lips, a stubby nose and dull eyes that flashed with anger and loathing.

The creature could have been a missing link from Earth's prehistory. But the Doctor knew it was not. He knew that it, and the others of its kind that were treading heavily through the hatch, were Ogrons.

8

Rampage

Spiggot pushed himself back against the wall of rock around the entrance of the cavern, desperate to maintain his cover. He watched as the first of the ape creatures aimed its gun at the Doctor, who was shaking his head to clear the effects of the blast. The security officer, that frumpy old girl who had been taken over by the Xais mask, was getting up too. And she didn't look too happy.

'No!' She pushed the ape creature's gun aside. 'This Normal must be kept alive.' She brushed a crease from her tunic and looked approvingly at the monsters, more of which were emerging through the docking port. 'Now. Where are your masters?'

To Spiggot's surprise, the first ape spoke, in a guttural, grunting monotone. 'Masters wait in ship.' To illustrate his point, the creature pointed a large hairy finger towards the docking port.

Xais nodded and went to the hatchway. The Doctor called after her. 'Er, would you mind telling me what's going on? At least introduce me to your hairy friends.' He tried to stand but a hefty boot blocked his progress. 'Excuse me,' he addressed the ape, 'you're standing on my scarf.'

He's pushing it, thought Spiggot. Why doesn't he just clam up and let them ignore him for a bit? That'd be the best approach.

The ape-being growled and clubbed the Doctor with the butt of its rifle. He groaned and his head jerked back and was still.

Xais clicked her fingers. 'Take him,' she ordered the

leading ape. He threw the Doctor's unconscious body over his shoulder and lurched off through the hatch and back to the ship.

Damn fool, thought Spiggot. But at least the Doctor's ill-advised bid for freedom had given him a chance to strike one for the home side. Xais had stopped in the hatchway to allow the ape to pass. Her silver face was still, the blank slanted eyes like those of an insect. He raised his blaster and aimed for her heart.

'That's it, darling,' he whispered. 'Now, don't move . . .'

He pulled the trigger and a bolt shot from his blaster with a crack that reverberated around the small cavern. But Xais had already turned to enter the hatch and the shot went wild, bouncing harmlessly against one of the metal struts that supported the docking port.

'A Normal!' Xais screeched, her arms thrown up in hatred. 'Find him!' she ordered her new servants. 'Find him and kill him! Kill all of the Normals!'

The ape creatures reacted to her words with enthusiasm. They snorted and whooped and started to run towards Spiggot's hiding place. The big lugs could run for sure, he thought, despite their bulk. It was definitely time to be leaving.

He sprang from cover and raced out of the cavern. The creatures pounded after him. The first of the pack let off shots from their rifles. The high-pitched zings of the energy charges rang in Spiggot's ears. But, he reflected as he led the chase back into the corridors, however big and nasty the apes might look, they were lousy shots.

The ship used by her partners was not up to the standards Xais had set herself. It was dull and grey and dirty and badly lit. The location of the Ogrons' quarters was made plain by the foul odour of animal excreta mixed with the heady fumes of Rigellian ale, that wafted down a passage leading from the central aisle. It was regrettable that she would have to deal with these creatures. But she needed

113

their strength and force of numbers to effect her plan.

The flight deck was cramped, with little space between the patched-up consoles and feebly flickering instrument displays. Despite the antiquity of its contents, the room was without a speck of grime. The control panels had been polished, the keyboards were clean. More than a suggestion of menace was lent to the scene by the positioning of two huge curved knives above the main navigation console. Underneath the knives was a framed black and white photograph of a middle-aged woman dressed in a housecoat and hat. It was titled in large black letters OUR MUM.

Xais noted that the g-stress chairs one would normally expect to find in such a spacecraft had been ripped out. They had been replaced with two domestic armchairs. Seated in these chairs were her accomplices, the Nisbett brothers.

There was a strong family likeness apparent in the brothers. Both were six foot five, powerfully built, with brilliantined grey hair and lumpen features that suggested ruthlessness, brutality and cunning. They wore black jackets, immaculately creased black trousers and brogues. But Eddie, the younger by eight years, although gigantic, was slender in comparison to his elder sibling Charlie, who wore a pair of black-framed spectacles that magnified his terrifying stare.

'It is good to see you again,' said Xais, stepping forward.

Eddie raised a finger to his lips and whispered, 'Be quiet. Charlie's having his steak meal.'

Xais looked to Charlie. There was a tray on his lap, and the check-patterned plate upon it played host to a dribbling steak, accompanied by generous servings of potatoes and carrots, smothered in stodgy gravy. Charlie was munching slowly at the meal, chewing each mouthful several times before he swallowed. The hilts of a four-pronged fork and murderously sharp knife were clasped in his podgy hands. He stared into the space ahead of him as if there was nobody else in the room, or indeed the universe.

'There is no time for these customs,' Xais said angrily. 'We have much to discuss.'

Eddie inclined his head slightly. His thick eyebrows knotted and he repeated, a little louder, 'Charlie's having his steak meal.'

Xais was becoming impatient. 'I did not summon you here to watch you eat. The hour of atonement is at hand.'

Charlie stood abruptly, sending the tray and the food crashing to the floor. He dabbed away splashes of gravy from the sides of his mouth with a napkin and said, 'I was having my steak meal. Nobody interrupts my steak meal.'

Xais suppressed her natural instincts, which were screaming at her to kill these ignorant idiots. A glance would be enough. She had to remind herself that they were not Normals, at least, not quite. She took a deep breath and said, 'I was unaware of the significance of this ceremony. It is one of the rites of your clan?'

Eddie looked puzzled and turned to his brother for guidance. 'What's she saying, Charlie?'

Charlie brushed him aside and extended a hand to Xais. 'Pleased to meet you again. And no, I just like to have my steak meal in quiet. Helps me to think.' His voice was very deep and very slow, each word a grave rumble.

'You kept your side of our bargain,' said Xais. 'That is good.'

Charlie shrugged. 'I knew you wouldn't let us down. I remembered what you said at our first meeting, back on Bervisto. Not to worry if you were captured, even if they said you'd been executed, because you had a way out. You're like us, my dear. Too clever to get caught.' He indicated her face. 'What's all that with the mask?'

Xais touched her metallic cheek. 'It is not important. In my escape from the reverser I suffered a disfiguring injury.'

This was her first lie.

Eddie produced a bowl from the food dispenser. It contained a block of something that let off sugary steam. 'You won't be wanting your crumble now, will you, Charlie? Not now you've been interrupted.' He looked down at the custard-smothered dessert. 'Shame to let it go to waste.'

'You've had your yogurt and now you want my crumble. It's not right to have two helpings.'

Eddie shifted uneasily. 'But I don't like yogurt, you know I don't.'

Charlie clamped a hand on his brother's shoulder. 'You'll have what you're given and like it.' He wrenched the bowl away. 'Whether it's yogurt or a clip round the ear. Mum told me to look after you. I know what's best.'

Unnoticed by the brothers, Xais's hands flickered over one of the flight system keyboards.

'But you've had a sponge and a mousse this week already,' protested Eddie.

'Shut up,' said Charlie.

Xais had spent years plotting her revenge and was surprised to find herself listening to such trivial discussions. She decided it was time to reintroduce her agenda to the proceedings.

'My friends,' she said. 'Let us discuss our tactics. First, your servants will sweep through this station and kill all the Normals. I note you are now employing Ogrons.' She hesitated, selecting her next words carefully. 'They are not the most intelligent of beings, are they?'

Charlie halted the crumble-filled spoon that was halfway to his big mouth. 'What are you saying?'

'I merely state what I have heard. The reputation of the Ogrons is not what it was. Once, they could strike fear into the hearts of Normals through the nine corners of space. Now, they are the butt of jokes throughout the human empire.'

The spoon wielded by Charlie had now returned to the plate. He tapped his portion of crumble with its underside menacingly.

'And the Nisbett firm itself,' Xais went on, well aware of the likely reaction to her words, 'the criminal organization that thirty years ago virtually ran West Coppertown. A network of professional businessmen. Reduced to this?' She indicated the rusty ship.

Charlie handed his bowl to Eddie and stepped forward threateningly. His bulk towered over Xais. 'This is a setback. A small setback. Don't make me angry, love. You wouldn't like it. I've handled myself with tougher nuts than you. I had Mad Mick the Tracksuit Atkinson cut in two for less than what you've just said.'

'We've got his kneecaps in a jar on the mantelpiece,' Eddie added. 'I get them out sometimes for a look.'

Charlie smoothed back his hair. 'So don't give us grief. You know how we fell on hard times. No fault of our own. We were betrayed.'

Xais congratulated herself on her understanding of exactly what motivated the Nisbetts. She had succeeded in steering the conversation to where she wanted. 'Quite. And remember, I know the identity of that informer. And I will give you the name, once you have given me what I require.'

She leant forward and straightened the collar of Charlie's coat. 'And we will then be a lot happier, and wealthier.'

Romana had unearthed a small toolkit from a well-stocked storage locker in a corner of the control centre untouched by the explosion of the central console, and was using the rudimentary tools it contained to attempt repairs on K9. The task was made doubly difficult by the lack of adequate lighting.

She tweaked at a junction of coloured wires with a pair of pliers and awaited a reaction. None came. The complexity of K9's internal circuitry baffled her. This model had been constructed by the Doctor after an original that he considered far inferior. Unfortunately, his modifications to the design had been carried out with his customary disregard for technical standards that everyone else in the universe, so far as it seemed to Romana, employed as common sense. She wasn't sure if this approach was born out of lack of skill or sheer bloody-mindedness. Whichever was the case, the innards of K9 Mark II were an amazing hotch-potch of items cobbled together by means that were the work of either genius or ineptitude.

'Come on, K9,' she urged the inert audio sensors of the dog. 'Power up. I've reconnected your fuse box.'

There was no response. Romana's shoulders slumped. 'I'll just have to start again,' she said. She was all too aware that K9 could come in very useful if they had been boarded by hostiles.

The technicians had fled the control centre when the Rock had steadied itself. The only other person left with Romana was Pyerpoint, who had pulled himself up with all the dignity he could muster and staggered over to an emergency unit. The arrival of the alien craft seemed to have shaken him. His immaculately coiffured hair had unwound from its beaded coil and his face was drawn and pale.

'What are they?' she heard him cry from the other side of the room. Romana abandoned work on K9 for a moment and went to him. He pointed at a small monochrome screen. It showed a group of uniformed security officers struggling to beat off an attack by three huge, hairy, ape-like beings dressed in rough sacking coveralls and purple jerkins. They watched as one of the creatures took one of the guards by the neck and snapped it in his mighty grip like a twig.

'Ogrons,' Romana replied, shocked. 'They're mercenaries. I wonder who they're working for?'

'Xais,' growled Pyerpoint. 'That's obvious.' He flicked a couple of switches next to the screen and sound was relayed to accompany the picture.

The voices of the Ogrons were gruff and deep. 'Come. We must attack. Or the Mr Nisbetts will not be pleased.' They ambled away from the security camera.

Pyerpoint's eyes widened. 'Nisbetts?'

'I've heard of them,' said Romana. 'Gangsters, aren't they?'

'Indeed. And in a different league to Xais. Why is she doing this?'

He reached for a large red button on the emergency panel. A klaxon began to sound loudly from speakers around the station. The recorded voice that made all the announcements aboard the Rock said smoothly, 'This is an emergency. This is not a drill. Evacuate. Evacuate. Evacuate.'

Although it had been designed by her sly mind to goad the Nisbetts, there was more than an ounce of truth in Xais's approximation of the Ogrons' abilities. They lumbered through the corridors of the building, and shot down any human that was unfortunate enough to cross their path. As far as this part of their task was concerned, they were efficient enough. The problems lay with the inability of the Ogron mind to grapple with the twisting geography of their surroundings. The architects of the Rock had endowed the complex with an unsettling lack of symmetry that confused even those who had lived and worked there for years. So it was that the Ogrons spent much of the time they had been allocated for the purpose of maiming and murdering wandering the echoing, empty corridors that wound around the building. A crucial mistake was that they had concentrated on reaching the centre, at the same time that the workers, lawyers and criminals, encouraged by the klaxon, were running for the stairway and the escape capsules, or making for the transmat, all of which were located on the far side of the complex.

K9's eyescreen flashed red for less than a second and died again. 'Good boy, K9,' Romana said. 'You can do it.' But there was no further response from the dog.

Pyerpoint had sunk into a chair, his head in his hands. 'You must leave,' he said. 'Your colleagues may be dead,

119

but you could still get away.'

Romana lifted K9, who was surprisingly light, from the console and joined Pyerpoint. She knew for certain that the best course of action for her to take would be to return to the TARDIS, where she could repair K9 with adequate tools.

'I know a place where we can hide,' she told Pyerpoint. 'Come with me.'

He remained slumped in the chair. 'No. You go. I must stay here.'

'They'll kill you.'

Pyerpoint looked up at her. To her surprise, there was anger in his eyes, the first time she had seen an emotion expressed so strongly there. 'I know what will happen to me,' he said. 'And I have to stay.'

Romana could tell there was no point in trying to reason with him. He probably had some grand notion about the captain going down with his ship. She hefted K9 in her arms and left the control centre.

As soon as Romana had gone, Pyerpoint stood. The normally impassive set of his features twisted into a snarl. He picked up the chair he had been sitting on and threw it across the room. It smashed into the damaged area and sent a shower of sparks flying.

He reached in his tunic and pulled out a red key, then crossed back to the emergency systems panel and inserted it in a small slot. A red light flashed and he spoke into a concealed microphone.

'This is High Archon Pyerpoint, broadcasting from asteroid 6KK Gamma, the Rock of Judgement. Our emergency is under control. Repeat, I have the situation under control. Caution. Do not approach. I say again, do not approach. Radiation hazard.'

He withdrew the key and pressed a button next to the slot. The message he had recorded would be repeated constantly until he saw fit to cancel it.

* * *

The first thing the Doctor's senses registered as he returned to consciousness was the smell. He possessed a large and very sensitive nose that identified sweat, filth and badly brewed alcohol in the recycled air around him. There was also a bruise throbbing on the back of his head.

He opened an eye to check his surroundings and saw a large boot. The boot's owner was standing guard over the Doctor's forlorn body, his unthinking, ape-like eyes trained on the opposite wall. For a moment, the Doctor considered tackling the Ogron and making a break for it. But the creature was armed and he was feeling rather beaten, so he decided to bide his time. He closed his eye.

Voices and footsteps drifted along a nearby corridor. The Doctor strained to make out what they were saying, which wasn't difficult, because they were heading in his direction.

The first voice he recognized as that of Margo, now submerged by the identity of Xais. 'I thought you might like to take a look at him, and ask him a few questions. He's an investigator of Five police.'

'What, you reckon they might be on to us?' This voice was male and sounded almost as deep as that of an Ogron.

'I'm not certain,' said Xais. 'But I think it's worth keeping him alive, for the moment.'

The Doctor gave an inward sigh of relief. He heard the small party move away from the doorway of whatever unpleasant room was his cell. Their voices carried faintly through to him and he rolled over very slightly in order to follow their conversation.

'About the deal,' said a third voice, male again. It was similar to the first, but contained a quality that made it somehow more threatening. 'We've got the items you requested, all that mining equipment. Before we go any further, I want to know more about the belzite you promised us. We've waited four years to begin this operation, remember. We want results. Where is the belzite?'

'That's easily answered,' said Xais. 'Planet Eleven. There is a rich seam of belzite there.'

'That can't be so,' said the first male voice. 'There's nothing down there. Besides, they can't scan the surface because of the storms.'

'Belzite,' Xais insisted. 'Up to six million credits' worth. I discovered it through a contact in McConnochie Mining, some years ago. The company are aware of it, of course.' She paused. 'They've been holding back from exploiting the planet until the economic conditions are right. I am aware of the exact location. Which I will divulge when we reach the planet.'

The stronger male voice spoke again. 'And the other information you hold?'

'Ah, yes, the identity of the man who betrayed you. I will reveal it when the mining operation is complete. That seems reasonable to me.'

The Doctor was unable to hear what was said next, as Xais and her accomplices turned a corner. He decided it was time to take a more active part in the proceedings and emitted a loud and theatrical groan before rolling over and snapping both eyes open.

The Ogron stared down at him. 'You are a prisoner. Stay still or I shoot.'

The Doctor took no notice and leapt up from the floor. The room of his confinement was now revealed to him as the Ogrons' mess. There had probably never been such an apposite use of the word. Personal hygiene was plainly not one of the Ogrons' primary concerns. When packed with the dirty creatures the place must have been frightful.

'Hello, I'm the Doctor,' he said, offering the Ogron a hand and grinning broadly. 'What's your name?'

As he had hoped, the Ogron was confused by his air of authority. It was used to obeying orders, following the commands of the strong in order to subjugate the weak. 'My name is Gjork,' it said.

'Gjork, eh? That's a very good name, Gjork.' He

fumbled in his pockets and produced a small paper bag. 'Now, would you like a jelly baby?' He took one of the sweets from the bag and bit its head off, then offered the remnant to his captor.

The Ogron snatched the half-eaten sweet from him and examined it with suspicion. 'Go on, try it, they're really very nice,' the Doctor urged.

Gjork raised the sweet to his lips and popped it into his mouth. He smiled and said, 'Give me another jelly baby.'

The Doctor nodded. 'Delighted.' He made to pass the bag to the Ogron and pretended to notice that it was carrying a rifle. 'I tell you what, I'll hold that, you hold this.'

For a moment it looked like the Doctor's plan was going to succeed. Just as Gjork was about to hand the rifle over, some working in the cumbersome muddle of his mind clicked and he pushed the Doctor back. 'You are a prisoner!'

The Doctor popped another jelly baby into his mouth and chewed resentfully. 'Aren't I just,' he said.

The corridors of the station were almost empty. The Ogrons had shut down the lift system and Romana had hurried to level three, K9 in her hands, down the emergency stairs. She found the recreation area, which was also deserted. The emergency klaxon had stopped sounding and now a silence had settled over the station. She might have believed she was the only person left aboard as she looked around at the sofas and the unattended bar.

Something crashed over, not far away. Heavy footsteps echoed along the corridor outside. Romana looked to the far door, which led to the TARDIS. She might just reach it in time. Hoisting K9 further up in her arms, she stepped from cover and raced for the door.

Too late. The other door crashed open and two Ogrons stumbled in. One of them saw her, raised its rifle, and fired. The blast whizzed past her ear and she threw herself the few remaining yards to safety. Her pursuers grunted and shouted and pounded heavily after her.

Romana pelted down the corridor outside, skidding round the corner that led to the panel the Doctor had cut through. The Ogrons might be stupid, she reflected, but they were surprisingly nimble. The distance between them was closing, and it would take only one bolt to blow her out of existence. She squeezed herself and K9 through the rough-edged hole cut by the sonic screwdriver and found herself back in the cavern where the TARDIS had materialized. It stood there, square, blue and reassuring. Now all she had to do was get inside.

The Ogrons were directly behind her. Her dilemma now was that she couldn't afford to stop at the door of the TARDIS, an action that would offer them a sitting target. A plan worthy of the Doctor presented itself to her. She would lead the Ogrons into the catacombs leading off from the station, lose them, which shouldn't be too difficult, and then return at her leisure.

She dashed for the exit to the cavern, a thin crack in the rock that was only just wide enough to admit her and K9. As she passed through, she appreciated how much that would delay the Ogrons. With luck, they might even give up and turn back. She sneaked a quick glance back at them. They raised their rifles and fired again in her general direction. Where usually she might have been pleased by their lack of accuracy, she was distressed to note the effects of this salvo.

A large portion of the cavern's roof creaked, wobbled, and collapsed, showering the Ogrons with rock dust. This had the less pleasing result of showering the TARDIS with huge chunks of rubble that blocked the door.

Upsetting though this was, it did not dampen Romana's determination to escape. She pushed herself on, noting that the Ogrons had already regained their sensibilities and were making their way through the cavern towards her.

The route she had chosen took her into a long, low tunnel, from either side of which several possible openings sprouted. She ducked through one at random, crouched behind a spar of rock, and listened for the sounds of pursuit. The Ogrons were clattering about nearby, but the confusing acoustics of the chambers of rock meant that she could not be sure of their location.

'I fear the darkness,' said one of the Ogrons.

'Yes,' his comrade murmured. 'One ugly girl is not important. Masters will not care. We will go now.'

Romana heard them moving away. She waited a few moments and emerged from hiding. Her only chance now, she knew, was to get K9 operational again. His nose laser would make short work of the boulders blocking the door of the TARDIS. She took the toolkit from the inside pocket of her jacket and got back to work. Perhaps it would be a better idea to cross his geostatic traction links with his power accelerator . . .

Thus engrossed, Romana was unaware of the large, lumbering figure moving through the shadows towards her.

9

The Plotters

'Ah! A friendly face, at last!'

Romana jumped at the sound of the distinctively plummy voice and gave a sigh of relief as the new arrival revealed himself. For this was an infinitely more reassuring presence than a returning Ogron.

'Mr Stokes! You made me jump!'

He waved a hand. 'I must apologize. I didn't intend to give you a fright.' Romana noted the genuine contrition in his voice. He walked into a shaft of light and she saw the streaks of grime that covered his big sweaty face and the disarray of his clothing. His suit, which had never been immaculate, was torn in places and the collar of his shirt was askew. 'Alas,' he went on, 'I was overcome by enthusiasm at the sight of your prettiness.'

He blew out his cheeks and sat down on a ledge that formed a perfect seat in the rock. 'What is that curious object?' he asked, indicating the inert K9.

'Never mind about him,' Romana said hurriedly. 'Tell me what happened to you.'

Stokes wiped his forehead and smeared an even longer greasy streak across it. 'It was horrifying, my dear,' he said. 'I was ruminating in my cell when I heard screaming and shouting. And shots. Then the door of my cell opened by itself and they were telling us to evacuate. For a moment, I thought I'd landed myself in the middle of a break-out. Until I saw one of those brutes with the guns.' He shuddered. 'Well, of course, everyone started running for the escape capsules or the transmat. Including myself. Except I got lost, didn't I?'

'You know the station well enough to find your way about, surely?' asked Romana.

'Oh yes, I know it very well, when the lifts are working. But all those stairs!' He took a dirty handkerchief from his pocket and coughed into it. 'Goodness, yes, with those hairy monsters lumbering about. I haven't run like that for many years.'

Romana felt he deserved an explanation. 'Yes, well these creatures are called Ogrons. They're a slave race. At present they appear to be working for the Nisbetts.'

Stokes's red face blanched white in less than two seconds. 'The Nisbetts? The psychotic brothers?'

Romana shrugged. 'I suppose so.'

The artist lurched to his feet and started to wring his hands. 'And I didn't believe things could get any worse! This is appalling news!' He looked about at the catacombs. 'I don't know whether my bladder can stand all this!'

'I hope it can,' said Romana. 'Because I think the Doctor's been captured by them. And we have to rescue him.'

A thought struck her. 'And Xais is involved as well. She's somehow reincarnated herself using that mask you made for her.'

'I won't say that's any more impossible than anything else that's happened today,' Stokes said. 'In fact, it seems almost reassuringly ordinary.' He shook his head. 'Oh no, my dear,' he told Romana, 'I'm afraid I'm not trained for this sort of thing.'

'No doubt.' Romana had to admit that Stokes was more of a liability than an asset. 'But I'm afraid we've no choice. We have to rescue the Doctor.'

Stokes backed away. 'I don't think so, my dear. I know he meant a lot to you, but if the Doctor has fallen foul of the Nisbetts, there is every likelihood that his internal organs are now scattered in small gristly portions. And I, for one, have no intention of joining him in that fate. I've often stated that the kidneys belong inside the body.'

He straightened his collar and started to walk away. 'Goodbye, my dear. I hope that your venture brings you success.'

Romana watched him depart. 'It's best if we stick together,' she called after him. 'Stokes!' But he had gone, without a backward glance.

She returned her attentions to K9. The breakthrough was near, she was certain. A green light showed that his power distributor links were almost powered up. Theoretically, he could come back on line at any moment, as long as nothing else had been damaged.

Stokes came crashing back through the catacombs. Romana jolted upright, terrified that he had led the Ogrons to her. 'What are you doing?' she whispered as he stumbled towards her.

He pointed dumbly behind him. 'It's coming,' he gasped at last. 'One of those great hairy Orgons.'

'Ogrons,' Romana corrected.

'Whatever they're called, it's right behind me,' he blurted. 'I bumped into the blessed thing, it's huge, covered in long filthy coarse hair. Ugh!'

'You idiot!' cried Romana as they heard the sound of approaching steps. 'You've led it here!' She looked around but there was nowhere to run. The footsteps grew nearer.

Spiggot emerged into the light, smoothing back his long permed hair and trying not to look too ruffled.

'All right there,' he greeted them confidently and lit a cigarette. 'I think it's about time we got this mess sorted out, don't you?'

Xais observed her allies closely.

Eddie was looking up at the high ceiling of level two of the station. Inscribed in gilt letters was a scroll that detailed the achievements of the Uva Beta Uva state since its foundation almost two hundred years ago.

'Look at that! We could strip that lot, make a fair few bob.' He squinted up at the letters. 'I can't make it out.'

Charlie glowered at him. 'It's in Latin,' he said.

'What's that, then?'

'It's the language the Romans used to speak. Besides, three grand of synthigold ain't nothing on three mill of the big B.'

'Quite.' Xais gestured ahead. 'Let us hurry, please.'

As they walked on, she looked approvingly at the deserted corridors and passageways and at their escort of two Ogrons. 'Perhaps I was hasty in my opinion of your new slaves. They have done well to clear this place of the Normals.'

Charlie nodded. 'They're not bad lads.'

'Where did you come by them?'

Eddie answered. 'After the firm was broken up, we were on the look out for some new muscle. We got them cheap, in a job lot from the labour pits.'

'What Edward means to say,' said Charlie, 'is that we purchased the Ogrons for a competitive price from the auctions on Ghelluris. Their previous owners had run into a spot of bother – they were planning to invade the galaxy but some bloke blew half of them sky high – and they had to sell up.'

'Charlie got us the ship into the bargain,' said Eddie. 'It used to belong to a warfleet, you know.'

'Oh really?' said Xais.

'Yes. But it isn't a patch on what we're used to, though. We had a luxury class star yacht, you know. The *Stellar Caprice*. Gone like all the rest of our stuff when we were grassed up.'

Charlie stopped and turned. 'Eddie, you know I don't like you talking about the old days.'

They had now almost reached the control centre. Xais had another question to ask. 'The man who betrayed you. You never met him, yet you trusted him. I always wondered. Why was this?'

'He was a good contact. Plenty of inside knowledge. We communicated in code, on pirate satellites. He always fixed things for us, told us if the coppers were sniffing round. In return, he got his cut. Thirty per cent, beamed down the credit line to an untraceable Platinumtown bank account. He called himself Sentinel.'

Charlie's hands clenched. 'The lying scum put the law on to us. He must have got greedy for the price on our heads. We had to break up the firm and run. None of our mates got away. Tony, Frankie, Dylan the leg. All gone to the particle reverser.'

'It is good that you understand hatred for this Sentinel,' said Xais as they reached the door of the control centre. 'Hatred is the purest, strongest, most beautiful force in the universe.'

The door to computer control was flung open from inside and Pyerpoint staggered out. She'd been wondering where he'd got to. He straightened himself and their eyes met.

'Well?' he said with surprising calm. 'I'm waiting for an explanation.'

Xais threw her head back and laughed. 'Gentlemen. Allow me to introduce High Archon Pyerpoint.'

'The reversing judge,' Charlie said. 'You passed sentence on my firm, old man.'

Pyerpoint faced him squarely. 'I would do so again. It is my duty.'

Eddie reached inside his jacket and pulled out a compact black blaster. 'Can I have him, Charlie?' he pleaded.

Xais stepped forward. 'No. I have good reason to hate this man also. It was he who sentenced me to death.' She stared at Pyerpoint. 'I want him to suffer ultimate humiliation before he dies.'

'Why not?' said Charlie. He came closer to Pyerpoint and fixed him with his fiercest stare. 'Bnorg,' he ordered the nearest Ogron. 'Take this old fellow back to the ship and put him in with the other one. In the guest suite.'

The Ogron grabbed Pyerpoint by the scruff of his neck. 'No guest suite on ship, Mr Charles,' he said, confused.

'The crew quarters.'

Bnorg nodded and grunted, his huge yellow teeth and rotting gums visible as he gave the Ogron equivalent of a laugh. 'Guest suite! It is a funny joke!'

'Shut up and obey your orders,' Charlie said. Bnorg quietened immediately and set off back down the corridor, almost dragging Pyerpoint along behind him.

Xais returned her attentions to the door of computer control. 'Now, to business. We must set a course for Planet Eleven.'

'Hold on. Why don't we take our own ship?'

Xais said patiently, 'No. You would not be able to land on its boggy surface. We will use this station to reach Eleven, transmat down to the survey base on the surface, and then release the security on their emergency launchpad.'

Charlie was pleased. 'You've got this well planned. Good.'

The Doctor had spent about three-quarters of an hour under the watchful eyes of the sweet-toothed Ogron and he was becoming bored. He took another look around the mess. In a corner stood a large food dispenser, of the kind that normally displays a variety of items from which the user makes a selection. This one appeared to contain nothing but meat pasties.

'Excuse me. This machine. There's nothing in it but pasties.'

The Ogron nodded. 'We like pasties.'

'Good job, really.' The Doctor squinted at something written in small alien script further along the wall. 'Product of the Kathok empire,' he read. 'Hah. Haven't seen one of these for years. I think your masters have been taken for a ride.'

'What do you say?' Gjork asked, puzzled.

The Doctor was glad of the opportunity to demonstrate his superior knowledge, even to an audience this limited and uncomprehending.

'The Kathok empire,' he explained, 'was an invention

131

of scrap merchants in the fourth quadrant. They'd had a few wars in that area, and were left with bits of old spaceships and not a lot of people left to sell them to. So they jammed all the bits together, spun some tale about a fallen empire, and sold them off to gullible souls in surrounding space. All very underhand. And dangerous, of course.' He patted the wall gently. 'These things tend to fall apart rather easily.'

Gjork frowned. 'Ship is good. You be quiet.'

The door of the mess slid open and Pyerpoint was thrown in. The Doctor hurried to his side and pulled him up. Another Ogron stood in the doorway.

'Gjork,' he said. 'Here is another prisoner. We must look after him.'

'Are you all right, old chap?' the Doctor asked Pyerpoint.

The old man straightened his clothes. 'I believe so.' He wrinkled his nose. 'What is that appalling smell?'

The Doctor watched as Gjork and Bnorg sauntered over to the food machine and removed their rations. 'Pasties, warm beer and Ogron doings,' he told Pyerpoint. He looked the judge in the eye. 'This is all a bit of a dog's breakfast, isn't it?'

They've rampaged through the station, Doctor. I think nearly everyone has got out, either by transmat or in the escape capsules.' He bit his lip.

'Your security isn't very good, is it?' the Doctor pointed out. 'Perhaps you should have listened to us, eh?'

Pyerpoint pinched the bridge of his nose. 'You are a police investigator, Doctor. I have learnt to distrust members of your profession over the years.' The Doctor noticed for the first time how angry Pyerpoint appeared, as if he was forcing down a torrent of rage. He had lost his career and nearly his life in the space of a few hours, but his concern seemed to be directed at something else. Something that wasn't yet clear.

'The involvement of the Nisbett brothers,' said the Doctor, 'has come as something of a surprise.'

'Indeed,' Pyerpoint said quietly.

'But I happen to have overheard,' the Doctor said confidentially, 'the details of their alliance.'

Pyerpoint became more alert. 'Yes?'

The Doctor outlined what he had heard about Xais's promise to lead the Nisbetts to a rich seam of belzite on Planet Eleven in return for the use of their mining equipment. When he had finished, Pyerpoint closed his eyes and sighed.

'She is lying to them,' he told the Doctor. 'There can be no belzite on Eleven. It's quite impossible, the entire planet is next to worthless. That's common knowledge.'

The Doctor rubbed his chin. 'So what's she really after, eh?'

Romana had moved back to the cavern where the TARDIS had materialized. It was easier for her to work on K9 in the light. She and Stokes were being treated to Spiggot's account of his escape from the Ogrons.

'I was glad of my training, I can tell you. Of course, training on its own's nothing. Instinct's important.' He stubbed out his cigarette on a rock. 'I guess that's my strength. And perhaps my weakness, too. Follow your nose, and it might lead you to your prey, or you might get it cut off.'

'I'm not sure how much of this I can stand,' said Stokes.

Spiggot misunderstood. 'Try not to get too uptight. I've figured my way out of worse situations than this. This is the easy side of my life.' He ran a hand through his hair. 'It's on the emotional side of things that my talents aren't suited. Take my wife, Angie. I lost her, didn't I, screwed the whole thing up.'

'Yes, I'm sure your marital history is fascinating,' Stokes said rudely. 'But at present my thoughts are, perhaps oddly, rather more preoccupied with my likely demise at the hands of those Orgon things.'

Romana looked up from her work on K9. 'Ogrons.'

To her delight, this word brought about a response from K9. His head raised, his audio sensors twittered, and he said, 'Ogrons. Simian humanoid ectomorphs, *homo ogronalis*. Natives of high gravity planet known as Braah, located in the outer extremity of Earth's galaxy.'

Romana couldn't help putting her arms around the metallic animal. 'Oh, K9, it's good to have you back.'

'Sentiments reciprocated, Mistress.'

Stokes crouched down next to K9. 'This is your idea of a weapon? What effect do you imagine that will have on the Nisbett brothers? Do you expect them to die laughing?'

Rather put out, K9 extended his nose laser. A bright red beam shot out and blasted a chunk of rock from the wall behind Stokes.

He leapt up. 'Perhaps I was rather hasty in my judgement, er . . . ?'

'K9,' the dog said proudly. 'Mistress, I am now fully recharged and ready to assist you.'

'Good boy, K9,' said Romana. 'How are your sensors? Do you think you can locate the Doctor for me?'

She looked on as K9 started to turn a circle, his antennae buzzing. 'It's no use, that thing can't have the range, it's too small,' Spiggot said.

'I don't consider it wise to underestimate K9,' Stokes reminded him. 'His little nose ray certainly seems like our biggest asset at present.'

'Survey completed, Mistress,' K9 reported, coming to a standstill. 'The Doctor Master is located inside the spacecraft docked to this station.'

'How is he, K9?'

'His heartbeats are steady, Mistress.'

Romana looked up triumphantly. 'I was right. The Doctor is alive and well.'

'He's on the Nisbett brothers' ship, love,' said Spiggot. 'I don't call that alive and well. I call it alive and being saved up for the toenail job later on.'

Romana turned back to K9. 'Listen, K9. I want you to

clear a way to the TARDIS.' She indicated the blocked entrance.

'Orders accepted.' K9 motored eagerly forward and started to blast away the rocks.

Romana stood up. 'I'm going to rescue the Doctor. Are either of you coming?'

Spiggot and Stokes regarded each other coolly. She could tell that each was waiting for the other to speak.

'My dear,' said Stokes. 'You surely can't contemplate such a mission, particularly not alone.'

'Those Ogrons'll blast you as soon as they see you,' said Spiggot.

'How gallant.' She turned to leave.

To her astonishment, she found Stokes following her. 'Wait, wait.'

She turned. 'Yes?'

He dithered for a few moments and said, 'I'll come.' He took her hand. 'There's something about you, Ramona, that I find rather reassuring.' He shot a look back at Spiggot. 'And if I'm going to die, I may as well do it in the best possible company.'

As they walked off, Spiggot called, 'Well, good luck. But I still think you're nuts.'

Alone, Spiggot knelt down and patted K9 on the head. 'Looks like it's just you and me now.'

K9 concentrated on his work and did not reply.

'I don't suppose,' Spiggot continued, 'a computer like you can understand what it feels like to be human. To have flaws, imperfections. All your reactions are printed on a circuit board. You'll never have trouble with the ladies, K9. Do you know, it's crazy, but it's at times like this, when my life's on the line, that I can't stop thinking about Angie and the kids, about where I fouled up. People think that I'm tough, that I can cope, just 'cause they see me beating people up now and then or drinking a bit. They don't seem to understand that I'm a man too, that I've got the feelings and the needs of a man. That I've got a sensitive side . . .'

Spiggot carried on. What he didn't know was that K9's audio sensors, which assessed all incoming data for relevance and possible future usefulness, had switched themselves off long ago.

The screen that dominated one wall of computer control showed the Rock of Judgement's present position in relation to its new objective. Xais sat before the row of shattered consoles, the short nails of Margo tapping navigational data into the guidance systems. Her task completed, she plucked the necessary codeword from Margo's memory, punched it in, and sat back. The screen flicked through reams of computation and settled on a pattern that snaked around the system towards Planet Eleven. Xais keyed in her assent and the giant thrusters embedded in the other side of the asteroid swivelled in their sockets. The floor vibrated as the new course was established.

Pleased, Xais turned to the Nisbetts. 'All is well. We will arrive in orbit around Planet Eleven in just under three hours.'

She flicked a button on her console and the screen switched to a view of the station's transmat terminal. It was an unexceptional structure, with a transmission platform raised before a control panel. A couple of Ogrons stood on guard. At their feet were the bodies of workers that hadn't made it to the transmat before it fell to the invaders.

'Good,' said Charlie. 'We may as well get ourselves settled in. I'll have the lads bring over the mining equipment.' He took a small communicator from his inside pocket and flicked the channel open.

'Now,' Xais said, 'I wish to interrogate the investigator. I want to know how much the police know of our operation. Bring him to me.'

The hard stares of the brothers reminded Xais that they were unused to receiving orders. 'If you would,' she added reluctantly. How she loathed having to abase herself before these insects.

'The Nisbett brothers are mutants themselves,' Pyerpoint told the Doctor. 'Recessives. They are allowed to live in certain areas, but they are not permitted to vote, or associate.'

'Then it's no wonder they're so impolite.' The Doctor sat on the floor of the mess, staring into space. He clicked his fingers. 'Worthless!'

'What is worthless?'

'Helicon. Everyone knows it's worthless. They mix it with Ball's ore and use it to line pipes.'

'I know that,' Pyerpoint said patiently.

'Exactly!' the Doctor cried. 'You know it, I know it. Everyone knows it. Apart from Xais. Because to her it's the most valuable thing in the universe. It's given her a kind of immortality, although I'm not sure how.'

Gjork, who had been listening to orders on his communicator, strode over to him. 'You, stand. You are wanted by Xais.'

'Ah! Well, it's always nice to feel wanted.' The Doctor stood. 'Let's go, my feet hurt, it must be all that sitting down.' He was led out by Gjork.

The Doctor was dragged along the deserted corridors of the Rock by Gjork. A further set of instructions from Xais, relayed over the communicator carried at the Ogron's belt, directed them up to level eight. They passed the rows of cells, empty for the first time since their construction. If he had been a lesser man, the Doctor might have grown fearful at this point, but dungeons had long ago ceased to worry him unduly.

At the end of a long and straight metal corridor, Gjork lurched forward abruptly and bundled the Doctor through a door set into one wall. It was a small and unimpressive door that led to a large room as bare and grey as everything else in this area of the station. It contained a row of seats, and a platform upon which stood Xais. Her hand rested on a large metal chair that had been bolted to the platform. Directly above it was a funnel-shaped structure that was bolted to the ceiling. The room was antiseptically clean, but it contained a sharp, sweet odour the Doctor recognized immediately as the smell of death.

'Hello,' said the Doctor. 'We must have a chat.'

Xais hissed. 'Do you recognize this chair, investigator?'

'Please, call me the Doctor. Investigator sounds far too formal.' He peered at the chair. 'I can't say I do. Is it important?'

She slapped him viciously across the face with the back of her hand. The blow drew blood. The Doctor winced and felt the wound tenderly. 'I don't think that was necessary.'

'Be thankful, Normal,' she warned him, 'that I do not unleash my power to crush you where you stand.' She ran her hand along the back of the chair. 'It was in this chair that I met my death, three years ago. They say the particle reversal process is painless. That is a lie, like much of what Normals say. I screamed as the rays from the reverser bathed my body and I was consumed. Dissipated to the cold winds. But they had not triumphed. I survived, my soul survived, and fled to the mask.'

The Doctor raised a polite finger, as if he were a keen student at a lecture. 'Er, yes, I wanted a word about that, actually. We can't have all this immortality, you know. It makes a mockery of the judiciary if people they've executed keep popping up again and carrying on where they left off. Fair dos and all that.' He trailed off, aware that Xais might be about to strike him again as she came around the chair.

'You talk like an idiot, Doctor,' she said. 'Why? You are not an idiot, I can tell that.'

'Perhaps I'm just curious. I'd like to know how you pulled off that trick with the mask, actually. And about your choice of material, helicon.'

'No doubt you would.' Xais clicked her fingers and Gjork threw the Doctor into the chair. 'Unfortunately, you are not in a position to ask questions.'

The Doctor settled himself in the chair and crossed his legs nonchalantly. 'I don't know. This is rather comfortable.'

Xais pressed a control built into a panel fixed to the wall and the Doctor found himself fixed to the chair. He cried out as a beam of force gripped him. With a tremendous effort he managed to speak. 'A force field.'

'Which will at least still your flapping tongue.' To the Doctor's pained senses, her voice seemed to come from far away. 'Unless you answer my questions, Doctor, I will operate the reverser. Every last atom of your body will be inverted. Your blood will bubble, your brain will expand until it seeps through your skull. Your suffering will be amusement to me. My hate is stronger than you could comprehend.'

The Doctor cried out. 'I'll answer your questions. I didn't say I wouldn't.' He twisted his head painfully in an attempt to face her. 'Pardon me for saying so, but you seem to take considerable pleasure in your work.'

She trailed her fingertips almost tenderly across his wounded cheek. 'Oh, foolish Normal, with your idiotic humour. I am going to make you scream for death.'

An Ogron paced up and down outside the docking port leading to the Nisbett brothers' ship, his rifle raised. Occasionally he yawned and revealed his black tongue and rotting teeth.

Stokes and Romana crouched at the entrance to the previously concealed docking port and looked down at the sentry. Their lack of armament did not inspire Stokes's confidence. 'We should have brought your computer,' he whispered.

Romana shook her head. 'One Ogron shouldn't be too much of a problem. I hope. Their evolutionary pedigree is rather fascinating, actually.'

'Yes?'

'Hmm. The climate of their planet went through a series of rapid changes. All the evolutionary paths they took got confused. Their instincts are a mixture of primate and carnivore. They're even more jumbled up than your own species.'

She emerged from hiding and hopped nimbly down to the entry hatch.

Stokes, terrified, shook his head at her gall. The girl was certainly brave as well as beautiful. He watched as the Ogron observed her approach and raised his rifle to cover her. 'You, girl!' he shouted. 'Stop or I fire!'

'Don't you know who I am?' she said haughtily.

The Ogron, who must, thought Stokes, be accustomed to being pushed around, cowered, lowered his weapon, and shook his head.

'I am Xais!' Romana shrieked, outraged. 'The partner of your masters, the Nisbett brothers. Now stand aside and let me pass.'

'The masters say no one allowed in ship,' the Ogron protested weakly.

'They will be displeased if you do not let me pass,' Romana blustered. 'Now, will you obey me? You know of my power to kill with one glance?'

The Ogron muttered feebly and scampered aside. Romana summoned Stokes. His heart in his mouth, he came forward and stumbled past the Ogron. 'I'm with her,' he stammered, rather spoiling the effect.

The dark entranceway of the ship gave onto a central corridor that ended in a flight deck, with doors leading off to either side. There appeared to be nobody about. Stokes and Romana crept along the aisle, trying to step as lightly as possible in case their presence was noted.

'I cannot believe I am doing this,' Stokes whispered. 'If yesterday you had given me the choice between breaking into the Nisbett brothers' ship or hacking off one of my own legs with a rusty saw, I would definitely have taken the latter.'

He noticed a rack of weapons built into the wall. Romana took down one of the compact rifles used by the Ogrons and looked it over. 'High impact, high range energy weapon. Causes displacement of internal organs through narrow channel photon bombardment.'

'Don't go on, I feel queasy enough as things stand,' Stokes protested.

'Ah, but there's a stun setting,' Romana pointed out. 'That could come in handy.'

She flicked the catch off the rifle and walked towards the nearest door. Stokes followed, peering over her shoulder. A transparent panel revealed a storeroom that contained several boxes and large metal containers. Romana walked on to the next door and looked into that.

'Don't tell me, it's the torture chamber,' Stokes muttered, his knees knocking. 'Replete with every device of agony known to humanity, and a few more besides.'

Romana beckoned him over and pointed through the panel. Stokes looked and saw Pyerpoint, sitting cross-legged on the floor. Standing on the other side of the large dirty grey room was an armed Ogron. 'It's the old scratcher,' said Stokes. 'Trust him to survive.'

He was alarmed to see Romana's hand reaching for the door control. 'Create a diversion,' she ordered him. He would have protested but the door was already open and the Ogron was lumbering over.

'Who are you? What do you want?' it demanded.

Stokes fumbled for an explanation. 'I – I'm an old friend of the Nisbett brothers,' he stammered. 'I thought I'd just, er, drop in.'

The Ogron looked him up and down. 'You do not look like friend of brothers.'

Trust my luck to get the clever one, thought Stokes. 'Yes, they said, do pop round if you're ever passing.' He tried to think of something else to say, but his mouth merely opened and closed a few times. His eyes kept flicking down to the Ogron's rifle.

Fortunately, this diversion was all that Romana needed. She leapt through the door and fired her stun charge at close range to the Ogron. He was knocked back and his rifle fell from his grip. The ape floundered on the floor, his eyelids fluttering a few times before they closed at last.

Pyerpoint sprang up nimbly. He stared at Stokes, who was fanning away the fetid air. 'What are you doing aboard this ship?'

'Rescuing you, you ungrateful old idiot,' Stokes said. 'You can thank Ramona for that, of course. If the decision had been mine, I'd have left you here in the lock-up. Given you a taste of your own medicine, as it were.'

Romana addressed Pyerpoint. 'What's happened to the Doctor?'

He stooped to scoop up the weapon dropped by the Ogron and settled it in the crook of his arm with ease. 'He was taken for interrogation. There was nothing I could do.'

Stokes threw up his arms. 'Interrogation? Oh dear, no. Right now the poor old Doctor's probably lying half in half out of a bath with electrodes dangling over the water. That was one of the firm's favourite methods, as I recall.' He rested a protective hand on Romana's shoulder. 'I really shouldn't discuss such things in front of you, should I? Try not to be too upset.'

She removed the hand. 'Thank you, but I shouldn't worry. The Doctor's been interrogated before. I think he enjoys it.'

'Listen.' Pyerpoint was at the door, looking down the corridor and out of the ship. 'In my office, up on level nine, there's an emergency beacon. Only I know the combination that will activate it.'

'What good will another silly old signal make?' said Stokes.

Pyerpoint angled the tip of his newly acquired rifle slightly towards Stokes and spat, 'It will transmit our exact position to the nearest police patrol. They could be with us in hours.'

'Right,' said Romana, steadying her own weapon. 'Let's go.' She hurried from the mess. Pyerpoint stalked out after her.

'Why do we have to do all this rushing about?' Stokes complained as he panted along the corridor after them. 'Can't we stop and have a rest somewhere?' But the others were not listening.

The door to computer control opened and a small party of Ogrons walked in. They carried gleaming silver crates that were marked with alien symbols. Charlie turned from the console he had been examining and inspected the equipment.

'Right, that lot looks all right. Three mini-rigs, a Kekkerson drill, and seven rubble crushers. Remembered the atmosuits as well, good.' He stepped forward and took a small cardboard box from one of the Ogrons. 'Take it all down to the transmat.'

The first Ogron inclined his head. 'Yes, Mr Charles.' He gestured to his colleagues and they started to shuffle out.

'Hang on,' called Eddie. 'What about the tea?'

He took a smaller box from one of the Ogrons, waved them away again, crossed to the console at which Charlie was seated, put the box down, and pressed a red button on its side. It flipped open. Inside was a steaming pot of tea, a jug of milk, sugar, and a china service that consisted of two small white cups and saucers. Gathered on a plate were a selection of icing-striped fondants in dainty, floral patterned paper cases and a couple of dry tough unsweetened biscuits.

Charlie watched as Eddie poured. In the old days, before the bust, one of the firm would have carried out this task. Old Frank McGhee or Andy the five-headed axe Wilkinson. It would have been beneath the brothers to pour their own tea. They had tried to teach a few of

143

the brighter Ogrons to wait at table, but the ungainly beasts had proved to be appalling butlers, particularly when serving smaller items such as new potatoes or sprouts.

Charlie slipped the pudgy index finger of his right hand through the small handle of his teacup and sipped at the boiling liquid. His other hand wandered over the fancies, weighing the charms of one against another. It settled on a pink oblong. He nibbled the edges of icing from the sponge. He liked to save the small nobble of cream in the middle of the top to the very last and eat around it.

'Just think,' he heard his brother say. 'With three million credits' worth of the big B, we'll be able to get ourselves proper tea again, none of this HL plantation stuff.'

Charlie settled his teacup on its saucer and finished off his fondant before speaking. 'Listen to the boy,' he said. 'It's a good thing Mum told me to look after you, Ed. "Three million credits' worth of the big B." My elbow.' He noted Eddie's eyes lusting for a fondant and passed him one of the unappealing biscuits.

'What, you don't think she's trying to spin one over on us?' Eddie's eyes narrowed.

'Do I reckon?' Charlie finished his tea. 'Do I reckon? If Dad could see you now, Ed. What would he think.' He leant over the console. 'There's no belzite on Planet Eleven. If there were, it'd have been stripped clear years back. And she knows as much about our old chum Sentinel as I know about keeping goats.'

'What, she's taking us for a pair of chumps?' Eddie slammed down his teacup and bit a corner off his biscuit. 'Let's have her!'

'Don't be hasty,' said Charlie. 'Think about it. Xais wants us to set up a little mine on Eleven, right? So there's got to be something worth her trouble down there. And if it's worth her trouble, worth waiting for us all this time, it's got to be worth a lot. I want to find out what it is. And

144

don't think I'm going soft, neither.' He reached for the other box he had taken from the Ogrons and flipped open its cardboard flaps. A row of small, dusty, bullet-shaped objects, painted a dull green, were inside, wrapped up in yellowing newspaper. 'Remember these?'

'They're those remote blast mines you bought off that bloke at the auction,' said Eddie.

Charlie replaced the flaps. 'Right you are. Insurance. We'll set them up down at this survey base. And when we've got what we want, we can clear out, "Yes, goodbye, my dear, lovely to work with you, perhaps we'll do it again one day", then sit back at our leisure, and blow the lot. No Xais, no evidence. Just us. And the loot.'

Eddie sat back in his chair, amazed. 'And you've had this all worked out right from the start? Four years back?'

'More or less.' Charlie poured himself a second cup of tea and went for another fancy, a yellow one with butterfly wings of halved macaroon. 'I've waited four years for this.' He took a bite of the cake. A pulse throbbed on his temple. 'Nobody uses the Nisbett firm.'

10

Traitor

Stokes was feeling sicker than ever. His stomach ached with cramp every time he took a breath. It had been easy enough for Romana to trick the Ogron guard at the entrance of the ship to let them pass back into the deserted corridors. Pyerpoint had led the way to the stairs and was now, rather irritatingly, striding up them. Amazing for a fellow of his age, Stokes supposed. Unnatural, in fact, tearing about like that.

He stopped at a junction. 'Please,' he wheezed. 'I have to rest. I was not built for speed.'

Romana turned. 'If you want to wait here, you can always follow us on,' she suggested sweetly.

'Oh, you are wicked,' Stokes said. 'This whole business is more than I can bear. When it's all finished, I shall seek reparations, you know.' He looked up the stair-well at Pyerpoint, who stood waiting impatiently on the next landing. 'This station was supposed to be totally secure. What a shambles. I expect compensation for this inconvenience, Pyerpoint. The destruction of my life's work, wrongful arrest, invasion by big hairy aliens. I don't feel very secure after that, I can assure you.'

'We have to move on,' Romana reminded him. 'There may be —'

She was interrupted by a cry from Pyerpoint as an Ogron appeared at the top of the stairs. The old judge leapt forward, angled his rifle up at the creature and fired three times into its chest. The charges blew the Ogron apart. Its death scream merged with the zing of the energy bolts that killed it.

Romana hurried up to join Pyerpoint. 'I'm going on,' he told her bluntly. 'I can't spare any more time on you or Stokes. My duty comes first.' He stepped over the body of the Ogron and hurried up the last flight of stairs that led to level nine.

Stokes joined Romana as she looked down at the remains of the Ogron. 'Enthusiastic, isn't he?' she said.

'I never trusted him,' Stokes said. 'I always used to say that he was the creepiest character aboard this tub. Shifty eyes. And you can never tell what he's thinking.'

'Let's get after him,' said Romana.

The Doctor called on the last reserves of his strength as the force beam tightened its grip on his body. He shouted up at Xais, 'Stop this! I've already said, I'll answer your questions!'

The agony lessened. He opened his eyes and saw a blurred vision of Xais and her Ogron slave. His legs were cramped and shooting with pain. The bones inside felt as if they had been stretched an inch or two. His fingers had lost their grip on the rests of the chair and flopped helplessly.

'That level of pain should kill a Normal,' Xais observed as she came closer, lifting up his head. 'There is something different about you. What should I have to do to finish you off, I wonder?'

For once, the Doctor, exhausted, was unable to think of a reply. He slumped back in the chair and said weakly, 'What has driven you to this sadism, Xais? This senseless hatred. Can't you see its inevitable end? Your own destruction.' He stared at the eyes behind the mask. 'Tell me. Would that really satisfy you?'

'My destruction? Oh no, Doctor, that day will never come. I have elevated myself above the mortal plane. When this body is exhausted, I shall take others. I shall endure until the skull of the last Normal rests on a sea of guts and bones.'

'I doubt that, Xais,' the Doctor taunted. 'Yes, that

147

mask trick of yours is very clever. But a strike of planetary missiles would make short work of it.'

'Empty threats, Doctor. Soon, I will be able to brush off your planetary missiles as easily as I swat an insect. I will be able to stand at the centre of a sun as it ignites and survive!'

The Doctor shook his head. 'No. That is not possible, Xais. You are a deluded sadist. You cannot justify your actions.' He let his eyes close again. He needed to prepare himself for the next wave of agony.

'I . . .' He heard Xais gasp. He opened his eyes and saw her standing back from him. One of her hands had raised itself to the mask in a jerky movement that belonged to Margo. 'I am . . .'

The Doctor strained forward in his bonds. 'You are Margo,' he urged her. 'You can fight her off. I will help you. Concentrate.'

The masked face slumped. 'No,' said Margo's voice. 'She has nearly . . . destroyed me. But there is something I can do.'

She lurched over to the control panel and pressed a button. The bonds securing the Doctor to the chair snapped open.

The last of the large boulders blocking the way to the TARDIS was being chiselled away by the concentrated laser power of K9's nose ray. He reported to Spiggot. 'Instructions completed. TARDIS is now ready for entry.'

The rock dust settled in the pink afterglow of the laser beam and Spiggot saw the blue door of the TARDIS for the first time. His face fell. 'What the flamin' heck do you call that?'

'Vehicle known as TARDIS,' said K9. 'Time And Relative Dimensions In Space.'

Spiggot sighed. 'There's hardly room to swing a cat in there!'

'Negative,' said K9. 'TARDIS contains sufficient area for centrifugal tests on felines.' He darted forward and his sensors quivered with indecision. 'There is a conflict in my programming. Orders were to return to TARDIS, but the Doctor Master and Mistress Romana may be in danger and it is my function to assist.' He clicked and whirred. 'I will return to TARDIS and wait.'

'I wouldn't hold out much hope for them, K9,' said Spiggot. He looked back down the tunnel towards the main body of the station. 'If you tangle with the Nisbett boys head on, you can only get creamed, sooner or later. No, I've got a much better idea.' He started off.

K9 turned at the door of the TARDIS. 'Wait. What is the nature of your plan?'

Spiggot looked back. 'And why should it concern you, eh?'

K9 trundled forward. 'All information is useful.'

Spiggot laughed. The thing had emotions, or programmed responses that simulated them. 'I get it. You're curious, aren't you?'

'Negative. I am not programmed for curiosity. Your input is required.'

Spiggot was pleased that somebody was paying attention to him again, particularly now that he'd worked out a plan. 'Right. Well, you see, what everyone's forgotten about are the engines. Throw a spanner in the works down there and their business, whatever it is, will be well and truly scuppered.' He stood up and set off for the hole in the wall of the cavern.

K9 called, 'This plan is inadvisable. Your technical knowledge is limited. You will wait here with me.' Spiggot walked away. He heard the robot's motors whirring as it followed him.

The long stone corridor adjacent to the courtrooms of level nine was deserted. Romana led the panting Stokes at a brisk pace to the door that led to the judges' chambers and Pyerpoint's office. As soon as the door was closed safely behind them, Stokes collapsed into one of the big leather chairs.

'Finally. Now, may I suggest we hold on here, for a while, at least?'

Pyerpoint was standing by a covered figure of Liberty on the other side of the office. The top had swung open and he was fiddling with some concealed controls inside. The weapon he had taken was still gripped tightly in one hand. 'Please be silent. I have to concentrate. This sequence is complex.'

Stokes snorted. 'And I thought he was getting us a drink.' He peered at the locked drinks cabinet opposite the desk. 'I say.'

Romana wandered over to the window and looked out. A small, dirty blue globe was appearing in the stars. 'We're nearing a planet.'

Pyerpoint finished his work and stepped back from the globe. The hatch swung shut. 'The signal has been sent,' he said evenly as he made for the door. 'You two, stay here.'

Romana turned. 'Where are you going?'

'That is not your concern,' Pyerpoint said. 'You are going to stay here.' He slipped out of the door and closed it. Bolts clicked over automatically.

'He's locked us in,' Stokes said unhelpfully.

'I know!' Romana shouted. She thumped on the thick wooden door with a gloved fist. 'What is he doing out there?'

Stokes sniffed. 'What does it matter, my dear? We are alone, but at least we are together. And,' he ran his fingers around the clear panel of the drinks cabinet, 'I can see some interesting things in there.' He pulled open a drawer of the desk and searched through the papers and files inside. 'The key has to be somewhere in here.'

Romana closed the drawer. 'That's very bad manners. And you'd never get it open.' She indicated a mechanism built into the top of the drinks cabinet. 'It's sealed by a personal recognition code, like the door. We're trapped. What is Pyerpoint doing?'

Stokes sank back into his chair. 'Well, my pet, we must

look for positive aspects to our predicament. We are alone, and untroubled.' He patted his lap and raised an eyebrow. 'I suppose you think an older fellow like me is past his prime, don't you?'

'You've been telling me that for several hours,' Romana said patiently.

He blew out his cheeks. 'Oh, don't listen to me.'

'I wasn't,' said Romana. She started to look around the office.

'No,' said Stokes, 'I meant, that although I may not be suited to yomping up endless corridors and stairs, there are certain physical activities that I consider myself to excel in.'

'That planet is coming awfully close,' Romana said from the porthole. 'It must be Planet Eleven.'

'You are cruel,' Stokes accused. 'One could be forgiven for thinking you weren't human.'

She turned to regard him. 'That's the nicest thing you've said all day.'

In the silence that followed her rebuke, Stokes heard a hissing noise.

A thin trail of yellow vapour was pouring from a nozzle in the globe. The vapour collected in a thick yellow cloud and began to catch at their throats.

'The old scratcher,' gasped Stokes as he toppled from his chair. 'He's trying to poison us!' He fell to the carpet, his big nose bumping the deep green pile.

Romana knew she had more time left. Her respiratory bypass would save her from the effects of the gas but would leave her as unconscious as Stokes. The moments she had would be best employed searching for a way to turn off the gas. She staggered into the gas cloud and stretched out her hands to the globe. The surface was smooth and unyielding. Her grip loosened as the vapour took its hold upon her. Her hearts pumped as if they were about to burst out of her chest.

She let herself fall to the floor of the office. The gas

continued to seep from the globe over her body and that of Stokes.

The Doctor raised his hand. His muscles creaked with the pain of the torture. His fingers touched the edge of the Xais mask. He pulled. The mask did not yield.

'It's somehow melded itself to your skin,' he told Margo. He was unable to keep the horror he felt from his voice.

'I know,' she said. Her body trembled with the effort it took to keep Xais suppressed. 'Please, Doctor, go. I cannot . . . hold her.'

The Doctor glanced at the door of the chamber and ran his tongue over his top lip. 'There are things I must know,' he said. 'Try to concentrate. The more I know, the more I can do to help you.'

'There is nothing you can do,' said Margo from behind the mask. 'This is my face now. She has taken . . . complete control.'

He steered her gently towards the chair and pushed her into it. 'Tell me how she took control. Tell me about her plans, Margo.'

'I saw her executed,' Margo began. 'She sat in this chair, a shield about her head, screaming her defiance. Even then, I felt something. As if a part of myself was dying. I can see into her mind now, see how it was done. I know all that she knows.

'Many years ago she carried out tests, using the power she controls to estimate the resistance of certain substances. She realized that helicon, in its liquid state, reacted uniquely.' She moaned and writhed in the Doctor's grip. 'It can record her mind, Doctor. Exactly. Emotions, memories, personality. The small amount she had was not enough. She planned to mine a vast amount of helicon from Planet Eleven.'

The Doctor frowned. 'How was she to know it was there?'

Margo's hands gripped at the rests of the chair, the

knuckles whitening. 'Her contact with the establishment told her. Pyerpoint.'

A bewildering flurry of thoughts flashed through the Doctor's mind. 'This is the point,' he said, 'where I feel I ought to say, "Goodness, I should have realized." '

'Xais worked with Pyerpoint. He arranged for her to destroy his enemies, or enterprises that threatened his own investments. He used her as a walking weapon. She used him to satisfy her own hatred of humanity. They were planning to mine the helicon together when she was arrested. And together they worked out how to use Stokes and his gallery to recreate her.'

'How does the process work?'

Margo struggled with the concepts in Xais's mind. 'The transfer process is achieved by Xais releasing a quantity of her power into a quantity of liquid helicon. The helicon is primed, it becomes almost alive. She can then fill it with her mind and her purpose. The more helicon, the quicker and easier the process. She was in contact with the small amount used to make the mask for only fifteen minutes. As a result, she estimated the transfer of her soul to the mask could take up to five years. I remember . . . she can remember lying back as Stokes took the mask. Then it lay dormant in the gallery, gathering strength, seeking a suitable host. It chose me. It amused her to select the woman who had put her to death.'

The Doctor sensed Margo's bitterness in her next words. 'And somehow Pyerpoint knew. He could see it in my eyes as Xais took hold of me. But,' she chuckled, 'he didn't know what she was planning as she took control of me. She forced me to steal a transmitter from stores. This was to signal the accomplices she had already briefed, before her arrest. Accomplices he knew nothing of.'

'What about the raid on the survey base?'

'Yes. Through my eyes, Xais saw reports of the survey on Planet Eleven. She was afraid that McConnochie Mining would commit themselves to mining the planet before her. One night, she summoned up all her energy

153

to take control of my mind. Using my body, she trans-matted herself to the survey base, killed their engineer, and switched off the life support systems. Back at the Rock, she used her technical skills to falsify the transmat records and introduced a creeping virus into the security system, to prevent her signals to the Nisbetts being detected. Then, when she was ready, she took full control and led them in.'

Margo twisted and shook as Xais struggled to return. 'Please, Doctor, you must go . . . she will consume me . . . help me . . .'

The Doctor made for the door and turned as some-thing occurred to him. 'I must know one more thing, Margo. Tell me, what does Xais intend to do with the helicon when she has it?'

'She wants to activate it using my mind as hers,' said Margo. 'The mask may soon be independent, her power over it is growing, but she still needs the mind of a living host to bring the helicon to life. When she has transferred herself, her power will be terrifying.'

'But what will she do with that power?'

The question triggered a series of spasms. Margo gasped as the voice of Xais choked at her throat. 'I will replicate myself a million times, Doctor!' she cried. 'I will be immortal, untouchable! An army of me will sweep through the universe. I will destroy all Normals!' Her head jerked up and he saw the eyesockets of the mask start to glow with a deadly fire.

He threw himself through the door and keyed in the locking command on the panel beside it. Then he hurried through the cells as quickly as he could.

Xais rose from the chair, her host body quivering with anger. She searched her thoughts for the mind of Margo, but it was gone finally, consumed in the pool of her consciousness. Still, what did it matter if she had freed the Doctor? He was one Normal and would perish soon enough.

No, she warned herself. As a police agent, the Doctor was dangerous. If he was able to escape from the Rock and reveal his findings to his superiors her plan could be in danger. A strike of planetary missiles could destroy Eleven and the prize it held for her.

The Doctor had to be found and killed as soon as possible.

The Nisbetts had detailed a couple of Ogrons to stand guard at the entrance to the huge cavern where the Rock's mighty engines were located. The ape beasts stood before the enormous metal door at the far end of level two, their weapons raised.

'We will soon be rich, masters say,' remarked one of the Ogrons.

'Yes. I will buy necklace for wife,' said his mate. 'And a big stone.'

The first Ogron grunted his encouragement. 'Yes, it is good to have a big stone.'

Spiggot watched them from the cover of a large container of spare parts on the other side of the hallway. On their journey through the corridors he and K9 had managed to dodge the Ogron patrols but this situation was different.

'How the heck are we going to get in there?' Spiggot looked across at the Ogrons' thick protective jerkins and then down at his blaster.

'Your concern is unnecessary. I will incapacitate these hostiles.' K9 extended his nose laser and moved from cover.

Spiggot caught his breath as the robot dog went into the open. He looked rather helpless and pathetic as his noisy motor carried him slowly toward the huge Ogron guards and their fearsome blaster rifles. Spiggot almost couldn't bear to look. K9 didn't stand a chance.

The first Ogron stepped forward suspiciously. 'What is this machine?'

The second scratched his head. 'Is it a robot?'

K9 fired a twin beam. The bright red stun rays sliced through the cold air with a high-pitched buzz. The Ogrons fell after a couple of seconds.

Spiggot emerged. 'Well done.' He looked down at K9. 'Who put you together, eh? The force could do with some like you.'

'Queries irrelevant.' K9 turned up the power of his ray and blasted the locking mechanism of the metal doors. They slid open. 'The engine room is now clear.' He went in.

Spiggot followed and found himself in a surprisingly small room that contained a dead engineer, a large and intricately labelled console, and a screen that displayed the Rock's present position in the system. Planet Eleven was now less than an hour away.

K9 was examining the console. It looked to Spiggot as if he was sniffing at it with his antennae. 'Engine system based on primitive fission reaction,' he said disapprovingly. 'Motor guidance uses hydraulics. Suggest disabling guidance unit.'

'Oh, decided to help me now, then, have you?' said Spiggot. He flexed his fingers and reached for a bank of console controls. 'Now, these must be for the guidance unit.'

'Halt!' K9 ordered. 'My sensors indicate that the console is protected by security devices.'

Spiggot withdrew his hand. 'Then how are we going to break into it?'

'Remove the inspection panel in the base,' K9 ordered.

Spiggot knelt down and with some difficulty unhooked the metal sheet from the foot of the console. A network of rods and tubes was revealed. Each was labelled a different colour.

'I am not familiar with these colour codings,' K9 admitted. 'But logic circuits indicate that the mechanisms serving the guidance system are those to the left.'

Spiggot nodded. 'Right. And are they safe to touch?'

'Negative,' replied K9. 'I will use my defensive laser to sever the connections.' He started to cut away at one of the rods. 'Estimate component will be destroyed in thirteen minutes four seconds.'

One of the several disadvantages faced by employers of Ogrons is that their servants are similar in appearance. It is difficult for non-Ogrons to tell Ogrons apart. When two Ogrons shuffled fearfully into computer control, Eddie mistook them for a couple he had sent on another errand. 'Hello, boys. Brought us breakfast, then?'

The Ogrons looked guiltily at the floor. 'No, master. You did not give us orders to fetch breakfast.'

Eddie frowned. 'Oh, right. You must be the lads that were on duty back at the ship. We sent the relief guard. Shouldn't you be on patrol?'

Charlie looked up from the book he had been reading. It was one of his books about classy works of art that Eddie couldn't understand. Charlie had always had fancy tastes. 'What's going on?'

The first Ogron looked as if he was about to wet his underpants. 'Sorry, master, but we lose prisoner, the judge man.'

Charlie slipped his bookmark gently between the pages of his book and rested it on the console. 'What have you done?'

'Ugly girl came to ship,' said the Ogron. 'She said she was Xais, your friend. Said you would punish if we did not let her in. With big bald man. They take judge man away.'

The second Ogron said boldly, 'They knocked me on head and I –' His explanation faltered as Charlie's stare bored into his primitive fear centres.

'What ugly girl?' asked Charlie. 'All the people here are supposed to be dead.'

Eddie spoke up. 'Perhaps we've missed some, Charlie.'

Charlie clenched his jaw and spoke very quietly. 'I do not like this. I do not like it at all. I look at this operation and do you know what word enters my mind? Slipshod. I am not accustomed to a lacklustre standard of work.' He addressed the first Ogron. 'What's your name?'

'It – it is Flarkk, Mr Charles. Your pilot.'

'Flarkk.' Charlie clamped a hand on the Ogron's shaking shoulder. 'If anyone says that they are one of our friends, and that they have our best interests at heart, and must be allowed through, do you know what to do?'

Flarkk shook his head.

'You kill them, Flarkk. Because we haven't got any friends. No one has our best interests at heart. In fact, everybody hates us. Got that?'

Flarkk nodded. 'Everybody hates you.'

'That's right. Do you hate us, Flarkk?'

Flarkk floundered. 'Er, no, Mr Charles. I like you. You are good to Ogrons.'

Charlie leant closer and whispered, 'Wrong, Flarkk. You hate us. We don't give you enough food, do we? Or enough room to sleep in? And your beer is warm and recycled from your own urine, isn't it?'

'I hate you, Mr Charles,' Flarkk said dutifully, although Eddie knew that the Ogrons were pleased enough with their lot.

Charlie crossed to the station's public address system and pressed a button. 'This is Mr Nisbett senior to all Ogrons. There are humans aboard this station. You are to search them out and shoot on sight. And get it right this time. Oh, and by the way, rations are halved until further notice.' He was about to break the link when something occurred to him. 'And would Miss Xais please return to computer control as we are nearing our destination. Thank you.'

He broke the link and waved the luckless Flarkk and his associate away, then returned to his chair and his book.

Eddie edged over. 'What do you reckon this ugly girl and big bald man are, then?'

'Dead,' said Charlie, finding his place.

At the intersection of corridors on level eight, Xais stood listening to the announcement. 'The idiots. Why did I ever choose to work with them?'

'A question I would like answered,' said a voice from the darkness.

Pyerpoint emerged, his rifle levelled in her direction. 'Our arrangement. You have broken it.'

She faced him without concern. 'I sent you to their ship for your own safety.'

'Did you?' He came closer. 'I played my part. I gave you the helicon. I've been waiting for you three years. Involving the Nisbett brothers was never part of our plan.'

She took pleasure in unsettling him. 'They were part of the operation from the start. I decided not to inform you that we would be using their mining equipment. I imagined it would displease you. But they are here now and we will be rid of them soon enough. Essentially, nothing has changed.'

Pyerpoint lowered the gun slightly. 'Perhaps. And the attack on the McConnochie base? The Doctor told me of it.'

'Necessary. I know your caution, Pyerpoint. These things had to be done but you would never have sanctioned them.' She curled the fingers of one hand over the tip of the rifle and angled it downwards. 'All will be well soon enough. The helicon is going to make your ambitions a reality. Remember the demonstration I gave you? The power of helicon can be yours.'

He grimaced. 'Why am I still alive, Xais? What use am I to you now?'

'You are the only survivor of the raid, Pyerpoint,' she said. 'As you will recall, the mining process will take two months. As High Archon, your account of events here will be beyond suspicion. In two weeks, you will be found aboard the smoking remains of this station as it drifts on the other side of the system. You will report that the Nisbett brothers mounted a raid. Fortunately, you learnt the whereabouts of their base, on Helta. The police will be tangled up for months in bureaucratic wranglings with the Heltan authorities. Their attentions will never turn to our activities on Eleven. With your influence you can make doubly sure of that.'

'You have staked a good deal on my cooperation,' said Pyerpoint. 'And my reward?'

Xais waved a graceful hand. 'Unchanged. You will receive half of the activated helicon, which I will imprint with your personality.' She walked away. 'I have your assent? You must see there could be no other way.'

'Perhaps not. I did not realize you were so resourceful, Xais.'

'It is nothing. Now, the Doctor. He is the danger now. If he reports to the police, they may move against us before we can extract the helicon. He must be found and killed.'

'He was your prisoner,' said Pyerpoint. 'You lost him?'

'An error that will soon be rectified,' she said confidently. 'I must return to the Nisbett brothers. They must know nothing of your part in this. So drop the gun and play your part well.'

In the engine control room, Spiggot felt in his pocket for his packet of lights. His fingers closed around an empty box. 'Dammit,' he snarled. 'No smokes left. What am I going to do about that, K9?'

At the base of the console K9 continued his work. 'Ingestion of nicotine substances is harmful.'

'Ah, shut up, you sound like a state health warning.' Spiggot clenched his fists. 'I feel so helpless, just standing here. But what can I do?'

'Exercise is recommended to relieve tension,' burbled K9. 'The physiology catalogue of my data bank offers two hundred and twenty-nine exercise routines for humans. Exercise one. Stand with feet together and knees slightly bent –'

'Look, will you give it a rest, all right?' Spiggot screamed. 'And I was just beginning to get used to you. Like you, even.'

'Your approval is irrelevant,' said K9, sounding slightly miffed. 'My – oh.' His voicebox emitted a curious groan and he motored back hurriedly from the console.

Spiggot asked, 'Hey, what's up?'

The dog's ear sensors twirled. 'I have made an error,' he said. 'Please cover your eyes.'

The innards of the console revealed beneath the inspection plate fizzed and crackled. Currents of vividly coloured static buzzed like angry hornets between contact points and sparks burst in trails along insulated cables. Levers and switches on the console above started to move of their own accord. A bleeper sounded.

The floor beneath Spiggot upended and tipped him over face first. K9 skittered across the room.

'What have you done?' Spiggot demanded as he pulled himself up. The ever present throbbing note of the engines sounded deeper and discordant.

K9 twirled about, sensors and probe extended, absorbing information from all sources. 'Regret error has been made,' he said. 'Linkage ignited has not placed engines in stasis mode. Failsafe mechanism has operated. Engines have stalled.'

'They've what?' Spiggot exclaimed. He hurried over to the small screen that displayed the Rock's relative position. Planet Eleven was dangerously near and they were dropping towards it like a stone. 'We're going to crash down there.'

'Inevitable,' said K9. 'Impact will cause massive explosion of inflammable gases on the planet's surface.'

Spiggot felt like tearing his hair out. 'So what does that matter to us? At the speed we're dropping, we'll be dead well before that!'

11

Planet Eleven

Scrambled eggs, fried mushrooms, kedgeree, triangular slices of fried bread, bacon, baked beans, sausages, brown sauce. All slid greasily from Charlie's plate as the Rock of Judgement tipped forward into its new and deadly course.

He steadied himself. 'What was that?'

Eddie hurried over to the navigation console and squinted to make sense of the readings. 'We're speeding up. Going into a close orbit.'

Charlie put his breakfast tray aside, wiped his yolk-stained lips clean with a napkin, and joined his brother at the console. A screen on top showed a computer projection of the likely outcome of the spiral in which they were locked. Blue animated lines converged in an urgently warbling red point at a range of mountains on the approaching world. Warning messages unrolled.

'We're going to crash,' Charlie exclaimed. 'Where is she?'

'What, Xais?'

'Who else?' Charlie's hand dipped into his pocket and his fingers slid into the grips of his knuckleduster. 'She's sprung her game quicker than I'd reckoned on.'

'No game of mine!'

The brothers turned as Xais stalked into computer control. She was accompanied by Pyerpoint, who looked convincingly cowed. Eddie leapt forward but Xais raised a forbidding hand. 'Leave him. He may still be of use.'

She flung her head back and a small liquid noise of disapproval issued from the back of her throat. 'Must I spend my time rounding up prisoners that you allow to escape?'

Eddie waved Flarkk and Gjork forward to watch Pyerpoint.

The computer room shook once more. 'The engines have been interfered with.' Xais pushed Charlie's raised fist aside and strutted over to the navigation console. She consulted the diagnostic systems and grunted at their response. 'Somebody has sabotaged the control linkage.'

'But we've got a couple of the lads posted at the engine room.' Eddie leaned forward and flicked the security channel of the display screen to the relevant camera.

A monochrome picture flashed erratically through belts of static. Charlie's eyes bulged. 'Who the hell is that?'

There was a man inside the engine room and some sort of robot with him.

'No!' Xais cried. Her silver face whirled to face Charlie. 'Your Ogron servants are pathetic. All the Normals should have been killed!'

Charlie's fingers tightened around the grips of the knuckleduster. 'What did you just say?'

Xais pushed his arm aside. 'Idiot! There's no time for such puerile distractions!'

The console clicked. The display screen sent up reams of navigational data and suggested emergency routines. Xais ran her eyes down the list and snarled.

'If the linkage is damaged,' Pyerpoint shouted over, 'there's no way to right the asteroid.'

Eddie whispered in his brother's ear, 'Why don't we kill her now?'

Deep rumbles issued from Charlie's stomach as the acids of his digestive system reacted to his confused loyalties. 'Soon,' he croaked.

Xais slammed her hand down on the console. 'Useless! The orbit will decay and we will impact with the surface. We have less than an hour.'

Eddie had a suggestion. 'Why don't we just transmat down?'

'We couldn't risk it,' Charlie replied. 'When this rock crashes it'll smash the planet apart anyway. Eleven's got a weak crust.'

A frustrated scream burst from Xais's shining lips. 'No! I will not be cheated of my vengeance!' Behind the eyeslits of the mask an orange glow started to build up. 'There must be another way. We could travel on in your ship, circle in space, and return to Eleven when the damaged area has stabilized.'

Charlie shook his head. 'No point. It'd take us a good hour to load the mining gear back aboard.'

Beams of hate sizzled from Xais's eyes and struck the security screen. The glass fractured.

The Doctor gripped the brass handle of a courtroom door as the corridor on level nine swayed again.

'Somebody needs driving lessons,' he said and righted himself. His head banged a concrete pillar. 'Definitely a refresher course at the very least.' The Rock shook up and down and he was flung up to the ceiling and then jerked back to the floor. 'Maniac! The spaceways aren't safe nowadays.'

The door of Pyerpoint's office was ahead. He steadied himself, waited for the shaking to stop, and then ran for it. It was locked. He fiddled in his pockets, whipped out the sonic screwdriver, brought it to the mark, and gained entrance.

An instinctive movement and his nose and mouth were covered with one end of his scarf. The air had been contaminated by thick yellow vapour. He coughed out the small amount caught in his throat and dabbed the tip of his tongue at the solid residue that stained his teeth. The substance was sharp with corrosive chemicals.

He backed away and was about to leave the office when he saw the fingers of a pale hand through a clearing patch of gas. The hand belonged to Stokes. The Doctor propped up the heavy body and searched for a pulse.

Fortunately the fellow had not been exposed for too long.

The gas was thickest on the other side of the room. The Doctor reasoned it must contain the source. He tightened his grip on the end of the scarf pressed to his mouth and dived into the dense heart of the cloud. The chemicals in the vapour irritated his eyes and gritted tears stung each time he closed his eyelids. His eardrums popped as he advanced.

The sonic screwdriver was still in his hand. He fumbled with the tiny controls on the side and extended the device into the cloud. It bleeped, leading him to the nozzle set in the side of the globe. Thin streams of the vapour poured from the tiny opening. A precisely directed channel of ultra-modulated sonic waves welded the concealed innards of the globe and the hissing ceased.

The Doctor staggered back to where he remembered Pyerpoint's desk to be and searched for the office's environment controls. He thumbed the air conditioning button and slats in the wall clattered open. Emergency vents started to suck the unfamiliar matter from the atmosphere.

The arms of one of the big chairs embraced the Doctor's aching body. Its back, solid and upright, soothed his spine. He took his hat from his pocket and wafted the gas away from him. 'Well done, Doctor,' he managed to say. 'Yes. Very well done, Doctor. How awfully clever and heroic of you.'

'Well done, Doctor,' said a familiar voice from beneath the desk.

He peered down. 'Romana! What on earth are you doing down there?'

She sat up and stretched, her long blonde hair falling immaculately over her shoulders. 'Being gassed and looking at your boots.'

Stokes moaned and raised his head. 'Ah. The errant Doctor. I've heard so much about you since our last meeting.' He climbed slowly to his feet, wiping yellow stained fingers on his coat. 'Now, let me guess. You've dispatched Xais, the Ogrons, and the Nisbett brothers, and we're safely on our way home.'

The Doctor gave a broad toothy grin. 'No,' he said. 'Disappointing, isn't it?'

'Pyerpoint locked us in here and turned on the gas,' Romana said. She examined the inert globe. 'Do you think he suspects us of being in league with Xais?'

The Doctor swung his feet up on the desk and popped his hat on his head. 'I very much doubt it,' he said matter-of-factly. 'Because, of course, he's in cahoots with her himself.'

'What?' Stokes spluttered.

Romana perched on the desk and said, 'What do you mean, "of course"? You had no more idea of that than anybody else.'

'Well, no,' the Doctor admitted. 'But I enjoyed saying it, anyway. A man has to have his simple pleasures.'

He pushed the hat from his face and continued, 'I think that before we do anything else, we ought to try and work out exactly what's going on here. Eh? That safe looks interesting, for a start.'

Romana picked up her cap and started to rearrange her hair. 'What safe?'

The Doctor leapt from the chair and swept a row of books from the shelf. Beneath was a metal hatch protected by a combination lock.

'Ah,' said Romana. 'That safe.'

'Imperative we return to TARDIS and vacate,' K9 said as he and Spiggot hurried down the corridors leading away from the engine room. 'Destruction of this environment is now certain.'

'Ah, what's the point?' Spiggot stopped. 'You know as well as I do that we haven't a hope.'

K9 swivelled to face him and beeped impatiently. 'Urgent. We must return to TARDIS.'

'I never thought it'd end like this, K9,' Spiggot said

wistfully. 'Well, we all have to face it, you know. And this is it, K9. The big one. The final curtain.'

He took out his wallet and flipped it open. Inside was a colour photograph of Angie and the kids. 'I'll never see them again. Funny, but I always thought I'd die a hero's death. I used to dream about it as a kid. But life's not like that, is it? Don't really know if this qualifies. Yeah, I suppose I'll be taking Xais and the Nisbett brothers with me. You could call that glory. But what's the cost? Is it worth it, eh?'

He looked back at the photograph. 'Hell, I just couldn't say no, could I? Maybe it had to end this way. Eh, K9?'

He looked up but K9 had gone.

In his place was an Ogron.

Spiggot yelped and jumped.

A wide red beam shot the Ogron in the back and it toppled heavily down. K9 trundled forward.

'You will accompany me to the TARDIS,' he said angrily.

'Thanks,' said Spiggot. 'Hey, you're the best partner I never had, K9.'

The robot dog whizzed off. 'Your input is unnecessary,' he said. 'Please conserve use of speech centres for relevant information!'

'That dirty little planet,' sighed Stokes.

Grubby blue chemicals whirled in stormy clusters over the surface of the ever closer Planet Eleven as observed through the porthole of Pyerpoint's office. 'One of the last places I'd have chosen to die.'

'Oh really?' asked Romana as she clipped her hair back into place. 'Where would you have chosen?'

He closed his eyes. 'Ooh, perhaps one of the pleasure centres outside this rotten system. Nothing like that here, of course. I've always found the people of these planets rather provincial in outlook. Tatty suburban tastes. They wouldn't know how to enjoy a pleasure centre if it leapt upon them. Not that it matters any more.'

He had managed to break open the drinks cabinet and returned to his chair where a tumbler and a half empty bottle of Solturian Scotch were waiting to soothe him. 'Ah well. After a few of these, perhaps I shan't feel the bullets when they strike. Or the dagger as it slits me. Oh, there must be something we can do instead of sitting here doing nothing!'

The Doctor looked up from a mass of charts and papers he had purloined from Pyerpoint's safe. 'You're the only one who's sitting here doing nothing,' he pointed out.

Stokes groaned. 'Today I have been attacked, robbed, jailed, gassed, and forced to run up miles of stairs. I hardly call that doing nothing. Not to mention being chased by those Neanderthal beasts.'

'That's hardly a fair comparison,' the Doctor said without looking up from his work. 'The Neanderthals were charming people. Much better mannered than their successors. And they could knock up a superb mammoth casserole.'

'Doctor,' called Romana from the porthole. 'I'm worried.'

'You're worried? Oh that makes me feel much better,' grumbled Stokes. He felt like crying.

'Shut up,' the Doctor told him. 'What vexes you, Romana?'

'That planet. I've calculated our new trajectory and it looks like we've entered a decaying orbit. We're going much faster than we should be.'

The Doctor hurried over and looked out. 'There's really no need to check,' Romana said frostily.

'Goodness,' said the Doctor. 'Romana, I think you're right.'

'I know I'm right.'

He leapt back to the desk, cleared a space among the papers and beckoned her over. 'Right. I think it's time for our little conference.'

'I suppose you're going to ignore me,' whined Stokes,

pouring another drink. 'I shall just sit here and quietly go insane, shall I?'

'I shouldn't think you've ever done anything quietly,' said Romana.

'Now, Pyerpoint is a very powerful man,' the Doctor began. 'With access to all sorts of information. As High Archon he has contacts in administrative bureaux throughout the government and military of the Uva Beta Uva system. And as we now know he's crooked. A rotten apple, a bad egg.'

Romana was looking over the papers. 'He's been trading in that information for his own benefit. He owns huge stakes in these companies, all of which have been granted excessive public funds.'

'Oh, a great discovery,' Stokes snorted. 'It's called corruption, dear. Everybody's at it.'

The Doctor went on. 'I imagine that's how he started out. But as he got more confident his ideas got bigger. Take a look at this.' He passed Romana a sheaf of print-out he had taken from the safe.

She ran widening eyes quickly down the list of figures. 'He's running about a quarter of the major crime syndicates on Planet Five. He supplies the information, they do his dirty work, he takes thirty per cent.'

'Pardon my interruption,' said Stokes, 'but High Archon Pyerpoint is hardly the sort of person that the average gangster is going to conduct business with.'

'There's no need to carry out direct business,' said the Doctor. 'He probably uses codes and signals to establish the link. And if he needs his partners out of the way for some reason, well, they'll never know enough to implicate him. It's a very tidy little racket.'

'But why involve himself with a fanatic like Xais?' Romana asked.

The Doctor considered this objection. 'Well, most fanatics never get past their front gates. Xais has the advantage of being very, very clever. Anyway, somehow they joined up.' He picked up the list of Pyerpoint's commercial interests. 'Now, as one of the directors of the Board of Mineralogical Extraction, Pyerpoint received news about new finds before almost everybody else.'

He passed her a slim blue folder. 'This report was compiled for Pyerpoint about five years ago. He hired a mineralogist to carry out an independent survey of Planet Eleven. Nobody had ever done that before because it's a very inhospitable place. It can't be surveyed from orbit or by remote sensors, either. Far too much atmospheric distortion.'

'We hardly need reminding of that,' Stokes said with a nervous glance at the porthole. 'Is all this chat really necessary? We're about to crash!'

'I'm determined to get to the bottom of this plot before we go any further,' the Doctor told him severely. 'Now then, Pyerpoint must have related the findings of the survey, incidentally, to Xais. And she noted that the property is rich in helicon. One point three per cent of planetary mass, in fact.'

'And she can use helicon to reincarnate herself,' mused Romana. 'But how is that possible?'

The Doctor shrugged. 'It has to be something to do with that energy from her eyes. It reacts to molten helicon, allowing her to record psychokinetic information along telepathic wavelengths. However it works, it copied her personality, her memories, even her physical attributes.'

Romana tutted. 'That's an irritatingly vague theory.'

'Well, it's the best I can do at the moment,' the Doctor snapped. 'You'll just have to accept it. So Xais and Pyerpoint hatched a plot to mine the helicon for themselves. She needed him to keep prying eyes well away.'

'But the helicon is worthless to Pyerpoint. He can't duplicate himself, surely?' asked Stokes.

'It's possible that she could do it for him,' said the Doctor. 'She promised him half the spoils from Planet Eleven. That's always been the deal. But then, the police struck lucky for once and captured Xais. It looked as if the game was up.' He leaned forward. 'Until you presented yourself, Mr Stokes.'

The artist drew back. 'Oh really? I suppose the blame for all of this affair is now to be laid at my door?'

The Doctor nodded. 'Yes, You gave them a legitimate reason to bring Xais into contact, very briefly, with just enough liquid helicon to cross herself over. Her original self was executed and her new half slowly took control of poor Margo through the mask. And that's when things started going wrong for old Pyerpoint.'

With help from his whisky glass, Stokes had put his immediate discomfort aside for a moment and had become engrossed in all of this double dealing and intrigue, which appealed to his macabre sensibilities. 'I see. Because he didn't know that Xais was chummy with the Nisbett brothers?'

'Quite,' said the Doctor. 'She'd planned to call them in from the beginning. She needed strong allies with mining equipment and they fitted the bill. She'd thrown them some wild story about belzite reserves and arranged to send a homing signal when she was ready. As Margo lost control, Xais got her to steal a transmitter from stores, ready to send the beam.'

'And what about the raid on the survey base?' asked Romana.

The Doctor nodded grimly. 'That came about because Xais was dormant in Margo's thoughts. When Margo read that the McConnochie Mining team were coming to the end of their survey, Xais panicked. Although the place is technically worthless, there's a recession on and there was a slim chance the company might have gone in before she could organize herself. She summoned up all of her power and took control for just one night. Margo transmatted herself to Eleven and killed the survey team. And that put the mockers on any plans McConnochie might have had for a while. Then Xais came back up here and fiddled with the computers to cover her tracks, as we know.'

'I see,' said Romana. 'Although Pyerpoint knew nothing about any of that. He was waiting here patiently for Xais, as agreed.'

'Hence his concern when Zy was killed,' the Doctor remarked. 'He must have known full well who was responsible, but he framed poor Mr Stokes. Even then he didn't realize quite how advanced his partner's plans had become. And the sudden Ogron attack was as much of a surprise to him as to all of us. Of course, he took the first chance he got to dispose of you two. That gas would have destroyed your bodies completely, he doesn't want any evidence around to implicate him. And . . .'

He raised a finger and lowered it again. 'And well, I suppose that's all, really. Got that? I can always go over it again for you.'

Stokes shook his head. 'They're a devious bunch, aren't they? I always preferred the hotheads. All this premeditation. Takes the passion out of the whole thing, really.'

'Well done, Doctor,' said Romana. 'That was an awfully clever piece of deduction.'

He smiled. 'Was it? Well, the time for deduction's over, Romana. This is the time for . . .' He scratched his head. 'Er, what is it the time for?'

'Tea?' said Stokes hopefully.

'Action?' Romana suggested.

'Yes, action!' He made for the door of the office. 'Now, keep close behind me and do exactly as I say and don't do anything stupid. Unless I tell you to.'

Stokes got up from his chair. 'Where are we going?'

The Doctor grinned. 'Where do you think?'

'Oh no,' Stokes pleaded. 'Not the Nisbett brothers, please.'

The Doctor stopped in the doorway. 'This asteroid is heading straight for that planet and I'm the only person aboard who can stop it.'

Romana coughed.

'Well, perhaps not quite the only person. Anyway, let's be off. We've wasted enough time talking.' He strode away with Romana at his heels.

Stokes considered his options. He could drink himself into oblivion, he supposed. Then again, he hated being alone. He picked up the bottle of whisky and followed them.

The asteroid roared just above the upper atmospheric belt of Planet Eleven. Heat insulation material on the buildings of the justice block flaked away as the friction caused by the decaying orbit increased and the pull of the small planet's gravity strengthened. Balls of orange fire shot from the rocket ports as the asteroid tumbled towards what seemed certain destruction.

The Doctor pressed his ear to the door of computer control. 'There's no alternative,' he heard Xais say. 'We must return to your ship and evacuate.'

One of the brothers replied, 'Our ship'd never reach escape velocity from this far down. We're finished.'

'Not necessarily!'

The Doctor threw the doors open and bounded in, followed by Romana and Stokes, whose normally sallow complexion had begun to turn a disquieting shade of green from a combination of drink, fear, exhaustion and spacesickness.

The Doctor rattled on before anybody had the chance to shoot him, a tactic that usually worked. 'Hello, everybody. It's nice to see you again, Xais, and you Mr Pyerpoint, and you charming Ogron gentlemen, and, ah, you must be the Nisbett brothers. You don't know me, I'm the Doctor, this is my friend Romana, and that's Mr Stokes, and do you know unless you listen to me I think we're all going to die.'

Xais sprang from her position at the navigation console, resentment boiling in her eyes. 'Your robot was responsible for this, Doctor!'

'What, K9?' The Doctor tutted. 'I sometimes wonder why I ever let him off his lead. Now, then,' he indicated the navigation console, 'that looks important, I think I'd like to take a little look, if I may?'

Romana followed him. 'It looks like their control linkage has blown. Were they using a reverse thrust reaction?'

'Constant blast excitation/suppression, more like.'

'What, in a static charged field with torpor balance?'

'Looks like it.' The Doctor entered a series of commands into the computer. 'This is going to take some working out. These engines weren't built for this sort of thing at all.'

'Neither was I,' called Stokes. He had found himself next to Pyerpoint and the Ogrons. 'Your scheme looks ended at any rate.'

Pyerpoint regarded him with contempt. 'You are supposed to be dead.'

Stokes shrugged and pointed a finger. 'And you are supposed to be a trusted bastion of the establishment. Oh, I wish I'd never come aboard this dismal chunk of rubble!'

The Nisbett brothers had been sufficiently taken aback by the Doctor's spectacular entrance not to react with their usual threats of violence. He heard Charlie ask Xais, 'What's going on here? I thought he was an investigator. What's he doing helping us out?'

'I don't like this,' said Eddie. 'There's something wrong.'

'He's trying to save his own life,' said Xais. 'But there is nothing you can do, Doctor.'

'Well, perhaps you've been approaching this problem from the wrong angle,' he called back over the steadily increasing roar of the engines. 'You may well be a mathematical genius, Xais, but sometimes what's needed in these situations is some good old-fashioned creativity.'

Romana prised open a hatch on the side of the console. 'What he means is that we're going to alter course by confusing the engines. If we can suppress the next blast in

174

the chain for a couple of seconds longer than usual, we'll overshoot the planet by several hundred miles.'

'I don't understand her,' said Charlie. 'Is she right?'

Xais nodded. 'They could blow us to pieces if the blast is kept down for too long. But it's our only hope.'

The asteroid tore open a dense belt of floating methane as it got closer and closer to the planet. A chain of brilliant blue explosions ripped away chunks of rock. A red haze began to form around the edges of the shaking Rock as it dived downward.

A blue acceptance light flashed on the navigation display.

'I've sent the command!' Romana heard the Doctor shout jubilantly.

He moved to complete the operation but was pushed back in his seat by the crushing g-force. Romana had been thrown to the floor by the impact but was now nearest to the open inspection shield. 'You'll have to release the zonal flow valve!' he called urgently.

She dragged herself up, passing Stokes, who appeared to have passed out. Xais had fallen on top of Pyerpoint. Nearby, the Ogrons were wailing with fear. The brothers had somehow managed to lose their balance with dignity and were seated smugly at control positions like successful players in the final round of musical chairs.

Romana pushed herself on. She flung out an arm and stretched for the valve control. It was mere inches from her grasp.

'Give it some welly, Romana,' she heard the Doctor cry.

Redoubling her efforts, she flung herself against the force pulling her away.

Her fingers brushed the enamelled surface of the button.

The claws of gravity loosened their clutch at the offered morsel. Incredibly, destruction was averted. The massive weight of the Rock lifted itself free and roared off, its confused engines howling in protest all the while.

The Doctor shook himself and brushed specks of dust from his coat. He put a hand to his head and frowned. Had he forgotten something?

'Doctor,' Romana groaned from the floor.

He smiled down at her. 'Do you know, you really should take a more vertical attitude to life.'

'Doctor, the capacital limiter!'

He viewed the offending control. 'Yes, what about it?' Almost before he had finished speaking he had leapt forward and flicked it to the on position. 'Well, yes, of course, the capacital limiter. You didn't really think I'd forgotten, did you?'

She pulled herself up painfully and drew a deep breath. 'Of course not.'

Apparently satisfied, the Doctor swivelled his chair to face his adversaries, who were climbing to their feet, and clapped his hands together. 'Well, there we are. We're safe. How about that?'

He found himself facing the tip of a compact black revolver. 'Get up and keep your hands where I can see them,' Charlie ordered. He passed the gun to his brother. 'Cover them.'

Romana and the Doctor stood up. 'Your manners are appalling,' the Doctor told their captors. 'We've just saved your lives.'

Xais was checking over the navigation console. She was joined by Charlie, who asked, 'Well? What's the score?'

'We're coming out of orbit but our course is still fixed,' she told him. A graphic curve on the screen picked out a path that would take the Rock away from Eleven and into interplanetary space. 'In about twenty minutes we'll be out of transmat range. We have to move fast.'

Charlie nodded. 'Right.' He turned to his brother. 'Ed. You and Flarkk, take the prisoners with you, get down to the transmat and set up the beam. Chivvy the lads along with the mining gear. We'll be down in a couple of minutes. Understood?'

'Understood.' Eddie gestured to the Doctor, Romana and Pyerpoint with his gun. 'Right. You heard. Get into single file. No tricks.'

'Nobody's even said thank you,' the Doctor grumbled.

Romana pointed to Stokes, who lay slumped in the corner of the room. 'What about him?'

'He's no use,' said Eddie. 'Get on.'

Romana found this instruction impossible to comply with. She knelt and slapped the cheeks of the unconscious artist. His eyes opened and he sighed. 'Not again.'

'We've got to leave,' Romana said as she pulled him up.

'Move!' Eddie barked.

The sight of the black-suited, broken-nosed Nisbett brother and the Ogron at his side caused Stokes to emit a mouse-like squeak. He swayed, but Romana caught him and they were ushered out after the Doctor and Pyerpoint.

'You intend to keep the Doctor and his colleagues alive?' Xais suspected the motives of her partner.

'For a while.' Charlie cracked his knuckles. 'Our mum always used to say, never chuck out anything that might come in handy one day. I reckon this Doctor bloke might be very useful on the scientific side. He got us out of that orbit, didn't he? And that was something even you couldn't do, my dear.'

Xais was anxious to turn the conversation away from the exact details of the scheme. 'The other Normals, Stokes and the girl. They are of no consequence and must die.'

Charlie reached for the public address system. 'Something else Mum used to say. Sometimes you can untie a man's tongue quicker by torturing his mates than by having a go at the man himself.'

'An admirable homily. Your mother sounds like she was a remarkable woman.'

A look of fervour crossed Charlie's face. 'Oh she was. Ran the firm for thirty-two years. Of course Dad got all the credit. She'd still be alive today if we hadn't been grassed on. It broke her heart.'

Xais laid a hand on his arm. 'Do not worry. You will soon have your vengeance.'

Spiggot, who had been knocked down by the gravity storm, was nudged awake by K9. The policeman shook his long permed locks. 'Hey, what was that? I thought we were going to crash for sure.' He held up a hand and moved it up and down, an elementary safety test he'd learnt at school. 'We've levelled out.'

'Affirmative,' said K9. 'The asteroid is now moving away from Planet Eleven. Probability is that the Doctor Master realigned the engines.'

Spiggot punched the air with glee. 'Well done, Doctor! So, the game's on again.' He patted K9 on the head. 'It feels good to be alive, K9, eh?'

'Empirical approach states that expression of joy in human condition is reliant on variable factors; social formation, physical gratification, et cetera,' K9 told him. 'In addition, concepts of awareness also variable and semantically complex. Request specification of your query.'

The request was to go unheeded. A chime sounded and the voice of Charlie Nisbett boomed from the station's public address systems.

'Attention, attention. Calling all Ogrons. I order you to go back to the ship. Go back to the ship right away and await further orders.'

'Could be they're cutting their losses and pulling out,' Spiggot said.

'Unlikely,' said K9. 'We must investigate and assist the Doctor Master.'

Gjork and the two Ogrons on duty at the transmat

had loaded the heavy boxes of mining equipment onto the platform, and were waiting anxiously for their next orders. Eddie stood guard over his captives before the control panel.

The Doctor glanced at the settings. 'Those coordinates might have slipped, you know,' he said. 'What do you think, Romana?'

'The slightest variation in the beam and our molecules could be dispersed,' she said casually. 'Perhaps we'd better take a look.' She stretched out an inquiring hand.

Eddie gestured her away. 'Step back, lady,' he drawled. 'Everything's set up right, don't you fret.'

'Well, it was worth a try,' the Doctor whispered. 'Better luck next time.'

Eddie chuckled. 'There isn't going to be a next time, Doctor. You're into your last few hours, believe me. We're only keeping you alive now 'cause we might want some fun later.' His lower lip curled at the prospect.

Stokes screwed his eyes up tight and made short, sharp gasping noises. Romana and the Doctor remained unperturbed.

The Doctor turned to Pyerpoint, who stood as tall and grave-faced as ever. 'For a man I'd say has a lot to worry about, you seem remarkably silent. The game's up, you know. We've seen the safe. Very careless, leaving all that stuff lying about.'

Pyerpoint said simply, 'I do not want to talk to you.'

The doors of the chamber slid open and Charlie and Xais walked in with Flarkk. 'Right,' Charlie said as he sent Flarkk to watch the prisoners. 'Eddie, send the gear down.'

Eddie threw a bank of switches and the Ogrons and the boxes on the platform shimmered and vanished with a pulsing electronic sound.

A few moments later a call note came from Charlie's inside pocket. He reached in and pulled out a mobile communicator. 'Yes?'

'Gjork calling from planet, Mr Charles,' an Ogron

voice said through heavy static. 'Down and safe. There is good air and gravity is on.'

'Right. Well done, Gjork. Standby.'

Charlie put the communicator away and turned to Flarkk. 'Right, lad. Go back to the ship and follow us down to the base. There's a landing pad. Just follow the energy trace of the transmat.'

Flarkk nodded eagerly, keen to make up for his earlier error. 'Yes, Mr Charles. We will follow. I will not let you down again, sir. I hate you.'

'Good. Now make sure you put down the right way round, air-lock to air-lock, right?'

'Yes,' said Flarkk. 'I will not make that mistake again, sir. It is bad to land with air-lock facing wrong way.' He saluted and stomped off.

Xais stepped onto the transmat platform. 'We must leave now,' she said urgently. 'There is little time before we come out of range.'

'Ed, set the timer,' Charlie ordered. He herded Pyerpoint and the other prisoners up on to the platform.

A countdown of fifteen seconds flashed up on the console. Eddie patted his pockets, and joined the others.

There was an uncomfortable silence. Even Stokes was quiet, his head bowed. Romana supported his shaking frame. Xais stood alert, hands on hips. The Nisbetts stood together, faces set into the familiar brutal impassivity. Pyerpoint remained aloof.

'Well,' the Doctor said happily, 'this is nice, isn't it?'

Nobody answered him.

The timer clicked down to zero, the transmat platform glowed with power, and they shimmered and faded away.

12

The Truth Will Out

The Doctor's stream of comment was almost obscured by the warble of televerification assemblers as the small party of miscreants and heroes reappeared on a platform inside the Planet Eleven mineralogical survey base. The transmat chamber was similar to the one used aboard the Rock, but smaller, darker, and with a lower ceiling. It was sited at the end of one of the three arms that led from the central dome of the base.

Gjork stepped forward to greet his superiors. 'Transfer complete.'

Charlie nodded and stepped from the platform. 'Good. Where are the others?'

'Other lads in survey room as you order, Mr Charles. With gear. Waiting for you.'

'There's no time to waste,' said Xais. She turned her blank glare on the four prisoners. 'What are you going to do with these?'

'Don't mind us,' the Doctor said.

'Shut up, you bug-eyed freak.' Eddie spoke evenly, but the tip of his revolver nudged the Doctor's ribs. 'You've done well to get this far alive. Shame to spoil it all now, eh?'

'We'll lock them away for the moment,' said Charlie. 'You know this place, Xais. You see to it. We've got work to do.'

He straightened his suit and set off down the corridor towards the dome. Eddie tapped the Doctor's chin with the handle of his revolver and followed his brother.

Xais cursed her allies in an obscure mutant tongue as they departed.

181

'Creative differences?' queried Romana.

The silver mask regarded her with disinterest. 'I will kill you shortly. You are unimportant.' She turned to the nearest Ogron. 'Follow the signs to storage area three. Put them inside and lock the door. Do you understand?'

The Ogron nodded. 'Yes, Xais.' He prodded Stokes with his rifle. 'Move, fat one.'

The artist shuffled off in compliance. The Doctor and Romana, mindful of the assembled firepower of the surrounding Ogrons, got into file behind him.

The Doctor stopped at the door and looked out through a large viewport streaked with dark blue grime. The valley outside was thick with dirty gases. The plastiglass of the viewport thrummed in time to the rumblings of a close storm.

'Oh, what very charming weather,' said the Doctor. 'So this is Planet Eleven. Stale, flat, but perhaps not so unprofitable, eh, Xais?'

The Ogron pushed him on before Xais had the chance to reply. She placed a hand on Pyerpoint's shoulder as he made to follow the others. 'Not you.'

He met her smooth silver face without fear. 'Your strategy failed.'

'No. I have decided that I want you with me. There may be unpleasantness. With the brothers.' She reached inside her tunic and brought out a small silver pistol. 'I liberated this from an Ogron.' She handed it to him. 'Of course I have no need of it. But you may find it useful.'

Pyerpoint tucked the weapon into his waistband. 'You trust me,' he said, watching her all the while. 'If you turn your back, I can kill you. I have reason to.'

She turned and walked on. 'I trust your ambition. Without me, you will never be able to activate helicon.'

The Ogrons hurried the Doctor, Romana and Stokes along the narrow and oppressively low-ceilinged corridors of the base. The only sounds were the distant crackle of shifting gas clouds and the barely discernible hum of the life support systems. The recycled air was still and smelt sour.

The small party reached a large grey hatch that was marked STORAGE AREA 3. One of the Ogrons thumbed a panel on the wall and the hatch swung slowly open. It revealed a small room filled with racks of crates and boxes. A single strip light flickered, casting a winking gridded shadow over the faces of the three prisoners as they were thrown roughly inside. The hatch shut with a definite-sounding clunk.

The Doctor tapped at the hatch with the tips of his fingers. 'It's megalanium. Even K9'd have trouble cutting through it.' His hand, which had been scrabbling instinctively for the sonic screwdriver, emerged from his pocket.

Romana sunk despondently onto one of the boxes. 'Things don't seem to be going very well, do they?'

The Doctor smiled. 'I wouldn't say that. They may have got us where they want us, and their plans may be proceeding smoothly, and we may have become separated from any effective means of resistance, but, er, no, you're right, things aren't going very well, are they?' He joined her on the box.

Stokes broke his long silence with a whimper. 'You think you're very clever, don't you?'

Romana looked over at him. He was standing on the other side of the room, twitching one leg like a horse at a starting post. The excesses of the past few hours had left him crumpled and forlorn, and his large face shone with sweat under the intermittent fluorescence. 'The both of you,' he went on. 'Sat there looking pleased with yourselves. All this ridiculous running about! You seem to find it very amusing.'

Romana said calmly, 'I can assure you we do not. But there's no point in losing your head. Try to relax.'

He shuddered. 'Are you insane?' He hammered on the wall. 'We're all going to die here!'

Romana crossed the small room in two long strides and grabbed Stokes by the shoulders. 'Stokes! Stokes, listen to me! We'll find a way out of here, but you have to keep your nerve.'

Stokes wriggled free from her grip and flopped down in a corner. 'Oh, leave me alone,' he said pathetically. 'Please, just leave me alone.'

Romana turned to the Doctor. 'Well? What is the way out?'

He hitched up his scarf. 'I'll think of something.'

The survey room at the centre of the base was cramped and dark. Contoured charts of the planet's surface shifted into new patterns on the row of screens set into one wall, a display of weather movements from distant areas provided through a network of relays. The consoles and computer banks always found in such places were beneath the screens. Broad-shouldered shadows were thrown onto the walls as the brothers prepared a group of Ogrons for the next stage of the operation.

Eddie unpacked the third helmet and passed it to Gjork. The leading Ogron clamped it down on his head. It connected automatically, with a loud hiss, to the clips on the neck of Gjork's atmosuit. Gjork and two others were now suited up and ready to begin the mining operation. During the long wait for Xais's signal, Eddie had trained these three specimens with the mining gear. The Ogrons' willingness to learn and practical skill, qualities that were a legacy of their confused evolution, were a considerable asset in a slave race.

'All set,' Eddie reported.

Charlie sat before the main computer display. The base's drinks machine had provided a cup of tepid coffee, from which he took measured sips. 'Right. Get down to the air-lock. Take the probe.'

Eddie was confused. 'We don't need the probe. Xais is going to tell us where to set up the rigs.'

Charlie patted the seat next to his in invitation. Eddie

joined him before the console, and was greeted with a powerful pinch on the arm.

'It's a good job Mum and Dad aren't here, you know,' Charlie said as he loosened his grip. 'What would they think of you, boy? "Xais is going to tell us where to set up the rigs." You don't think, that's your trouble. No sense.' He leant closer to his luckless brother and whispered, 'With the probe we can have a good look at this planet for ourselves. Find out what she's really after.'

'Well, we're going to kill her anyway, aren't we?' Eddie protested.

Charlie nodded and reached for a nearby box. 'Yes.' He pushed open the lid of the box and produced one of the bombs. 'Let's get this set up.'

The bomb fitted snugly between the console and a free standing unit beneath. Charlie pushed a tiny button on one side of the device and a red light flashed on.

Eddie jumped up. 'It's not going to go off, is it?'

'Not yet.' Charlie closed the lid of the box. 'But now it's armed. So, whenever I'm ready I can detonate.' He leant back in his chair. 'Right. Get down to the air-lock. Proceed as drilled.'

Eddie leapt up and selected a particular crate from the pile. He beckoned to the three atmosuited Ogrons. They followed him as he left the survey room and headed for the air-lock.

Spiggot put out a hand to steady himself as the Rock of Judgement swayed slightly. A further series of bumps followed before the corridor steadied. 'Hey, was that what I hope it was?' he asked K9.

K9's antennae twitched and he replied, 'I am unable to answer your question until you tell me what you hope for.'

'Well, I hope it was the Ogron ship splitting off.'

'It was what you hoped it was,' K9 said. 'The Ogrons have left the Rock of Judgement. My sensors indicate that two transmat transmissions have been made recently. Inference is that Doctor Master and Mistress Romana, along with Xais and the Nisbett brothers, have used transmat to reach Planet Eleven.'

'Let's get after them, then,' Spiggot said. 'The transmat's only down one level from here.'

'Unnecessary,' K9 said primly. 'Travel by TARDIS more efficient.'

'Oh, not that stupid box?'

K9 trundled off towards the nearest lift without comment.

Stokes was slumped in his corner. He looked over resentfully at the Doctor and Romana. She was sighing, he was staring ahead and cogitating in that irritating way of his. She sighed again.

'Romana, will you stop that, please?'

'Stop what?'

'Sighing.'

'All right. But I feel so helpless, sitting here.' She slid off the crate and her eyes widened. 'Doctor!'

He stayed still. 'Yes?'

'What have we been sitting on all this time?'

'Our bottoms?'

She pulled him away from the crate and pointed to stencilled lettering stamped where they had been sitting. Stokes peered across. The letters read DANGER!!! BLASTING MATERIALS.

As one the Doctor and Romana prised the lid off the crate. Stokes shuffled over to them. 'What have you got there?'

The Doctor whirled round. He helpd up a small red device decorated with a couple of yellow stripes and said, 'Our deliverance, Mr Stokes. A Z7 hermite pack. This little beauty packs a punch that'll blast our way out of here.'

'In a space as small as this it might also blow us to pieces,' Romana pointed out.

'Well, have you got any better ideas?' the Doctor said bullishly.

'It is my idea,' Romana said.

'Well, then you should feel very proud. Now then.' He examined the controls attached to the blast pack. 'This must be the timer. I'll give it a few minutes.' He twisted a dial and fixed the pack to the hatch. 'I suggest we all get behind the crate.'

Braah, home planet of the Ogrons, was a massive grey ball some light years from the central spaceways. The bulky Ogron frame had been designed for the high gravity of that enormous world, and was well equipped for the deadening atmosphere of Planet Eleven. Gjork and his two colleagues moved through the thick grime with powerful, loping strides, the tough rubber joints of their atmosuits creaking at the knees.

Gjork had been drilled in the use of some of his suit's more basic functions, and he stopped to consult his wrist read-out. A line of neon numbers glowed beneath a panel that was kept clean by an automatic sprinkler. 'Stop,' Gjork told the others. 'We have walked enough metres now. Unpack the probe.'

One of the others slung a carrying case from his shoulder and unclipped a row of bolts on its side. The lid whirred up and the Ogron removed the probe, a fat silver tube about half a metre long that was packed with sensor circuitry of the highest calibre. The tube tapered to a snout at the front and a couple of glowing red power-packs were attached to the rear. Gjork reached over and took the device. He pressed a button on the snout and it tingled against his gloved hand. Carefully, he bent over and angled the probe like a spear at a soft piece of ground nearby. It beeped three times and shot from his grip into the slimy soil, disappearing within seconds.

Gjork nodded, pleased, and opened his communicator frequency. 'Mr Charles. Gjork here. I have activated the probe as you ordered, at,' he consulted his wrist read-out again, 'distance of 1401.'

'Good,' said Charlie. He checked the position of the Ogron mining team on the map of the locality displayed above him, and made an approving noise. That was far enough out from the more solid ground where the base had been built for a general reading to be trusted. 'Were there any complications?' he asked Gjork.

'No complications,' Gjork replied. 'We wait for probe to come back now, yes sir?'

'That's right. Call back upon its return. Out.'

Charles heard footsteps behind him. He turned to see Xais, who must have overheard the exchange. She stiffened and threw back her head. 'You've sent down a probe? Why? There is nothing of value in this region.'

The far door hissed open and Eddie walked in. 'It won't hurt to have a look, though,' he told Xais. 'Just a general survey of the region. To see what's about.'

'You are wasting time,' said Xais. 'There is nothing here.'

Charlie took a checker-patterned vacuum flask from a crate and unscrewed its lid. His nostrils twitched at the tempting vapours of the steamy broth within. 'Like Eddie says. We're just having a look. No harm in that.' He took a sip of broth. 'And we've got the gear, remember. You won't get far without it. From now on you do as we say.'

Xais battled with the urge forming behind her eyes, a familiar sticky hotness that was pushing at her brow and tugging at the pulses in her forehead. One glance could crush these recessives. But she had to remain calm. They had to remain allies until the rigs were set up and programmed and the helicon gathered. It would take at least two months. Two months of this. At least she had the lives of the Doctor and his Normal friends to feast upon while she waited.

The lives of the brothers, though, were what she wanted. It would be so good to feel their agony and fear. She imagined Charlie's brain bursting through his head and suppressed a lustful chuckle.

A louder roar burst over the rumble of the gas clouds. Eddie looked up. 'That must be the lads coming down.'

Charlie stood up. 'I've cleared security on the pad. Tell them they can set down.'

Eddie nodded. 'Base to Flarkk,' he transmitted. 'You're clear for landing.'

Xais watched as Charlie noted Pyerpoint's silent presence in the survey room for the first time. The old judge had slipped in behind her, his face still as ever. 'What's he doing here?'

Xais faced Charlie. 'Pyerpoint has specialized knowledge. Security codes, and the like. We may need him.' She noted Charlie's suspicious expression. 'Don't worry. My eyes are upon him at all times. He can do nothing.'

Charlie frowned and stalked away.

Pyerpoint's hand moved down to the bulge in his tabard where his laser pistol was concealed. 'No?' he whispered to Xais with a glance at the brothers.

She curled a hand over his and said, 'No. Not yet.'

The boom of the ancient, spitting motors of the landing Ogron ship concealed the detonation of the hermite pack as it blew open the hatch of storage area three. Despite Romana's fears, the hermite had exploded outwards into the corridor, leaving the occupants of the storage area unscathed. The Doctor's head popped up from behind the crate and he removed his fingers from his singing ears. 'There we are.'

Romana looked up and blinked away the smoke from her eyes. A pleasantly sized hole had been blasted in the hatch. Flames danced around the glowing edge of the gap. 'Well done, Doctor.'

He leapt up and made for the hole, but stopped as if he

had forgotten his manners. 'Please, ladies first.'

Romana nipped through the scorching ring of fire and called back, 'It's all right, Doctor. It's quite safe.'

He followed her, dusted himself down and rearranged his scarf. 'I know it's safe.'

The Doctor turned at the sound of Stokes's voice. 'Where are you two going now?' he asked from the other side of the hole.

'Well, we're going to defeat Xais, of course,' said the Doctor. 'Or try to.'

'Why don't you stay here?' suggested Romana.

Stokes took a little run-up and jumped through the hatch. 'Oh no,' he said, looking up and down the corridor. 'No. I shall return to the transmat. As would you, if you had any sense remaining to you at all.'

Romana frowned. 'Don't be ridiculous. The Rock's probably drifted out of range by now.'

Stokes backed away. He appeared genuinely afraid of them. 'It doesn't matter. I'm prepared to take a chance. I'd rather I were scattered painlessly into the ether than have my spleen squeezed until it pops by a gang of psychopaths.'

He gave Romana a little wave. 'Farewell, my angel. I wish only that your level of sanity was equal to the magnitude of your attractiveness.' He looked less fondly at the Doctor and added, 'You are obviously as mad as you appear.'

Romana watched as he scurried off. 'Doctor, we can't just let him go like that.'

The Doctor was already striding in the opposite direction. 'I think we just have. Now, which way to survey control, I wonder?'

'Now this has got to be some sort of trick,' said Spiggot as he entered the brightly lit control room of the TARDIS. He looked back at the big white double doors, which were decorated with a pattern of indented circular panels. He was sure the door he'd pushed open had been wooden, and blue, and had belonged to a box large enough to hold four people at most. There was only one way to check. He stepped back through the white doors —

— and was back in the cavern, standing in front of a tall blue box. He pushed open the door, stepped through slowly —

— and he was in the huge white room. 'No, this has got to be some sort of trick. You've got a teleporter rigged up or something, yeah?'

K9 whirred forward. 'Please mind the doors.' The big white doors swung shut with a low electronic hum.

Spiggot shook his head and marvelled at his new surroundings. 'So, this is your TARDIS, eh? I guess I was wrong to doubt you. But how do you get,' he waved a hand about, 'all of this inside that little box?' He gestured to the hexagonal control console which bulged with knobs, switches and levers of various shapes and colours. 'And how does all this work?'

'Relative dimensional stabilizer maps interior dimensions onto exterior outlet,' K9 replied. 'Number of relational components of TARDIS inestimable, therefore detailed report on its workings is unavailable.'

A particular device at the base of one of the console panels caught Spiggot's eye. It was a golden grille with a couple of switches at either end. 'Ah, right,' he said, stretching out a hand, 'this'll be your guidance and local hazard warning system. Looks like it, anyway.'

'Caution!' K9 squeaked. 'Do not touch TARDIS controls or I may be forced to stun you. Unauthorized handling of systems is very dangerous.'

Spiggot withdrew his hand. 'I get it. Like, only the Doctor knows how to fly this thing, yeah?'

K9 replied, 'I am fully integrated to TARDIS systems. I will operate this flight by remote.' He beeped a signal and the central column of the console began to rise and fall. An unearthly trumpeting noise sounded from deep within the console.

'And I thought I'd seen it all,' said Spiggot. 'This could be a fun ride.'

Stokes scampered along the darkened corridors of the survey base. Hearing guided him, away from the side of the base where he judged the Ogron ship to have docked. The thought of bumping into a horde of those rampaging brutes in pitch blackness was not comforting.

At every one of the creaks and rumbles that rattled the metalwork about him, his head jerked up, his nostrils twitched, and he flushed a deeper shade of purple. This beastly place was alive. Alive with shadows, muffled noises and the distant conversations of the shuffling dead; a ghost base, a snare for the souls of the gruesomely dispatched miners.

Perhaps, thought Stokes, slippery hands twisting, there was something on this planet. A dark, ancient force more powerful than death itself. Something that could hide in the dark. Something that could lurk in the mind, feeding off your fear, something you could never shake away. A twisted white thing, spattered with warm blood, with thirty eyes, and seven giant claws. At the moment it was content to rattle a panel or shake a loose inspection covering or two. Just to let him know it was about. It would strike later, when it had brought him to his knees. A tap on the shoulder. He would turn. There it would be, half covered by shadow. It would jab its claws into his chest and bring out his beating heart, sink its teeth into his head and suck the juices from his brain. It was worse than Xais or the Nisbett brothers ever could be. Worse than Ventol, the three-headed killer of the lower City. Worse than Strapping Jack or the Zinctown Cobbler. Perhaps it was here.

He could feel its breath on his neck, but of course when he turned round it had dashed back into cover. It was playing with him. He had to escape from it, get through the door up ahead, set the timer on the transmat, climb up and disappear.

His outstretched fingers felt along the cold metal wall, leading him around obstacles that his failing eyesight could not detect. He bumped into something and cried out, but it was only an abandoned trolley. Alarmed by his own cry of distress, he ran recklessly ahead in a wobbling frenzy.

A shaft of light fell over the door at the end of the corridor, now only a few metres away. Yes, this was the transmat. He threw himself forward onto the metal hatchway.

The door to the transmat chamber refused to open. It was sealed. Stokes thumbed the opening panel but it failed to respond.

Stokes's vision started to wheel. He shook. His legs almost gave way. He tottered from wall to wall, desperate to stay upright. Hunger and fear and exhaustion were pressing him down. Shivering pangs of fever creased his shoulder blades. His mind and body were screaming for rest. He was transformed into a creature compounded wholly of terror.

He stumbled away, choking and spluttering. There had to be somewhere to hide. Somewhere safe, away from this madness.

Romana tapped the Doctor on the shoulder as he sped down the corridor. 'What are we going to do when we get to the survey room, Doctor?'

He stopped and she almost cannoned into him. 'Stop Xais. I think the Nisbett brothers ought to be told a few truths.'

'Is that wise? We don't know how they'll react.'

The Doctor shook his head. 'No, we don't. We'll just have to hope, won't we?'

He ran ahead again.

A bubble of mud swelled up and burst over the boots of the mining Ogrons. The probe shot back a second later, now coated in glistening blue soil. Gjork caught it and wiped clean the snout-nosed end.

He reported to the base. 'Gjork to Mr Charles. Probe is back.'

Xais tapped a foot. 'This is unnecessary. Why are we wasting time?'

Eddie frowned. 'Wait. Just stand there and wait.'

Charlie put down his soup and brought out the probe's relay unit, a large red box, from a crate. He flipped up a small screen and a series of results started to flash up.

PORTIZOL	0.00000012%
GOOMINUM	0.00000000000003%
VIBLIUS	0.000000000000000000014%
BALL'S ORE	0.000000000000000000000000000000023%
BELZITE	0.00000000000000000000000000006%
HELICON	*residual ??????*

'There,' said Charlie, satisfied. 'Not much we didn't expect.' He turned to Xais, who was studying the probe's findings over his shoulder. 'Right. You'd better give us the coordinates for these mountains, then, and we'll get the lads sent out.'

Xais raised a hand as he made to close the screen down. 'Wait. The helicon. Explain the reading for helicon.'

Eddie shrugged. 'It could be a freak reading for this area. It doesn't matter.'

'A residual trace of helicon?' said Xais. 'Impossible. Jarrigan Voltt's initial report estimated helicon at one point three per cent of planetary mass. A residual trace suggests that the helicon has been sucked away by selectively programmed mining bugs.' She turned to Pyerpoint. 'Yes?'

He looked away. 'The reading must be false.'

Xais clenched her fists. 'No! What has happened here? Where is the helicon?'

Curious, Spiggot removed one of the Doctor's coats from

the stand in the TARDIS control room and examined the label inside. 'H.J. Barber and Son, Aylesbury,' he read out. 'Aylesbury? Isn't that one of the outer worlds?'

'Aylesbury unimportant,' K9 replied. 'TARDIS now entering hover mode. Activating force field.'

There was a slight change in the ambient hum of the TARDIS's engines. The central column rose to its full height and stopped.

'Have we arrived then?' asked Spiggot.

K9 trundled forward officiously and operated the shutters over the scanner. Spiggot saw a close view of the atmosphere of Planet Eleven, flecks of which were already starting to adhere to the scanner lens.

'We are stationary above planet's surface,' said K9. 'I will now carry out sensor survey to locate mining base.'

'What about the atmospheric interference?' Spiggot asked. 'Nobody's ever surveyed this planet from space, it's impossible.'

'Gallifreyan technology superior.' Lights on the input panel on K9's back started to flash and his eyescreen flickered as he interfaced with the TARDIS computer. The picture on the TARDIS scanner shifted into scan mode, and topographical details became visible. After a few seconds, a green light started to flash over one area. The focus sharpened and Spiggot made out a couple of familiar shapes.

'Ah, right. That'll be the survey base and there's the Ogron ship.' An orange glow clung to the rear of the smaller object. 'It must have just touched down, there's still a heat shadow.' He looked down at K9, who was still flashing and beeping anxiously. 'What's up?'

K9's tail wagged in bemusement. 'TARDIS sensors register a secondary generator on planet's surface.'

'Don't be daft. It must be the distortion, playing up your fancy galliwhatsit technology,' said Spiggot. 'There's nothing else down there.'

In reply, K9 pulled the scanner image back and zoomed in to another point. The enhancers strained to

195

pierce the cover of a dense typhoon of gas. Peaks of a mountain range became visible, cramped and irregular. The spectrum of the image switched to negative, and Spiggot saw it. A tiny patch of black against bright green. 'What is it?'

'Insufficient data. Structure has been built under cover of mountain range. Patina of energy traces suggest there is an impulse-powered generator beneath structure. Smaller energy trails also present. This suggests use of processing machinery.'

Spiggot rubbed his chin. 'What, mining machinery?'

'That is possible.' K9 conferred again with the TARDIS. 'I have completed a rapid mineralogical analysis of planet. There is evidence of recent extraction of mineral alloy RL225, common name helicon.'

'There are pirates down there,' said Spiggot. 'Got there before Xais. It can't be one of the big companies. But who the hell would have the money to build a place like that down there? And what do they want with the helicon anyway?'

He knelt down and addressed K9. 'Hey. Why don't we take a nose at that place, eh? Give it the once over?'

'Your idioms are not in my phraseology bank,' said K9. 'If your suggestion is to travel to this mining base, I have already programmed a suitable course.'

'This cannot be!' Xais screeched. She threw the probe relay down and advanced on Charlie. 'Your equipment has malfunctioned.'

Charlie folded his arms and stared back implacably. 'Does it matter, eh? Who needs helicon?' He signalled to Eddie. 'Perhaps you'd like to tell us why you're getting upset about it.'

Eddie levelled his revolver at Xais's back. Pyerpoint, watching from the corner, reached for his own pistol.

'Because I like to have all the facts, dear,' Charlie went on. 'I like to have everything tidy and on the table and in its place. So, tell me. Why are you so interested in helicon?'

'One glance from my eyes and you are dead,' Xais warned. Her voice was becoming louder and more tremulous. 'I merely wish assurance that your equipment is functioning correctly. If we are to proceed with the extraction of the belzite, everything must be in good order.'

'So where is the belzite?' demanded Charlie. He spat out the last word of the sentence sceptically. 'Tell us. Now. We've fulfilled our part of the bargain.'

The tension in the survey room had lessened for the moment. Eddie lowered his revolver. Pyerpoint's hand moved away from his laser pistol.

Xais strode past Charlie and tapped out a series of figures into one of the consoles. A symbol flashed on the contoured map of the planet's surface. 'There. The Jilharro mountains. The range is almost impassable, but your Ogrons can reach the seam, I'm sure. All they have to do is set up mini-rigs at five points. I will program them by remote, and the belzite seam will be extracted and refined in two months.'

'At last,' said Eddie. He moved towards the communicator. 'I'll call Gjork back in and brief him.'

'Wait a second.' Charlie raised the flat of one hand. 'Xais. There's another thing I want from you. The name of Sentinel.'

Xais laughed. 'Do you think me such a fool? That information will be revealed to you only after the operation is over.'

'Then no deal,' said Charlie. 'You're going to tell us. Now.' He raised his hand to the mask. 'I don't like being kept behind. I've never had to do it before. I'm too old to start now.'

Eddie raised his revolver again.

Xais snarled. 'I'll tell you nothing until our business is complete.'

The main door slid open and the Doctor and Romana breezed in. 'Hello, all!'

'Not you again!' Xais exclaimed.

'You're not very good at locking people up, are you?'

the Doctor said politely. 'It's no wonder you prefer to kill them.' He turned to the brothers. 'Gentlemen, before either of you do anything rash, like shooting anybody, I think it's time you found out a few facts.' He coughed. 'Er, Romana.'

Romana stepped forward. 'There isn't any belzite on this planet,' she said simply. 'We've seen a mineralogical survey. There's none here.'

'She's lying,' Xais said. 'Believe nothing the girl says, she's an investigator!'

Charlie turned his black eyes on Xais. 'They expect me to be surprised.'

'We know that,' said Eddie, his mouth trembling with confusion and anger. 'But this mountain range. What's she after there? It's got to be worth something.'

'Only to her,' said the Doctor. 'You see, Xais is interested in helicon, which I dare say is to be found in the mountains, but isn't going to be much use to you. Unless you're thinking of going into the pipeline-making business.'

Xais, torn between priorities, swung her face towards him. An orange beam shot from her eyes and he sank to the ground slowly, hands covering his face.

'Doctor!' cried Romana.

'Nobody puts one over on us!' Eddie aimed his revolver at Xais and steadied his trembling gun arm.

Aware of his action, Xais turned instinctively, freeing the Doctor from the deadly beam of her eyes.

Eddie fired. The shot went wide of Xais.

Xais's angry stare transfixed Eddie. The revolver fell from his hand. The beam of pure hate lifted him off his feet. His eyes bulged with agony.

A second later, what was left of his body squelched to the floor.

Charlie pulled his own revolver from his jacket and fired four bullets into Xais. She was thrown back by each blast but still clung to life, the mask forcing her on. 'Fool!' she screamed.

Romana helped the Doctor to his feet. They watched as Charlie fired another three bullets into Xais's chest. Bloody holes opened up all over her white tunic. Still she advanced.

'Do you think you can kill me?' she taunted Charlie.

The lips of the mask moved. The face of Xais lived again. It twisted into an expression of grotesque silver hate.

'I exist!' the mask shouted. 'The transfer is complete! I cannot be destroyed!'

More bullets tore into the body beneath the mask. It crumpled and fell in a gruesome red heap. The mask screamed its defiance and closed its eyes.

Charlie ignored the Doctor and Romana and moved to the smashed remains of his brother. 'No,' he said through gritted teeth. 'No. Not Ed. My own . . .' He faltered at the sight of the splattered body. 'My own flesh and blood. I'll bring the lot of them down for this.' His eyes glistened. 'The whole lot of them.'

On the other side of the survey room, the Doctor was picking himself up. 'Are you all right?' asked Romana.

'I think so,' he said. He blinked rapidly and wiggled his fingers. 'Yes, I think I had a narrow escape.'

Pyerpoint had remained perfectly still during the blood-soaked altercations of the last few minutes. Suddenly he sprang into life. He leapt across the survey room, bent over the body of Xais, and ripped off the mask.

'Where are you off to with that?' the Doctor called.

Pyerpoint fired two beams from his laser pistol in the Doctor's general direction and sped out of the survey room.

The Doctor shuddered. 'It's just as well, Romana, that the people who try to kill me are all such bad shots.'

They looked down at the body of Margo. Romana knelt and turned it over. The arm flopped pathetically.

Where the mask had been, where the face should have been, was a flat lump of pink flesh. There were no features.

Romana recoiled. 'What happened to her?'

'She was absorbed,' the Doctor said sadly. 'Xais transferred totally.' He shook his head. 'The powers of activated helicon are more terrible than even I had dared to imagine.' He indicated the door. 'Let's get after him.'

Romana ran from the room, picking her way around the corpse of Eddie. The Doctor turned for a last look at the survey room.

Charlie's massive hand clamped on his shoulder. The other hand still held the smoking revolver that had stopped Xais.

'Scum!' Charlie spat. 'Why don't I shoot your knees away right now?'

The Doctor backed away, but the grip on his arm was alarmingly strong. 'Please,' he said, trying to sound as sincere as possible. 'I understand how you must feel. But you don't want to do anything hasty. I mean, it's always better to allow for a sensible interval of grief before taking any rash action. After all, you're not one of those people who gets into a rage and starts killing whoever happens to be about.'

A moist clicking sound came from the back of Charlie's throat.

'Well, perhaps you are,' said the Doctor.

Pyerpoint kept to the better-lit areas of the base, and followed them to a round junction halfway along one of the outer arms. The mind that had kept ahead through forty years of deliberation in the service of the law had already formulated a new plan to cope with the altered situation. If this base had been constructed to standard design, the section he was searching for would be just here.

An open door ahead led to a room that smelt of fuel fluids. He stepped through and saw his own face reflected in the plastiglass window of the base's skimmer.

He looked about. Neatly arranged on a rail nearby were a row of protective suits. He set the mask down on a work surface and pulled at the laces of his tunic. In under a minute he had changed into one of the featureless grey plastic suits. His own clothes he kicked away into a corner.

'Pyerpoint,' a voice whispered.

He looked down and licked his lips. The mask was speaking to him. Its eyes had opened and its lips were pouting. Without a host to draw from its voice was high-pitched and metallic, pure and chiming.

'Pyerpoint. You know what you must do. You will never learn the secret of helicon unless you wear my face.'

He took a pair of grey gloves from a pouch on the suit and pushed his hands into them. Then he picked up the mask by its edge and held it away from him as if it were radioactive. 'No,' he told Xais. 'There is an alternative.'

'Yes,' said the mask. 'Yes. Bring me another host.'

The sound of tentative footsteps came from the corridor outside the garage. Pyerpoint crept over to the door and looked out.

The girl Romana was standing in the middle of the corridor, her hands on her hips, looking about. 'Pyerpoint!' she called. 'You may as well show yourself. The operation's over.'

Pyerpoint felt the mask jerk in his hand. 'Yes,' it whispered. 'Yes.'

He stepped from the garage and advanced on Romana. She whipped round to face him and saw instantly what he intended to do. He gripped her by the shoulder and tried to bring the mask forward. Her strength was surprising, and her long legs kicked at his midriff. If they had fought under more usual circumstances she would undoubtedly have come off better.

But the mask was too strong. It gave Pyerpoint greater strength and determination. He pushed Romana against the wall, held her there, and pressed the mask over her face. The cap fell from her hair.

She flinched, slumped, and was still.

13

Sentinel

For once, Flarkk had followed his pilot's training with accuracy. The inner air-lock of the base clicked open and the Ogron crew barged through noisily. If there was one thing a group of Ogrons could be relied upon to do well, it was to barge noisily through an air-lock.

The guard Ogron gave a clumsy salute of greeting to his comrades. 'Welcome to Planet Eleven. You have good journey?'

Flarkk nodded. 'Journey good and safe. Where are the Mister Nisbetts?'

'In survey room. I will lead you.' The Ogrons followed him away from the air-lock.

On the opposite side of the base, halfway along one of the arms that faced away from the landing pad, a large hatch set a few metres above the ground slid back and the base's skimmer emerged. It had been used by the survey team on computer-guided reconnaissance missions in the locality of the base. It was about twenty metres long by ten wide, and its silver paintwork was scarred and soiled by the various tasks it had undertaken. The upswept tail section contained two large rocket thrusters, designed to provide maximum resistance against the dense atmosphere. At the front was a clear bubble of plastiglass which was doused constantly by automatic sprinklers.

Inside the bubble, at the guidance controls of the skimmer, sat Pyerpoint. His long bony fingers tapped confidently at the navigation panel, keying in a sequence of coordinates he had memorized for just such an eventuality. Next to him on the padded seating lay the body of Romana, still unconscious, her head thrown back. The glittering mask of Xais, unmoving, was framed by her long blonde hair.

The skimmer's motors responded to its new instructions and turned the tapered snout of the vehicle to face its destination. The rocket ports glared red and the skimmer shot through the gas clouds.

On the second row of seating, behind Pyerpoint and Romana, a bulky, irregular shape was covered by an oil-spattered tarpaulin. As the skimmer rocked and banked, the tarpaulin lifted for a second.

Stokes's terrified face was revealed.

The Doctor was still leading Charlie Nisbett in a macabre pas de deux around the survey room, neatly circling around the remains of Margo and Eddie.

'Who tipped you off about this operation?' Charlie snarled. 'Was it the judge man, old Pyerpoint?'

'Oh no,' said the Doctor. 'Nobody tipped me off, I'm just a natural blunderer. If there's trouble, I'll find it.' He coughed nervously. 'As for old Pyerpoint, well, he's the man you want to be chasing about with a gun.'

Charlie stopped and straightened up. 'Perhaps you're right.'

'Thank goodness,' the Doctor said, and pointed over his shoulder. 'He went that way.'

'I'd better tidy up in here first, though,' said Charlie. He raised his revolver and pointed it directly at the Doctor's left heart. 'You talk too much. My old Mum used to say empty sandshakers make the most clatter.'

The Doctor prepared himself to jump Charlie. Just as he was about to spring, a crowd of Ogrons burst in to the survey room.

Flarkk stopped in shock at the sight of the two bodies. 'Mr Edward!'

Charlie turned to face his boys, the Doctor momentarily forgotten. 'Where have you been?'

Flarkk wrung his huge hairy hands. 'We had trouble with the docking clamps again.'

'I don't want to hear about your flaming clamps,' Charlie stormed. 'My only brother is lying dead on that floor! We've got to nail the villain that did it.'

The Doctor used the opportunity of this distraction to pick up the probe relay unit discarded earlier by Xais. He consulted the read-out screen, did a few mental calculations, and shook his head ruefully. 'That villain has done a lot more than any of us anticipated.' He wiggled the device at Charlie. 'Somebody has sucked this planet clean of helicon. Mined out the seam in the Jilharro mountains, and cleared up the rest of the planet using selective gathering bugs. Before this survey had even begun. Now, the only person with the information, the opportunity and the motive to do all of that is Pyerpoint.'

'But he's the law,' Charlie said. 'And what would he want with helicon?'

The Doctor decided to take advantage of his temporary favour and sat down before the main console. 'Well, he's totally corrupt, for one thing,' he told Charlie. 'A greater danger to the system than your firm ever was or ever could have been, precisely because he was working from inside the law. And as for helicon . . .'

He punched up a picture from one of the base's external cameras. The rear of a skimmer was ploughing away through the grime. 'Through Xais, he can use it to unlock powers more dangerous than anything this sector of space has seen. I think he's off to collect it.' He looked around, a worried expression creeping over his features. 'Where's Romana?'

'Coordinates are aligned with course program,' K9 pronounced grandly. 'Materialization commencing.'

The central column of the TARDIS ground to a halt. Spiggot, who was getting used to some of the time ship's more basic functions, twisted the scanner control and the big shutters slid open.

Their immediate environment was a large and apparently empty room that was lined with quiescent mining technology. Large drills sat upended on a central work table, their coils blunted and smeared by overuse. A twisted rubber belt five feet wide was wrapped around a stanchion on the floor. Smaller tools were ranged in clips along the facing wall. Light came from a phosphorescent disc in the ceiling.

'Ah, a storage and repair area, right?' mused Spiggot. He reached for the door control. 'All set for a look about, K9?'

'Life support systems inactive, but residual oxygen and temperature sufficient,' the dog replied. 'Open doors.'

His blaster raised, Spiggot stepped cautiously from the TARDIS into the repair room. 'Ah well. Nobody about.' He crossed to the table and picked up an engine part that was covered in flaking rust. 'This looks like it could be part of a centrifuge. Ore separator or something.'

'Your analysis is likely,' said K9.

Spiggot replaced the component. 'You don't have to sound so surprised.' He noticed a communicator system as he crossed the room to a large machine that stood in the corner. The machine was ten feet tall, painted white, and was featureless, except for a central section of flashing controls and two slits just above.

'What d'you reckon on this, though?' Spiggot asked. He reached up and patted the machine. 'It's a big one, whatever it is. Could be a recharger.'

K9 trundled forward and extended his probe. 'Caution,' he said. 'Function of this machine is to supervise the sorting of ore. It has reasoning intelligence circuits and is programmed to resist unauthorized interference.'

Spiggot waved a hand dismissively. 'Ah, get off, K9. It's a recharger, right enough. I've seen some like this before. They have to be big to channel so much energy.' He tapped the machine's central panel. 'See, you put your charge leads in these sockets, right, and press this button here.'

'Danger!' K9 shrieked. 'Do not activate this machine!'

Spiggot pressed the button. The slits on the machine's top section flashed bright green. A whirring noise came from deep inside it.

'It's just a recharger,' Spiggot said, a little less confidently. 'Don't worry about it.'

There were a series of short, sharp clicks from inside the machine and it started to unfold like a living deck chair. Three white blocks appeared and formed arms, at the end of each was a different mining tool; a scoop, a saw, and a long serrated implement that quivered menacingly. The entire lower section sank down on an inflating circular base. The head swivelled from side to side, a pneumatic hiss accompanying its movements.

'I suppose I was wrong,' said Spiggot. He leapt back towards the TARDIS, to which K9 was already retreating.

The robot advanced. It seemed to know what they were trying to do, and a green ray shot from its eyes and bounced off the TARDIS. Apparently irritated by this disappointing result, it advanced smoothly on its circular base and fired again, this time directly at its opponents.

Spiggot ducked and followed K9 towards the door of the repair room. They tumbled through and the door closed. Spiggot thumbed the locking panel beside it and leant panting against the wall. 'K9,' he said. 'You have official permission not to listen to a word I say.'

'I do not need official permission,' K9 said testily and set off along the adjoining corridor. Spiggot raced after him.

The door of the repair room was blasted off its hinges moments later. The mighty robot pushed itself through the doorway and set off after them, its eyes flashing fiercely.

Gjork and his two colleagues in the mining party stood waiting for further orders from their masters. They were used to long delays between sets of orders. It was always the same, whoever you were working for.

A roaring engine noise was suddenly overlaid on the rumble of the swirling gas clouds. Each of the Ogrons heard it through his helmet and looked up curiously to its point of origin. Their eyes widened in astonishment and they gave puzzled grunts. A dark shape was swooping down through the clouds at alarming speed.

Confused, Gjork took a couple of clumsy atmosuited strides forward. It wasn't their ship coming in so low. And the masters would have said if they were coming over. The flying shape was turning round now, but still heading directly at them. The other two mining Ogrons panicked and started to run.

Gjork stood his ground. He decided to call his masters and find out what was going on. They were sure to have an answer.

'Mr Charles,' he began. 'Gjork is speaking.'

The thundering rocket ports of the vehicle came closer.

'There is a big thing here, sir, with big flames coming from it. What is it?'

A ball of jettisoned fuel waste dropped from the rocket ports of the skimmer. It ignited in the atmosphere immediately and Gjork and his colleagues were swallowed up by the conflagration within seconds. The fireball spun and sizzled for a few moments, then folded in on itself, trailing a squall of black fumes and cinders that were the only remains of the Ogron miners.

'What's going on out there?' Charlie called into the microphone. 'Gjork? Report!'

The Doctor pointed up at the screen that displayed the local weather conditions. A sequence of figures was flaring over the reference point of the mining party. 'I'm very much afraid there's been a hit and run.'

Charlie stiffened. 'Gjork and the boys? What do you mean?'

'Pyerpoint,' the Doctor said bitterly. 'He's a malicious

old stick. He burnt them away just because he felt like it.'

Charlie stood up. There was a determined set to his features again. 'Right,' he said.

The Doctor looked up at him. 'You've decided on a course of action, I can tell.'

Charlie turned to the nearest Ogron. 'Bnorg. Tie him to the chair.'

The Doctor spluttered and attempted to rise, but a firm Ogron hand pushed him down again. Bnorg unwound a length of white plastic flex from his belt pouch and wrapped it around the Doctor's waist and the chair, taking care to keep the hands of the prisoner apart by use of a simple but very stubborn looking knot. 'This is very ungrateful of you,' the Doctor protested.

'I know,' said Charlie. 'But you're the law.' He tapped the Doctor on the shoulder. 'No hard feelings.'

'I shall feel much better knowing that. Just what are you up to?'

Charlie scrabbled in his pocket and brought out a small black box with a red button mounted on top. 'Know what this is, Doctor?'

'Well, it looks like a signalling device to me.'

'It is.' Charlie tossed the box from hand to hand. 'And when me and Bnorg and the rest of the lads are far enough away from this planet, I'm going to use it to detonate that.' He pointed.

The Doctor saw the outline of the bomb underneath the main console. 'It doesn't look very big,' he said.

'Size is unimportant,' said Charlie. 'That bomb contains enough fine hermite to blow this base apart. And that's not all, you know. 'Cause this place has a fission generator beneath it. And when that catches light – well, there's not going to be much left of the planet after that.'

Stokes lifted the tattered edge of the tarpaulin again and raised his head slightly. From this position he could see out of the clear bubble on top of the skimmer and onto the surface of Planet Eleven. The place looked fairly much as he had imagined it. Dirty and blue. Occasionally a brighter splash of chemical would flash up in the greasy slow-moving clouds they were pushing through, but these were soon swallowed by the prevailing stodge. Stokes vowed that if he lived to take up oils again, blue would never form part of his compositions. He had seen more than enough of the wretched colour.

The skimmer was moving at an incredible rate, he thought. Its preset course was leading it towards a large black shape that loomed up ahead. As they came closer, he saw that there was more than one of these shapes. They were no higher than tall hills, but given the flatness of this planet's surface they reared up like mighty mountains. Their foremost peaks pointed solidly up from the gas clouds.

His stomach lurched as the skimmer banked and began to slow. A structure at the foot of the nearest mountain came into view. It was small, about half the size of the McConnochie base, and hugged the slope of the mountain with coiling metal pipelines. Its central section was oblong. It had no windows or external markings, and the rigours of the planet's atmosphere had covered it with dirt. The side facing the approaching skimmer had been partly buried under a cascade of sand, but the rudimentary docking port, little more than a large hole surrounded by a ring of securing clamps, had fortunately escaped the avalanche.

Stokes raised his head as high as he dared and peeked forward through the gap in the seating. He saw Romana's outstretched body and Pyerpoint's hand reaching out to make manual guidance corrections. Trust that old fraudster to take a young woman as a hostage.

If Stokes had been a more valiant man, he would have been planning the rescue of the girl. But he was not, and so he slunk back into cover and gnawed his knuckles in terror as the skimmer slid to a halt and he heard the clamps swing out to secure it.

* * *

In their flight through the darkened, stuffy corridors of the illegal mine, Spiggot and K9 had seen many more dormant robots standing among the machinery. It was just as well, Spiggot reasoned, that he had seen fit to activate the one that was in for repair. The thought of confronting a fully functional member of this robotic race would have brought him out in a sweat, if he hadn't already been sweating from the exertion of running.

He grasped hold of a staircase that ran along one wall, and swung himself under it. He panted and collapsed against the wall, trying to catch his breath.

K9 turned. 'Query your stopping. We must avoid pursuing robot.' The clank of the approaching machine echoed down the corridor towards them.

'Hold on,' Spiggot gasped. 'Why don't we set up an ambush? Lure it along this way, then you blast it with your nose ray.'

'Plan impractical. My defensive capability may be ineffective against mining robot. Insufficient data on its design.'

Spiggot waved a hand desperately. 'That control panel on its chest. Try blasting that away, eh? It's our only chance.' He wiped his brow. 'And sometimes you have to take a chance in life, K9. Follow your instincts. It's how I've survived all these years.'

K9 regarded him sceptically. 'My logic circuits refute your argument.' His sensors swivelled. 'However, a check on my power reserves indicates that at present speed, utility will cease in twenty-five minutes. To preserve power, I must take action.'

Spiggot watched as K9 turned and settled himself in the middle of the corridor. The nose blaster slid from his muzzle.

'Good boy, K9,' Spiggot called. 'Don't let me down now.'

K9's eyescreen flashed angrily. 'This unit has never failed you. Your inefficiency has impaired my actions at a rate of eight five point four three —'

The robot appeared at the end of the corridor, wobbling uncertainly on its base. Its serrated probe sliced the air ahead of it, and its head whirred from side to side, searching its prey.

'Interesting,' said K9. 'Inferior design of close tactile sensors. I have the advantage.'

The robot came closer. Its stare fixed on the immobile K9 and it stopped for a moment, apparently confused.

The delay was all that K9 needed. He aimed for the robot's chest unit, and let off a concentrated laser blast.

The mining robot's appendages went haywire. Smoke started to issue from its shoulders. It managed to release a feeble response to the attack from its eyes, but the twin beams succeeded only in scorching the floor. The machine clicked, groaned, and sagged.

K9 cut off his own laser beam and beeped proudly. 'Robot deactivated.'

Spiggot emerged from his hiding place. 'Hey, well done, little feller.'

Suddenly a distant clang sounded, followed by a scraping noise. Spiggot nodded. 'Sounds like we've got visitors.'

Stokes waited until he heard the door of the skimmer slam shut after Pyerpoint and Romana before he dared lift his head. The vehicle had come to rest in a small bare metallic chamber that adjoined the air-lock. Pyerpoint, carrying the supine form of Romana, was standing before a door that obviously led to the main section of this place, whatever it was. The old judge raised a finger to the chamber's entry coder and tapped in a recognition code. Stokes squinted to make out the letters that appeared on the tiny screen. They made up the word SENTINEL.

The door clicked open and Pyerpoint stepped through.

Stokes would have been quite prepared to remain in the skimmer, but he noticed a dial on the air-lock's atmosphere gauge swinging from green to red. A poor spacefarer he may have been, but he knew enough about basic safety to realize what was happening. In minutes, the air would be sucked out.

He pushed open the door of the skimmer and tumbled out, clutching at his throat, which already felt dry and constricted. His only hope was that the door would respond to the same code being used twice. He hurried over and slowly punched in the word SENTINEL.

The door swung open and he darted through. Fortunately, his fellow passengers had already moved off and he was alone in a corridor that was even darker and less comfortable than those of the survey base.

He barely had time to register the unpleasant details of his surroundings before a strange whirring noise issued from the darkness up ahead. He looked about frantically, but there was no exit except for the air-lock door.

He sank to his knees and clasped his hands together. 'Please, please,' he murmured to whatever celestial force might be listening, 'make it as swift and as painless as possible.' He screwed his eyes tight.

'Fear unnecessary,' said a high-pitched electronic voice.

Stokes opened an eye curiously. 'K9! How did you get here?' Despite his exhaustion he found his lips curling upwards in a grateful smile. Perhaps things weren't so bad after all. At least now he had company.

Another figure appeared from the shadows. 'I hadn't expected to be seeing you again,' said Spiggot. 'Thought you'd probably been blasted by those Nisbetts.'

Stokes pulled himself up. Oddly, the presence of this uncouth upstart galvanized him far more effectively than the terrors of the past few hours. The fellow was such a bore. All he ever did was talk about himself.

'I have come here in pursuit of our true enemy,' Stokes said grandly. 'The Nisbett menace is as nothing when compared to the improbity of High Archon Pyerpoint.' He relished in the revelation of the name.

'Pyerpoint?' queried Spiggot. 'What's he got to do with it?'

'He has come here, carrying the fair Ramona as his captive,' Stokes explained. 'He has led Xais and the Nisbetts, not to mention the great Doctor himself, a pretty dance.'

K9 spoke. 'Sensors indicate presence of the Mistress. However, her psychospoor trail is obscured by a rogue trace.'

'Exactly,' said Stokes. 'That'll be the Xais mask. She is wearing it.'

Spiggot laid a heavy hand on Stokes's shoulder. 'I think, mate, before we do anything else, all three of us had best find a quiet corner, sit down, and try to sort out just what's going on here.'

'It is not possible for me to sit down,' said K9. 'But I concur with your strategy. More information is needed before rescue plan can be devised.'

One of the large mining robots stood dormant before a plain metal door further into the mine. As Pyerpoint, who was still carrying Romana, advanced, its eyes lit up and one of its arms shot up.

'Sentinel,' said Pyerpoint wearily. 'Grant access.'

The robot slid to one side and the door slid open.

The room beyond had been designed for a specific purpose. It was dominated by an angled dais that had four metal clamps built into it. Above the dais, bulging from the ceiling, was a complex array of machinery. Sprouting from its centre was a slim metal probe. Above this device was a transparent panel built into the wall.

Pyerpoint arranged the body of Romana on the dais and secured her arms and legs in the clamps. When he was satisfied that she was safely tied up, he left the room.

Romana began to stir uneasily in her bonds. The jowls of the living mask twitched with hate-filled dreams.

Bnorg marched into the survey room. 'Mr Charles. Ready to leave, sir.'

A large pulse had started to throb in Charlie's thick

neck, making his shirt collar dance in time to the vein pumping on his forehead. He finished off his soup and screwed the lid of the flask back on. 'Good.'

Bnorg saluted and gestured to the gathered Ogrons. They started to file noisily back out of the survey room. Charlie made to follow them.

The Doctor coughed politely from the chair where he had been bound. 'Aren't you going to say goodbye?'

'No.'

'If you were a real gentleman, you'd shoot me. Pressing buttons and blowing people up, it's all a bit modern, isn't it? Rather gauche, wouldn't you say?'

Charlie sauntered over. 'Well. One thing this experience has taught me, Doctor. The old days are finished.'

He knelt and whispered in the Doctor's ear. 'As a lawman, I'm sure you appreciate it, too. When the Nisbett firm was in its prime, the streets were safe. You can't deny it. Now there's hooligans and punks and God knows what running riot in the streets, and bent judges and coppers playing at rackets, and all the big companies busting each other up.' He wiped a small tear from his eye. 'My Mum and Dad would cry to see things today, they would. All the lies and tricks. It was always the golden rule. Never mess on your own patch.'

'Crime isn't what it was,' the Doctor agreed.

Charlie stood. 'You're right there. Well, goodbye. You're a decent bloke for a copper, you know.' He took a last look at the body of his brother and left the survey room.

Left alone at last, the Doctor decided it was time to deal with his bonds. He held in his breath and shrugged his shoulders, but the knots remained as tight as ever. Surely the Ogrons couldn't be that good at tying knots? Far cleverer people had tied him to things and he'd managed to escape.

He strained to free his wrists, but had no success. This was going to take time.

* * *

Xais's eyes opened, the fluid silver sockets of the mask framing the clear blue eyes of Romana. Her exultant sneer became a frown of alarm as she felt the clamps securing her to the platform in the small room, and saw the thin probe angled directly at her.

A voice that she recognized came from a speaker somewhere close by. 'So you have woken.'

'Pyerpoint!' she screamed and tried to sit up. 'You will release me immediately!' Above the machine facing her was a faintly illuminated gallery. Seated within was her supposed ally.

'I want the formula for the activation process, Xais,' Pyerpoint said calmly. 'You will give me the formula now.'

Xais laughed. 'You are such a fool. I have the power to burn through these bonds and crush you where you stand.' Already a glow was forming around her eyes.

She saw Pyerpoint lean forward and press a button on the console before him. A blue light flooded the chamber accompanied by a strange, unwavering note. 'The room you are inside has now been charged with Stavender's radiation. If you release one rad of your own powers, the reaction will weaken the structure of your host body.'

Xais twisted and turned in frustration. 'No!'

Pyerpoint continued, his smooth tones as untroubled as they had ever been when pronouncing judgement in the courtroom. 'And you need a host to activate the helicon, Xais. Without a living mind you cannot power the transfer of your consciousness. Am I right?'

Xais grunted and struggled in her bonds.

His voice became mocking. 'You thought you were in control, Xais. Bringing in the Nisbett brothers behind my back. The alliance was doomed from the start. As was our own arrangement. I realized how you intended to use me. I knew you would never work with a Normal.'

'Release me,' growled Xais. 'This new host has closed her mind to me, but I sense great powers there. We can share them.'

Pyerpoint shook his head. 'I want the formula, Xais. All these years I have been preparing for this moment.' He gestured around him. 'I have mined the helicon from this planet. You will activate it for me, or die.'

'I cannot die!' Xais wailed up at him.

'But without a host,' he taunted her. 'What then? You are powerless.'

Xais drummed her fists on the platform. 'When I am free, old Normal, I will strip the flesh from your bones and bathe myself in your blood!'

The Ogrons' spaceship may have been old, but it was dependable enough. With a mighty roar that blew gathering dirt from its rocket ports, it lifted from the launchpad outside the McConnochie base, turned to steady itself, and soared up and away.

On the cluttered bridge of the ship, Charlie settled himself in his armchair and looked across to its empty counterpart. His eyes flicked up to the portrait of his mother.

'They're going to pay, all right,' he vowed.

'Preparing to depart atmosphere of Planet Eleven,' called Flarkk from the flight position.

'Good,' said Charlie. 'We'll give it ten minutes and then blow the charge.' He sat back in his chair, took hold of the arm rests, and closed his eyes, breathing deeply in an effort to calm himself.

Spiggot, Stokes and K9 had found shelter back in the repair room where the TARDIS had materialized. Stokes had shown particular interest in the police box, which had proved the claims made for it beyond doubt, but had been persuaded by the others to relate the complex story of Pyerpoint's plan as far as he understood it. As Spiggot listened, K9 had wandered off into a corner and was sniffing out what appeared to be some kind of long-range transmitter unit.

'I always reckoned he was a strange old guy,' said Spiggot. 'To devote himself totally to the law like he did. I mean to say, even I've found time for a personal life over the years.'

'I know,' said Stokes hastily. 'What puzzles me is how he managed to set this place up.'

Spiggot shrugged. 'Well, he's got the contacts and the money. Probably hired a pirate.'

'Wait a moment.' Stokes thought back to the last set of terminations. 'Now I come to think of it, Pyerpoint had some rogue miner chap sent to the reverser the other day. Veltt, or somebody. Who's to say he didn't construct this place on orders from Pyerpoint, who then had him framed to keep him quiet.'

'You're probably right,' said Spiggot. 'Funny thing, but I thought Pyerpoint had principles. He's an old-fashioned type. The last of his breed, probably.'

'Repressed,' was Stokes's judgement. 'And probably quite insane. All those years dishing out death sentences convinced him that he was God and could do anything he liked. He appears to have been running our entire system for the last fifteen years, at any rate. From both sides of the law. And just look at that code name he uses. Sentinel, pah! The arrogance.'

Spiggot looked up abruptly. 'Sentinel?'

Stokes nodded. 'Yes. Unbelievable, isn't it? He sees himself as some sort of guardian for the rest of society, I imagine.'

Spiggot licked his lips. 'When the Nisbett firm were brought in,' he said, 'some of the smaller fry cracked under questioning. They came out with a story that they'd been betrayed by some contact in the establishment. Nobody believed it.' He gripped Stokes's arm. 'And the code name they had for this guy was Sentinel!'

'I suppose it's likely,' Stokes said. 'The Nisbett firm were rather more successful criminals than their appearance would suggest. They could well have had help.' He coughed. 'Would you mind taking your hand away?'

Spiggot let go and clapped his hands together. 'Pyerpoint was behind the Nisbett firm. And he betrayed them when it suited him.' He smiled. 'I bet they wouldn't mind finding that out. They might even do our job for us, eh?'

Before Stokes could reply, K9 turned from his examination of the machine in the corner. 'This device is a long-range transmitter,' he said. 'I intend to use it to contact the Doctor Master at the McConnochie Mining survey base and request assistance.'

'Hold on a moment,' said Spiggot, his eyes gleaming with enthusiasm. 'I think I might have a better use for it.'

The Doctor tensed his arm muscles and tugged again at the knot around his left wrist. He felt it give way slightly, but realized there was no way he was going to get free before the bombs went off.

Perhaps there was another way. With difficulty he wrenched the chair he was tied to from its holding and hopped, still attached to the chair, over to the console under which the bomb had been placed. He knelt down as far as he was able, took a look at the device, and tutted. 'Even with the sonic screwdriver, I couldn't defuse it in time.'

At such moments, he was used to some miraculous means of deliverance to present itself. None seemed to be forthcoming on this occasion. 'My only hope,' he told himself, 'is to stop Nisbett sending the detonation signal.'

Spurred on by the desperate nature of the situation, he tugged once more at the knots around his wrists, and this time succeeded in freeing his left hand. He hurried over to the communications console, and tapped out a frantic all-frequencies alert. A red light started to flash, indicating that the call had been picked up.

The Doctor sighed with relief and waited for the channel to open. 'Come on, come on!'

At last a guttural voice came from the communicator, masked by heavy static. 'What do you want?'

'This is the Doctor, calling from the survey base. I need to speak to your master about something rather important.'

There was a prolonged pause.

Flarkk looked over his shoulder. Mr Charles was leaning back in his chair and sleeping. He could not be disturbed, whatever the problem. It was not done to wake the boss. And he needed his rest, after all.

'No you can't speak to him,' Flarkk told the Doctor. 'He is resting.'

'But this is urgent,' said the Doctor. 'I've just remembered something I must tell him. I'm speaking with his interests at heart.'

Flarkk's brow creased. 'You speak as friend?'

'I suppose so.'

'Mr Nisbett has no friends. Everyone hates him. You are lying and I shall not listen.' Flarkk clicked off the call.

The Doctor thumped his fist down on the communicator console. It seemed there was no way out.

Another red light started to flash on the console. Somebody else was transmitting a message from the planet's surface.

'Detective Inspector Frank Spiggot to Charles and Edward Nisbett,' a familiar voice said from the console.

'Who are you? Are you an enemy of Mr Nisbett?' came the voice of Flarkk.

'Well, you could say that,' said Spiggot.

Charlie Nisbett's dreams were taking him back to the old days. He and Eddie were standing together under the canopy over the main doorway of the Imperial Club in West Coppertown. Their shining black shoes sank deep into the plush red carpet. The punters were queueing up along the street, all in line, the lads in their smartest suits and the girls in their prettiest frocks. It was going to be a good night. One of the best bands from Capital were inside just striking up. There'd be drinks aplenty, and the finest nosh. And then later, the firm were going to take a van over to the Cog and Centrifuge and collect some money that was owing.

The town clock struck ten and the boys stepped forward to admit the first group of punters into the lobby.

A distant voice said, 'Mr Charles, sir. A message from the planet.'

Charlie looked around the crowd. Standing right at the front of the queue was a right ugly. Covered in hair, it looked like an upright ape. 'Mr Nisbett, sir,' it said. 'There is a message. For you.'

He jolted upright in his chair and was immediately transported thirty years forwards in time. Flarkk was tugging nervously at his sleeve. For a moment, Charlie thought he was going to shout at the hapless Ogron for waking him up. Then he realized that the pilot was about the nearest he could now call to next of kin. There was something oddly familiar and comforting about that huge, brutish face.

He rubbed the sleep from his eyes. 'A message? From where?'

Flarkk pointed to the console. 'From planet, sir. Comes from man called Spiggot.'

Charlie raised a suspicious eyebrow. 'Never heard of him. Patch it through.'

'I hear you've been casting about for a chap calling himself Sentinel,' the Doctor heard Spiggot say.

The Doctor tried to put his hands to his head in alarm, but of course he was still tied to the chair, and he succeeded only in pulling the muscles of his upper back. 'No,' he cried. 'The idiot!'

Charlie straightened in his chair. His eyes narrowed. 'What if I am?'

'What if I told you, Mr Nisbett,' Spiggot continued,

'that I know exactly where you can find this person. You'd be interested, eh?'

'I'd be very interested.'

The Doctor hammered frantically at the communicator controls in the survey room, desperately searching for a way to block the frequency connecting Spiggot with the Ogron ship.

The control panel before which Pyerpoint was seated bleeped urgently. He took his eyes from the writhing form of Xais below, and checked the reading. He frowned. 'A message being sent from this base?' he asked aloud. 'That is impossible.'

Concerned that an instrumentation failure might have occurred, he broke into the transmission frequency to check the reading. The voices of Spiggot and Charlie Nisbett came through clearly.

'You claim to know the identity of Sentinel?' Charlie was asking.

'Oh, better than that, Charlie, my mate,' Spiggot replied. 'I know where you can find him.'

Pyerpoint leapt up.

The sound of the conversation had carried from the gallery to the room below. Xais looked up, deep frown lines forming on the forehead of the mask.

And then she smiled.

'Where?' Charlie barked into his communicator link. 'Where can I find him?' He shuddered with emotion. 'You'd better not be messing me around, copper.'

Spiggot said confidently, 'I wouldn't mess your sort about. No, I've got Sentinel right here, Charlie. You'd know him better as High Archon Pyerpoint.'

Stokes looked on anxiously as Spiggot made his revelation. He whispered to K9, 'I'm not altogether sure about this. Something about this message makes me feel extremely uneasy.' He took another look at Spiggot. 'An uneasiness that probably has something to do with the fact that the person sending the message is a total and absolute idiot.'

'I am not programmed to express critical opinions,' said K9.

'Pyerpoint!' Charlie clamped his hands on the arm of his chair, his knuckles whitening. 'Pyerpoint! But he – but he –' His mind filled up with an explosive mixture of feelings. The first raid on the firm's premises. The lads being led away. Him and Eddie fleeing to Ghelluris. Reading in the papers about the executions of his oldest mates.

'But I've had him next to me,' he spluttered. 'All this flaming time.' He spat. 'No wonder that filthy cow Xais wanted to keep him alive. It wouldn't surprise me if they were all in it together. Pyerpoint, Xais, the Doctor.' He turned back to the communicator. 'You say he's with you, Spiggot?'

'At his secret mine. Why not come and get him? I bet you've got plenty to talk about.'

Spiggot broke off the call.

'There we go,' Spiggot said confidently, turning to face his colleagues. 'Now we can just pop back into the TARDIS over there, and wait for the brothers Nisbett to deal with our problem for us.'

Stokes shrugged. 'I suppose it sounds reasonable enough.'

The communicator bleeped. Surprised, Spiggot re-opened the channel. 'Hello, Mr Nisbett? Any details you want clearing up?'

'Spiggot,' said the Doctor's voice. 'You are a total and absolute idiot!'

Xais chuckled. 'Well, "Sentinel"? What is your plan now?' She smirked up through the glass at Pyerpoint, who was pacing the gallery in agitation.

'It doesn't matter,' he said. 'Even if their ship was able to make a landing here, which I doubt, it doesn't possess the weapons necessary to break in. This mine is protected by neutron cannon. I am secure.'

Charlie Nisbett's voice crackled over the communicator link. 'Pyerpoint,' he thundered. 'This is Nisbett.'

'I have nothing to say to you,' said Pyerpoint.

'Scum!' Charlie's voice broke with emotion. 'You're behind all of this. I wish I was there to bust you open with my own hands. I want you to suffer like my family suffered. It's too bad it's going to have to end this way.'

Pyerpoint stiffened. 'What do you mean? You cannot reach me here. Go away.'

'You're wrong on that score. See, the survey base is wired up to blow when I give the word. There's enough hermite stored there to crack open the reactor core.' He paused. 'And when that goes, the planet goes.'

'I do not believe you,' said Pyerpoint.

'You know what? Of all the people I've ever met, I hate you most of all.'

The transmission ceased.

Charlie's warning had been overheard on the open channel by Spiggot. 'Oh damn!' he said. 'Can he really blow up the planet like that? He can't, can he?'

'I'm afraid he can,' said the Doctor from the base. 'And as I happen to be sitting directly on top of the bomb, I'm not too happy about it.' He tutted. 'Really, Spiggot, I was just about to win Nisbett over. Couldn't you use just a little intelligence?'

'How was I to know?' the detective protested. He flinched under the accusing glare of Stokes. 'Well, at least the galaxy will be a better place without Xais and Pyerpoint, anyway.'

Stokes slapped him and turned his back.

K9's head dropped and he trundled away.

* * *

'If the reactor at the McConnochie base blows, you will die,' Xais called up to Pyerpoint. 'The base is built on the junction of faultlines that will bring the Jilharro mountains down on this place. You are finished.'

Pyerpoint drummed his fingers on the console before him. 'You will die with me.'

Xais shook her head. 'No. The mask will resist the explosion. And besides, you have gathered the helicon here. When it is released, I shall activate it and my plan will succeed. Only you will have failed, a victim of your own cunning.' She waited, and then added, 'There is an alternative, of course.'

He stood up and stared down at her. 'What?'

'Release me,' she said, gesturing to the clamps securing her wrists and ankles. 'Free me and I will save you. I can use the helicon you have gathered to protect you. I will activate it, and transfer your consciousness, in minutes. We will both become immortal. Or would you prefer to die?'

'Why should you want me alive?' Pyerpoint asked her.

'You'll never know until you release me,' Xais pleaded. 'You must release me.'

Pyerpoint, unsure but aware of the desperate nature of his predicament, leant forward and pressed a button. The hum of the radiation probe stopped, and the lighting in the room below returned to normal. The clamps on the platform clicked open.

Xais sat upright.

A beam shot from her forehead. It shattered the glass of the gallery. Pyerpoint, taken by surprise, threw himself back, his left arm raised to protect himself from the blast. He fell forward over the console, his body shattered.

Xais laughed cruelly and stepped from the platform. The long blonde hair of Romana cascaded down her back as she put her hands on her hips in a characteristically arrogant pose. She looked up.

'Goodbye, Nisbett,' she said.

* * *

Flarkk lifted his head from the flight position. 'We are ready to make warp jump, sir.'

Charlie gripped the detonator box in his hand. He looked up at the picture hanging above the bridge. 'This one's for you,' he told its subject. A tear trickled down one pudgy cheek. 'This one's for the firm. Rev down for warp, Flarkk.'

The Ogron nodded and flicked over a series of switches. The ship's engine noise altered in pitch to a protesting grumble. Flarkk cocked his head. 'Something is wrong,' he said. Smoke started to waft from the panel in front of him.

'I will check the computer.' He consulted the ship's fault tracer diagnostic system. A long list of faulty components flashed up. At the top a string of numbers flashed in red. Flarkk gasped. 'What? Computer is not working right. Engines are not working. Rockets won't stop.'

Charlie leapt up from his chair. 'Close 'em down! If we try going into warp with rockets still active, we'll be —'

The program set by Xais activated the moment the ship's warp engines were primed. A command tripped the safety checks on the rocket motors.

The explosion ripped through the Ogron ship in less than a second, as the warp stress tore open the active rocket fuel. The ship's black, skeletal frame was revealed in the moment before the fireball blossomed, sending the now unrecognizable mass of twisted metal hurtling back down through the atmosphere of Planet Eleven.

Gravity delivered it to the grasping gas clouds, which burst around it and consumed it with sky-splitting fury.

14

Activation

The energy flare from the explosion of the Ogron ship sent needles kicking crazily across their scales on the consoles in the survey room. The Doctor, still uncomfortably attached to his chair, took a look at the base computer's diagnostic reports as the readings settled. It looked as if Charlie and his servants had met with an unpleasant end. The Doctor would have taken his hat off to mark his respect, but it was still in his pocket, and it would have been too much trouble to take it out, put it on, and then take it off again, particularly in his current circumstances.

He flipped open the communicator channel. 'Spiggot,' he called. 'Spiggot, can you hear me? It's the Doctor.'

The static-coated atmosphere of the planet had been further tainted by the explosion, and the reply frequency was blocked by a quivering sonic howl.

'What to do, what to do?' The Doctor looked about him. Firstly, he could have a go at disarming the bomb. The signal would never be sent, but the thing had an antique appearance to it that was deeply unsettling. It might go off at any moment.

He hopped over to it, whipped out his sonic screwdriver, and set to work.

Xais sensed the destruction of the ship. She looked up at the gallery. Pyerpoint's body was slumped over the console. He was covered in his own blood. The injuries must have been fatal.

Xais took a deep breath. At last the situation was back

under her control. The Nisbetts and Pyerpoint were dead, and the latter had been foolish enough both to free her and to provide her with the helicon, ready-mined and ripe for activation.

'Now,' she whispered. Her eyes snapped open. The glow had already started to form. 'Time to begin.'

A mental image came to her. She saw herself standing in the middle of a burning city. Coppertown, perhaps. The air was rich with the satisfying odour of charred corpses. Death was all around her. The Normals were burning in their own filth. She had sterilized the area.

Soon.

Xais left the room where she had been imprisoned, and walked briskly along the corridor outside. She could feel the helicon, gathered and waiting, calling for her. Her flesh tingled.

Stokes tapped the door of the TARDIS. 'We appear to have evaded death once again,' he said. 'If this unlikely contraption can do half of what you claim for it, Spiggot, I suggest we make ourselves scarce.'

'Hang on a moment.' Spiggot peered through the entrance of the repair bay. 'She's coming this way.' He readied his revolver as the sound of hurried footsteps came closer.

K9 motored forward eagerly. 'That is the Mistress.'

'Don't, K9,' Spiggot warned. 'You've got to forget about Romana. There's nothing much we can do for her now.' He raised his blaster. 'This way may be the kindest.'

K9's laser shot the weapon from Spiggot's hand. Without a word, the automaton shot past the startled policeman and into the corridor outside.

Xais stopped at the sight of him. 'Ah,' she crowed, 'the dog. Your mistress is very fond of you. So stupid, the obsession of Normals with inanimate objects.'

K9 growled. The venomous features of the mask contrasted oddly with Romana's flowing blonde hair and stylish outfit. 'Release my Mistress, Xais.'

'Get out of my way,' Xais said. She opened her eyes wide and prepared to deliver the burst of energy that would crush the small machine into a smoking heap of sticky components.

Something stopped her. She gasped and clutched her stomach. Her head jerked back at an odd angle. The voice of Romana shouted out suddenly, 'K9! – Find the Doctor! – Find him! –' She doubled up.

Xais reasserted herself and Romana's body straightened. She pushed past K9 with an angry scream and ran down the corridor.

K9 followed her.

Spiggot, who had overseen this exchange from the doorway, emerged into the corridor. Although he was now without a weapon, he was determined to see this case, the most baffling of his career, through to the end. He set off after K9.

Stokes hung back. He looked longingly at the TARDIS. 'Why don't I,' he told himself, 'just wait in there?'

He squinted to read the notice on the door of the time-space craft. 'Pull to open. Right.' He grasped the handle on the right-hand door and pulled. The door refused to budge.

'I knew that was going to happen,' said Stokes. 'Oh well.' He hurried out of the repair bay.

Gently, the Doctor eased out the last of the thin red rods that formed the core of the bomb. He returned the sonic screwdriver to the pocket of his jacket, and exchanged it for his somewhat battered paper bag of jelly babies. With difficulty, he popped a yellow one into his mouth, and chewed to aid his concentration. The outlook was bleak.

'Well, Doctor,' he told himself. 'You're stranded in a survey base, away from the action. You've lost Romana, K9 and the TARDIS, and your only means of escape is to walk across two hundred miles of sludge in an atmosuit that'll increase your bodyweight threefold. Shouldn't take you a week. Landed, stranded, diddled, dished and done.'

The sugar released by the now chewed jelly baby raced through the Doctor's metabolism to where it was most needed. Instantly inspiration came. 'Ah!' he cried. 'Now, what about the transmat?'

With renewed enthusiasm, he hopped out of the survey room.

In the gallery above the room where he had imprisoned Xais, Pyerpoint stirred. He was covered in shards of glass that tinkled off as he righted himself. His left arm flopped, broken and limp, at his side. He fought down the pain and stood up, grunting with exertion.

His head throbbed, and blood smeared the left side of his face where the sharp point of a fragment of glass had opened his forehead, but these appeared to be his only injuries.

He felt for the laser pistol tucked into his waistband and staggered from the room.

The hum of active machinery led Xais to the mineral stores. The end of the corridor widened out to form a small, brightly lit chamber. One wall was white and featureless. The other was lined with about thirty small storage hoppers, arranged in three storeys. Each hopper had a clear panel at the front. Each container was filled almost to capacity with silver dust. Raw helicon, sucked from the mountains and the surrounding rocks and pools by robots and bugs, and sifted clear into the hoppers by automated shakers.

Xais let out a moan of ecstasy. She crossed to the nearest hopper and leant her head against it. She could hear the helicon inside calling to her. The itch in her forehead returned and her eyes reddened. The time was approaching. The problem of how to flee this planet afterwards remained, but she knew she would find a way.

And in just a few hours, the activation process would be complete. Every last molecule of the helicon stored here would be infused with her life-force. She could shape it however she chose. Then would begin her revenge on the Normals.

She reached out for the environment control panel next to the storage computer and instructed the hoppers to decrease their internal temperature by hundreds of degrees. The computer reported that the helicon would reach liquid point in six minutes.

'Mistress,' an irritating, tinny voice called from behind her.

She turned from the hoppers to see K9 and the two Normals approaching. She was amused to see that one of them was the cowardly artist from the Rock.

'Stokes. It is fitting that you should be here at this moment in history.'

'No it bloody isn't,' Stokes said.

Xais ignored him. 'I may need you to shape the pattern for a new body.' She raised a hand to her mask. It responded to her touch, moulding itself under her fingertips like wet clay. 'My skills with this substance are improving. I am starting to wonder if there is anything I cannot achieve, given time.'

Spiggot put his hands on his hips. 'Come on, Xais. The game's over. You'd best come quietly.'

'Idiot.' Again she tried to send a beam of energy towards them, and again failed. The host was blocking her, conserving its energies for moments of stress in a skilled way that Margo never had.

Frustrated, Xais reached for a control on the wall beside her. With a solid clunk, a massive shield slid down across the entrance to the storage chamber. K9 darted forward but was too late.

Xais nodded, relieved, and returned her attentions to the helicon. Bubbles were forming already at the bottoms of some of the containers.

* * *

Spiggot slammed the flat of his hand against the shield, howled, and sucked his fingers. 'She's got us licked.'

Stokes asked nervously, 'What exactly is she doing in there?'

K9 answered. 'My sensors indicate that she is lowering the temperature of the inert helicon in order to effect a chemical change in its constitution. This change will render it suitable for activation by the,' he clicked and whirred, searching his vocabulary, 'radiation that she is able to release.'

'So what are we going to do about it, then?' cried Spiggot. 'Stand here talking about it?' He collapsed against the wall. 'There's nothing we can do.'

K9 inspected the shield separating them from Xais. 'Negative. This shield is composed of steel. My laser can penetrate.' He extended his nose laser and started to cut away.

The beam moved with frustrating slowness. To Spiggot it seemed as if the ray was having no effect at all.

Back at the McConnochie Mining base, the Doctor completed his one-handed adjustments to the transmat. He hoped to divert the beam in the direction of Pyerpoint's mine.

'Hmm,' he observed, 'direct non-terminal transmat travel's a good few centuries ahead of this lot. If they only knew it was a simple matter of cross-hatching the pentalion drive with the guidance assemblers, and adding a verification tangle after the seventy-seventh pulse. But people never can see the obvious.'

He flipped up the transmat's timer controls, set the beam to activate in fifteen seconds, and hopped enthusiastically onto the transmission platform.

A dreadful doubt entered the Doctor's mind. 'I hope I remembered to step up the scale on the proton screen. It would be very undignified to be stuck to this chair for the rest of my days. Still, too late to check now.'

He felt the familiar tugging sensation of transmat travel

and the warble of the disassemblers. He shrugged his shoulders. 'Oh, that this too too solid flesh would melt . . .'

And was gone.

Stokes tugged at Spiggot's sleeve. 'Why don't we just go back to that TARDIS?' He gestured to K9. 'He hardly seems to be having much luck on the shield. As you say, we're finished here. There's nothing we can do.'

'You're right.' Spiggot knelt to address K9. 'We've got to evacuate. Let's go back to your box, right?'

'Negative. I must rescue the Mistress.'

Spiggot tapped him on the head. 'You know that's dumb. But me and Stokes are getting out of here.'

'Impossible,' said K9. 'The door of the TARDIS is locked. And if I were to open it, you would not be able to operate the systems.'

Spiggot frowned. 'You're coming back with us, K9. That's an order.'

'I am not programmed to accept your orders.'

'The robot revolution has come at last,' said Stokes. 'And, of course, I have to be right in the middle of it.' He crossed to K9 and shouted down, 'I hope you rust.'

'That's no way to address my dog,' said a voice from behind them.

Spiggot and Stokes whirled round. K9 clipped off his beam and swung about joyously. 'Master!'

The Doctor nodded a greeting. 'Hello, K9. Hello, Mr Stokes.' He turned his most withering look on Spiggot. 'Hello, cretin. Ruined any good plans lately?'

'Now, come on, that was hardly my fault,' Spiggot protested.

The Doctor waved him into silence and crossed to the shield. 'The Mistress is behind this barrier, Master,' K9 informed him. 'She is possessed by Xais. I am endeavouring to break open the shield before she can activate the helicon.'

'Good dog. You carry on.' The Doctor looked about.

On the wall to the left of the shield was a small microphone. He reached up with his free hand and unclipped it.

'Here, Doctor,' said Spiggot. 'You're tied to a chair, you know.'

The Doctor ignored him and switched on the microphone.

The helicon was starting to reach activation point. A gentle percussion of freezing bubbles against glass filled the storage chamber. Xais smiled. Her eyes opened. They were now a vivid blue. Her concentration was absolute. In just a few moments she would begin the process.

An amplified cough disturbed her serenity. 'Er, hello, testing, testing, one two three.'

Her mouth twisted. 'Doctor!'

'Hello,' said the friendly voice. 'That sounds like Romana. How are you, old thing?'

'Your attempt to reach her is futile, Doctor,' said Xais. 'I have total control.'

When the Doctor's voice spoke again it was with considerably more gravity. 'Xais. Listen to me. I know you have endured much. Your entire people were wiped out.'

'I do not want your sympathy,' she called back. 'You are a Normal. Your words mean nothing.'

'Well, at least do this for me, Xais, if you can. Use Romana's skills to work out the likely consequences of your actions. Can you control so much of that stuff? I doubt it. Even if you can, what then? There's no way you can leave this planet, Xais. Your escape route is gone. You'll be trapped here forever.'

At a junction not far away, Pyerpoint stood nursing his broken arm. His blood-soaked face was turned to a screen built into the wall. It displayed the interior of the storage chamber.

Pyerpoint shook with delight, remembering the plans

of the mine passed to him by its designer, his former accomplice Voltt. Xais was exactly where he wanted her. He could still triumph.

He licked his lips and hurried towards the storage chamber, gun in hand.

The Doctor looked anxiously down to where K9 had almost blasted through the shield. The hastily improvised plan he was about to put into action was gambling all their lives. But he could see no alternative.

'Here's the deal, Xais,' he said. 'You give me Romana, unharmed. I'll give you another host and transportation off this planet in my ship, the TARDIS. I'll take you out of this system. And don't imagine you'll be able to kill us and leave in the TARDIS. You'd never be able to operate it. It contains a field that nullifies all hostile action. Ask Romana to verify that.'

A few seconds passed as Xais considered. 'It is so. But these terms are not good enough, Doctor. You must take the helicon also.'

The Doctor licked his lips. He had anticipated this request, and deliberately not mentioned the helicon in his offer so that he would now appear to be giving ground. 'Very well,' he said with feigned reluctance. 'We'll load it aboard.'

'And my new host form,' Xais continued. 'I want you, Doctor, to wear my face. That way I will know there will be no tricks on your part. Is that agreed?'

The Doctor, surprised, clicked off the microphone and thought over the stipulation.

'You can't do it, Doctor,' said Spiggot. 'Let me be the host. I reckon I could show Xais a thing or two. I've been programmed to resist brainwashing.'

'You haven't a brain to wash,' said Stokes.

The Doctor reopened the channel. 'All right, Xais. I'll give myself as host. Until we reach the planet of your choice.' He paused. 'Now, why don't you open the shield and we can begin?'

Before Xais could reply, a high-pitched squawk came from behind the Doctor. He turned to see Stokes, who was held in an arm lock by Pyerpoint. The thin end of a laser pistol had been jammed against the artist's flabby neck.

'Don't move, Doctor!' Pyerpoint warned. 'Or I'll kill him.'

'Oh God, oh God, oh no, oh no,' Stokes wailed.

'Shut up,' Pyerpoint ordered him, jabbing him with the pistol to underline his point.

It looked as if Spiggot might be about to jump Pyerpoint, so the Doctor pulled him back hurriedly. 'What do you want exactly?' he asked.

'What I've always wanted,' Pyerpoint replied. 'A return to decency and social order.'

Stokes yelped again.

'Pardon me for saying so, but you've gone a very funny way about that,' said the Doctor.

'You are a symptom of the social malaise, Doctor. You would not understand. It was necessary for somebody to take a stand. If I had not become Sentinel, the law would have crumbled and crime would have run amok.' He tightened his grip on Stokes. 'Permissiveness and licence have allowed degenerates like this repulsive creature to flourish. With helicon, keyed to my personality, I intend to return this system to order. Forever.'

A crazed glint had entered his eyes. 'I am the natural leader. Without me, our society will turn to dust in less than a generation, I promise you. I must have – I *will* have – ultimate, eternal control if we are to survive.'

'I thought it would be something like that,' said the Doctor. 'Unfortunately, I fear you are labouring under a massive misapprehension.' He inclined his head slightly. 'You see, I've given it some thought, and I don't think helicon can be used by anybody but Xais. She can't work some formula on your behalf. That would be quite impossible. The transfer process is based on her personality, her soul if you like, travelling along a telepathic wavelength. Unless you share her psi-powers, such a transfer would be impossible to duplicate.'

'You're bluffing,' said Pyerpoint. 'Xais demonstrated the process for me, four years ago. At our first meeting. She activated helicon and gave it my personality. I spoke to myself!'

The voice of Xais came from the microphone still clutched in the Doctor's hand. 'The Doctor tells the truth, Pyerpoint. The demonstration was faked. There is no formula to recreate the process.'

Pyerpoint released Stokes, who fell panting to the floor, red-faced. He grabbed the microphone from the Doctor and yelled into it, 'No, Xais. I spoke to myself!'

'You spoke to a computer projection,' she replied. 'You were so easy to manipulate. So desperate to believe. In the end, whatever you planned, I knew I could always better you. You are a Normal.'

Pyerpoint's legs shook. 'This is . . . this is . . .'

The Doctor put a restraining hand on his shoulder. 'Steady on, old chap.'

Pyerpoint knocked the Doctor aside and spoke into the microphone.

'Sentinel,' he said. His eyes were rolling. 'Activate. Destroy intruders.'

Xais turned as a clicking noise came from the white wall behind her. An entire section of it slid out slowly. The white block unfolded with incredible speed. Its appendages − a long, vibrating knife, a whirring saw, and a spiked mace at the end of a chain − were revealed at the same time as the circular base inflated and detatched itself from the wall.

The huge mining robot bore down on Xais.

She was startled for a second, but the speed of her reflexes allowed her to duck under the nearest block as it crashed into the hopper behind her. The robot turned to finish her off, but she rolled herself nimbly under it.

She stood facing the hoppers. The helicon inside was

now ready for activation. This could be her only chance.

The robot whirred and turned, struggling to orientate itself.

Xais gathered all her energies. She closed her eyes, concentrated, and then opened them again.

A glittering yellow haze cascaded from her eyes like a shower of golden stars. The energy cloud was attracted to the helicon and slipped through the glass fronts of the hoppers.

The reaction was immediate. The helicon roared.

Xais screamed with pleasure.

Disorientated, the robot's sensors swung from the hoppers back to Xais. It advanced again, extending its vibrating knife with a view to impaling her.

Xais backed away and stumbled into a corner. In her exultation she dismissed the deal she had made with the Doctor. What did it matter now that her own existence was absolute and indelible? This host was unimportant, anyway. There were other Normals to be used, nearby. Pyerpoint would be a fitting host.

Romana had been conserving her energies. With an enormous effort of will, she forced Xais to raise her hand and throw off the mask – and suddenly found herself pressed into a corner with a robot bearing down on her. She took advantage of its lumbering movements to slip around its side.

She was tired and disorientated, but she realized instantly that she had no time to collect her wits. The robot turned again, its mace swinging for her and missing her by inches.

The temperature gauges on the hoppers shattered with successive tinkles of glass. Freezing steam poured from emergency vents, almost blinding her and confusing the robot.

K9 had almost cut through the shield. The Doctor, now freed from the chair, paced up and down, desperate to know what was going on on the other side. The microphone had relayed a confusing variety of sounds. 'Come on, K9, come on!'

'Estimate success in twenty-four seconds,' said K9. The red ray was now angled downward, carving out the outline of a man-sized arch.

Pyerpoint was slumped against a wall, giggling to himself. 'I will have control soon,' he said. 'Helicon will give me control!'

Stokes, who had picked himself up and dusted himself down, huffed. 'Madman.'

The ground started to shake and the lights flickered.

'What the hell is going on behind there?' cried Spiggot.

K9 shot back from the shield as the section he had carved out fell backwards into the corridor with a clang that all but deafened the Doctor, who was standing closest. A cloud of dust and smoke was released from the storage chamber beyond.

'Romana!' The Doctor covered his nose and mouth with the ends of his scarf and leapt through the hole. Romana staggered into his arms and he pulled her back.

Pyerpoint brushed past them. He dashed into the storage chamber and looked about at the hoppers. Each of them looked as if it was about to burst open and release the straining helicon inside. The robot, thoroughly confused, was spinning around wildly.

'Xais!' cried Pyerpoint. 'Xais!' He strayed too near a steam vent and scalded his good hand, which dropped the laser pistol. He screamed.

'I am here,' said the voice of Xais. 'I am here, Pyerpoint.'

His foot touched something. It was the mask. The lips moved. 'Pyerpoint. You must wear my face. Wear it! I will give you the activation formula. I was lying to the Doctor, of course!'

Pyerpoint, desperate to believe, picked up the mask. Slowly, he brought it down on his face.

In the moment that followed, Xais and Pyerpoint

exchanged the horror and the sickness of their personalities. Each struggled to take control.

The robot advanced and pushed its vibrating knife up through Pyerpoint's ribcage. He coughed and choked. The robot withdrew and ambled off.

Pyerpoint's body collapsed. The mask clung on, its host's blood dribbling through its lips. 'No!' it cried. 'No, Pyerpoint! You must not die! You cannot die! I need you! You are to be my new host! Without a living mind, I cannot stabilize the helicon! You must live!'

He died.

Xais felt his soul recede and then disappear.

'No!' she cried. 'Doctor – Doctor, help me! You must help me, Doctor!'

The robot lurched through the gap in the shield and advanced on the Doctor. He bundled Romana into Stokes's arms and shouted, 'K9!'

The dog rolled forward slowly. 'Reserves exhausted, Master . . .' He ground to a halt.

'Oh dear,' said the Doctor. The robot's whirring saw slashed out, slicing one of the ends of the Doctor's scarf.

Spiggot dashed forward. He lunged for the concealed control panel under the robot's flailing arms and fumbled for the activator button.

The saw halted an inch from the Doctor's face.

He stepped around it cautiously and shook Spiggot's hand. 'Do you know,' he told the policeman, 'I think your entire life has been leading up to that moment.'

'Doctor!' Xais called from the storage chamber.

The Doctor shook himself, nipped through the hole in the shield again, and answered his enemy. He had to shout over the rumble of the helicon. 'Yes?'

The mask, still attached to the dead body of Pyerpoint, pleaded with him. 'Please, Doctor. You must wear my face. I was able only to activate the helicon, to prepare it. I need a host to complete the transfer. The helicon is dangerous, aware but mindless. Without my direction it will consume the planet.'

'I'm sorry, Xais. If I give you what you ask, I condemn millions of innocent people to suffering.'

'You will obey me!' shrieked the mask. 'I order you! I will consume you! You will wear my face! Doctor!'

Romana came to stand beside the Doctor. 'We'd better leave, Doctor.'

'I know.' He took a final look at the hate-filled features of the snarling mask and followed Romana through the shield.

'Then die, Doctor!' Xais called after him. 'Die! The helicon will consume you, but I shall live forever!'

The hoppers exploded.

'The TARDIS, now!' cried the Doctor. He picked up the inert K9 and set off down the corridor at a furious pace.

Spiggot hurried after him, with Romana and Stokes bringing up the rear.

A wave of expanding silver burst from the hoppers, filling the storage chamber and swallowing up the robot, the body of Pyerpoint and the protesting mask of Xais in seconds. It flowed down the corridor and into the mine, roaring and moaning, a formless mass, sentient but with no soul.

Guided by a powerful homing instinct, the Doctor bounded into the repair bay. Spiggot, Stokes and Romana followed seconds later. The mine vibrated as the roaring tide of expanding helicon poured along its corridors.

The Doctor was ferreting in his pocket with his free hand. 'Come on, Doctor!' cried Romana. 'Let us in.'

'I can't find the key!' he shouted back. 'And we can't use K9, he's dead to the world.'

The helicon swallowed up the corridor outside the repair bay.

'When we were interrogated, back up on the Rock,' the

Doctor said desperately. 'I didn't leave it up there, did I?'

'No,' said Romana as coolly as she could. 'I remember you picking it up.'

Stokes pounded his fists on the door of the TARDIS. 'Let us in, let us in!'

Spiggot glanced over his shoulder. 'Oh, no!'

The helicon was flowing into the repair bay.

'Got it!' The Doctor held the key aloft. He jammed it in the lock, opened the door, and pushed the others inside.

He waved at the gushing helicon. 'Goodbye!' Then he threw himself inside the TARDIS. A moment later it dematerialized.

The helicon consumed the repair bay and went on to swallow the mine. Unsated, it burst open the walls confining it and splashed out onto the surface of Planet Eleven.

It spread in all directions at unbelievable speed. The highest peaks of the Jilharro mountain range were buried in less than five minutes.

The gobbling mass continued to expand, absorbing the thick gases in the atmosphere, seeping down and damping its tiny core, and covering the surface of the small planet.

15

Farewells

With some deft handling of the controls, and some help from Romana, the Doctor brought the TARDIS into a hovering orbit at a safe distance from the rapidly altering Planet Eleven. The police box materialized soundlessly.

Aboard the craft, Spiggot and Stokes were slumped against a wall of the control room. Stokes had decided merely to accept the impossible dimensions of the interior. His concern from the very start of this deplorable business had been to escape, and it would be ill-mannered to complain about the means. And he was quite simply beyond gaping.

'D'you know,' said Spiggot, 'if there's one thing this affair has taught me, it's this.'

Stokes raised a sarcastic eyebrow. 'Never doubt the word of a time-travelling robot dog?'

Spiggot ignored the quip. 'It's shown me that when it really comes down to it, when your life's on the line and the odds are against you, well, perhaps there's something more important than just staying alive.' He nodded. 'Soon as I get back to Five, I'm going after Angie and the kids. I'll find them, no matter how long it takes.'

Stokes frowned. 'I don't understand. Surely you'll find them where you left them?'

'Er, well, I didn't actually leave them,' Spiggot confessed. 'I came back from a case one day and they'd upped and left me. I still don't really know why.'

'Don't you,' said Stokes, rather amused. He let his large bald head fall back against the curiously warm and humming wall.

At the console, the Doctor was removing a set of leads from K9. 'How are you feeling?'

The dog's head snapped up and his eyescreen glowed a healthy red. 'Fully recharged, Master. Energy banks at eighty-nine per cent capacity.'

The Doctor rubbed his hands. 'Excellent. And how about you, Romana?'

She looked up from the read-out she was studying. 'Oh, fine. There's no need to worry. It was an unpleasant experience, but I remembered my training in resistance to outward telepathic interference.' She held up a hand before her eyes. 'I threw up a screen. She could use my body, but she couldn't see into my mind.'

'How jolly clever.' The Doctor patted her on the back. 'It's nice to know that the Academy are passing on useful information like that. Things were very different in my day, you know.'

'Oh, I didn't mean my Academy training, Doctor.' Romana smiled. 'I meant my training from you.'

K9 spoke. 'Master. Materialization in hover mode has now been achieved and TARDIS is stable.'

'Good, good.' The Doctor twisted the scanner control and the shutters slid open.

Planet Eleven lay below them, its entirety revealed by the scanner's powerful image translator. Its transmutation was complete. The stodgy blueness had been replaced by a layer of shining silver that coated the surface completely, and it now resembled a Christmas bauble or ball bearing, spinning helplessly in its orbit.

Intrigued, Spiggot and Stokes joined them before the screen. 'Is it really living?' Stokes asked.

'Not as such,' Romana replied. 'Not what you'd call life.'

'Hmm.' The Doctor looked less certain. 'But life, like death, is a very difficult state to define.' He reached out to close the shutters, but Spiggot laid a hand on his arm and pointed, in wonder, at the image.

'Doctor, look!'

On the surface of the planet, a shape was forming. Indistinct at first, the swirling helicon surged upward in a huge, but recognizable, pattern.

The face of Xais. Twisted, snarling, and spread across half the surface area of the planet.

Somehow, they all heard her voice as her mouth, larger than the mountain range, opened. Her angry voice echoed telepathically up to them from the planet.

'NO, DOCTOR! I ORDER YOU TO RETURN. PUNY NORMAL, I WILL CRUSH YOU! YOU WILL BE MY NEW HOST! I SHALL CREATE AN ARMY FROM THE POWER GATHERED HERE!'

Sadly, the Doctor reached out and twisted the scanner control. The shutters slid to and the voice faded with the image.

Stokes shuddered. 'Well, she looks rather active.'

The Doctor smiled. 'Don't worry, she's trapped there. Without a host, she's got no hope of going anywhere. And her telepathic powers aren't strong enough to reach out at that distance.'

He turned to the two men. 'I think it's time we saw about getting you gentlemen home.'

The main hall outside the courtrooms was much as the fleeing crew of the Rock had left it. Evidence of the Ogron attack was limited to an occasional beam-scarred pillar or bust, and it could have been that the sabotage attempt engendered by Spiggot and K9 had caused more damage to property.

A blue beacon began to flash in mid-air, and a few seconds later the police box shell of the TARDIS had solidified from transparency. The doors opened and the Doctor, Romana, K9, Spiggot and Stokes emerged. All of them looked rather battered after their recent ordeals.

The Doctor extended a hand to Stokes. 'Well, I'm afraid this is where we must say goodbye. I hope your artistic career continues to flourish, despite the obvious drawbacks.'

Stokes shook the hand warmly and said pettishly, 'A good craftsman will succeed in whatever circumstances.'

'That's exactly what I meant.'

The Doctor patted Spiggot on the shoulder. 'Goodbye. Try to keep clear of any trouble in future.'

'Hang about,' said Spiggot. 'What about Planet Eleven? What are we going to do about that? We can't have Xais shouting at passers by, it'll put the tourists right off.'

'A good point.' The Doctor ferreted in his pocket and produced a scrap of paper and a stub of blunt pencil. He scribbled down a complex formula and passed it to Spiggot. 'Tell your boffins to have a go with that. Should break down the helicon molecules fairly quickly.'

'Provided that the beam is directed at a convex angle,' Romana reminded him.

There was a clatter of booted footsteps along the corridor. Two men in black uniform were approaching. The taller of the two raised a blaster and cried, 'Halt! Who are you?'

Spiggot reached inside his jacket and brought out his wallet, which he flipped open to reveal his warrant. 'It's OK, boys, Frank Spiggot here. I've got the whole situation under control.'

The uniformed policeman lowered his gun. 'Hello, sir. Who are these people? Have you seen the High Archon?'

'Don't worry, they're friendly enough.' Spiggot stepped forward. 'As for old man Pyerpoint, well, you won't be seeing him again. Polished off, along with Xais and the Nisbett brothers.'

The officer boggled. 'Xais? And the Nisbett brothers?'

'Right enough. These people were kind enough to help me, and I recommend the highest civilian citation.' He turned to indicate the others, but the Doctor had already stepped hurriedly back into the TARDIS, K9 at his heels. Romana gave a little wave to Stokes and followed them.

The officer scratched his head. 'Why are they going into that box?'

The answer came a moment later as the TARDIS dematerialized.

'Well, it's not important,' said Spiggot, thinking quickly as ever. 'You'd never believe me if I told you. The important thing is, the menace is over. And I can tell you a thing or two about what's been going on out here.' He walked away with the officers.

Stokes lingered behind, listening to Spiggot beginning to relate the story of how he personally had dealt with the biggest criminal conspiracy of the decade.

'Finally, finally, I am going to be sick,' he said.

'Do you think Spiggot will pass on the formula?' Romana asked later, a little worried.

The Doctor was riffling through some yellowing star-charts. He held one up triumphantly, peered at a particular area, and grinned. 'Yes. Here, look.'

Romana examined the chart. 'The Uva Beta Uva system, surveyed fifty years after we left. And Planet Eleven is just a ball of rock. Good.'

K9 trundled forward, tail wagging anxiously. 'Master, Mistress,' he said. 'We have not finished the game.'

'Ah yes, the Monopoly.' Romana looked over to the board and reminded herself of the state of play. 'I'm just about to win.'

The Doctor unwound his scarf, shook off his coat, and draped them over the stand. 'The trouble with Monopoly is that it's far too simple. The mind wanders.'

'It won't take a moment,' said Romana.

The Doctor made for the inner door. 'I've more important things to do, anyway.'

'Oh really?'

'Yes!' the Doctor retorted. 'For a start, there's the . . .' He grinned. 'Well, I'll think of something.'

Available in the Doctor Who – New Adventures *series:*

TIMEWYRM: GENESYS by John Peel
TIMEWYRM: EXODUS by Terrance Dicks
TIMEWYRM: APOCALYPSE by Nigel Robinson
TIMEWYRM: REVELATION by Paul Cornell
CAT'S CRADLE: TIME'S CRUCIBLE by Marc Platt
CAT'S CRADLE: WARHEAD by Andrew Cartmel
CAT'S CRADLE: WITCH MARK by Andrew Hunt
NIGHTSHADE by Mark Gatiss
LOVE AND WAR by Paul Cornell
TRANSIT by Ben Aaronovitch
THE HIGHEST SCIENCE by Gareth Roberts
THE PIT by Neil Penswick
DECEIT by Peter Darvill-Evans
LUCIFER RISING by Jim Mortimore and Andy Lane
WHITE DARKNESS by David A. McIntee
SHADOWMIND by Christopher Bulis
BIRTHRIGHT by Nigel Robinson
ICEBERG by David Banks
BLOOD HEAT by Jim Mortimore
THE DIMENSION RIDERS by Daniel Blythe
THE LEFT-HANDED HUMMINGBIRD by Kate Orman
CONUNDRUM by Steve Lyons
NO FUTURE by Paul Cornell
TRAGEDY DAY by Gareth Roberts
LEGACY by Gary Russell
THEATRE OF WAR by Justin Richards
ALL-CONSUMING FIRE by Andy Lane
BLOOD HARVEST by Terrance Dicks
STRANGE ENGLAND by Simon Messingham
FIRST FRONTIER by David A. McIntee
ST ANTHONY'S FIRE by Mark Gatiss
FALLS THE SHADOW by Daniel O'Mahony
PARASITE by Jim Mortimore
WARLOCK by Andrew Cartmel

The next Missing Adventure is *The Ghosts of N-Space* by
Barry Letts, which will feature the third Doctor, Sarah Jane
Smith and Brigadier Lethbridge-Stewart.